Dear Mystery Reader:

W9-CHR-320

Philadelphia's Main Line is known as an enclave for the city's elite. Enter Ginger Barnes. Sassy, smart, and decidedly down-to-earth, Ginger is back in Donna Huston Murray's fifth DEAD LETTER offering, A SCORE TO SETTLE. This time, Ginger's taking her sleuthing skills on the road to solve the murder of a pro football quarterback.

After a game against the Houston Hombres, Tomcats' backup quarterback Tim Duffy is found dead in the locker room. Ginger's cousin Michelle, who's married to the Tomcats' starting quarterback, summons her to Norfolk, Virginia, and the home of NFL Films. An inside hit? An unhappy fan? Her own brother-in-law? As the list of supsects grows, so do Ginger's suspicions. Suspicions that may or may not lead her to the truth.

Whether you've been a Ginger Barnes fan from the start, or have just joined the DEAD LETTER team, one thing's for sure, you'll be waiting in the stands for Donna's next book after reading A SCORE TO SETTLE.

Yours in crime,

Joe Veltre

Joe Veltre
Associate Editor
St. Martin's DEAD LETTER Paperback Mysteries

Other titles from St. Martin's **Dead Letter** Mysteries

Dead Letter is also proud to present these mystery
classics by Ngaio Marsh

A SCORE TO SETTLE

Donna Huston Murray

St. Martin's Paperbacks

A SCORE TO SETTLE

ISBN: 0-312-96951-1

Printed in the United States of America

St. Martin's Paperbacks edition/April 1999

10 9 8 7 6 5 4 3 2 1

NOTE TO READERS

This is a work of fiction. All the characters and events portrayed in this book are fictitious, and any resemblance to real people or events is purely coincidental. The National Football League, NFL Films and any other real organizations portrayed in this novel are used fictitiously.

This book and its contents have not in any way been authorized or endorsed by the National Football League or NFL Films.

ACKNOWLEDGMENTS

First of all, I am immensely grateful to Billy Driber, Vice President in Charge of Production for NFL Films, for the fascinating tour of his workplace. The exposure to such a creative atmosphere literally inspired this book.

One notion naturally led to another, and soon I found myself on the doorstep and the mercy of Patty and Kurt Kunkle of Chesapeake, Virginia. Their input and guidance proved indispensable, and I thank them profusely, too.

Thank goodness Hench, my in-house football expert and University of Pennsylvania color commentator, switched to play by play for the duration. I am grateful—and amazed—that his patience survived.

Other friends and friendly folks helped me understand lots of things I really needed help understanding: Karen Lynch; Dr. Frank Manfrey, Catherine Howley, and Linda Mackie; Ellie Smith, Norma Sheward, and Paige Rose.

Also, the following people provided anything from the perfect spot for a stadium to the perfect pastry to describe it: Denise Nebb, Rosanne Murdock, Carol and Bill McConaghy, Carol Cepregi, Peter Johnson, Jim Frazer, Al Bagnoli, and Charlie Kurz. You'll all recognize your contributions when you see them; and I thank you very much, too.

—Donna H. Murray

Acknowledgments

V.I.P.S. (Very Important P.S.):

Originally I fantasized about giving every single person significant to my writing career their own book. Each dedication would be worded so perfectly that no one could fail to know how much I've appreciated their help.

However, even if my good luck should continue (never a safe assumption), the reality seems to be that I will never be able to write fast enough to acknowledge my growing list of benefactors—even if I were to leave off honoring my family and dearest friends, which certainly wouldn't do.

So herewith I formally thank my writing mentors, listed in the order I made their acquaintance.

Harold Brecht, who wrote successful literary fiction in the 1920s. Harold taught me much about characters, but most of all he was one.

Harriet Mae Savitz, leader of the women's writing workshop I attended for four years. Harriet endured my question-everything phase with humor and patience, and I highly value our friendship.

Barbara Bates, ''The only teacher I never questioned.'' Barbara gave me the great honor of graduating me to stay home and do my own work, a compliment I greatly prize, along with her continuing friendship.

Robert J. Randisi: Bob was the first person to welcome me into the world of professionals at just the time when acceptance—of any sort—was what I needed most.

And final thanks (for now) to my agent, Robert E. Tabian, for seeing something there, editing that shaky beginning, and launching me into this strange and wonderful business.

D.

ONE

"**Y**ou realize," I pretended to lecture my groggy husband, "your doctor only told you to read the sports section because it's so boring." Razzing my husband at breakfast was my way of reminding him that life wasn't just teenagers threatening suicide or teachers undergoing chemotherapy—the stuff of his days as head of Bryn Derwyn Academy.

"Box scores and statistics . . ." I continued to withhold the newspaper while pouring us more decaf, ". . . who got arrested for mouthing off at a night club. Bor-ing."

Rip's blood pressure had been up a little at his recent physical, and our doctor actually advised him to read the sports page more often. Since most wives would regard that as a boondoggle, the man had actually written a prescription. Naturally, I felt compelled to demonstrate that I wasn't most wives.

Rip ignored my ribbing and ate a piece of toasted waffle.

"There's another reason?" I inquired almost innocently. "Hormones in the ink?"

"You wish," responded my mate, finally grinning outright.

I slapped Monday's *Philadelphia Inquirer* onto his outstretched palm.

"Thank you, Gin," delivered with exaggerated gratitude.

"You're welcome," I replied.

1

After a moment, my husband inquired mildly, "Just out of curiosity, did you collect this from the driveway in that outfit?"

I glanced down at my pink bathrobe and duck slippers, which, I had reasoned, were much less revealing than a bathing suit. "Sure," I admitted.

Rip grunted something noncommittal, but his observation prompted me to reconsider my behavior, a habit I'd acquired a few years ago when Rip's job opportunity relocated us to this side of the Schuylkill River. Although our street was unusually casual for the area—which was the only reason we could afford it—Beech Tree Lane was still located squarely in the middle of Philadelphia's enviably upscale Main Line.

So maybe tomorrow I would wear an overcoat to run out for the paper.

Then again, who was around to care? Certainly not Letty MacNair, the zany recluse who lived to our left. Her whole wardrobe had improved tenfold when she discovered sweatsuits at Kmart. And nobody else could even see our drive through the assortment of unkempt bushes and trees that dominated the immediate landscape.

Still . . .

"From now on you go out and get your own paper," I concluded, rendering the bathrobe question moot.

"Doc said you wouldn't get it," my husband groused thoughtfully as he rattled the paper smooth and reached for his coffee.

"The paper?"

"The sports-page thing. I shouldn't have told you."

"Nonsense," I said. "Just because I think it's soap opera fodder drenched in testosterone doesn't mean—"

"Gin," he interrupted; and if I hadn't been so carried away, the change in his tone would have registered immediately.

"... that you can't read it to your ..."

"Gin!" Rip pulled me down onto the table's side bench. "Just listen a minute, will you?"

Down at eye level his hardened features and paled skin stunned me into silence.

"What?" I rasped through a clenched throat. Fear had swallowed me whole.

Rip turned the newspaper toward me. "TOMCATS' QUARTERBACK FOUND MURDERED" screamed the three-inch type, so naturally I assumed my cousin's husband was dead, and with her expecting, too, a multiple tragedy.

My lightened head lolled on my neck, revealing my mistaken conclusion to Rip.

"No, no," he said, patting my hand to secure my attention. "I thought that, too, but it's not Doug. Keep reading."

The subheading said "Tim Duffy Shot in Stadium Training Room."

I couldn't help it; I felt relieved. Michelle's husband was alive. His backup quarterback was the one who got shot.

Still, I couldn't shake the feeling that this tragedy skated perilously close to our family, and for that reason my eyes gobbled the printed word, absorbed the essentials in one gulp.

"After the Tomcats' 28–20 victory over the Houston Hombres, Tim Duffy apparently lingered in the training room to use the whirlpool ... body discovered by a security guard closing up ... police theorize that a crazed fan hid in the stadium ... no suspects as yet ... shocked the sports world ... great loss ..." blah, blah, blah.

A man was dead and they had nothing but frothy words and skeletal facts. And as usual, my ire kicked in when sympathy and grief might have been more appropriate.

Instinctively I fixated on the color photograph of the deceased football player.

Kneeling in the upper right-hand corner of the sports page, Tim Duffy held a blue-on-blue helmet under his arm and stared off into two-dimensional distance. A worldly shrewdness emanated from his shadowed eyes, plus a blatant ruthlessness most ambitious people were wise enough to hide. Otherwise he was just another extremely fit, brown-haired athlete who would never see his thirtieth birthday. Even his publicity shot was already obsolete.

My indignation segued easily into a weighty remorse.

"Too close," I murmured to Rip, who nodded that he agreed.

"What's up?" asked our thirteen-year-old daughter as she glanced uncomfortably between Rip and me. Narrow black slacks enhanced her lithe young figure and a yellow pullover highlighted the nutmeg-colored hair she had (for better or worse) inherited from me.

"Football player shot," Rip summarized.

Chelsea's onyx eyes widened as her eyebrows shot up and down, briefly curious why the event meant so much to her parents.

"Wow," Garry piped up, throwing his backpack on the floor at his sister's heels. Genetics had given him his dad's hazel/green eyes and dark, straight hair, but at eleven our son mostly remained an awkward, ingenuous child with occasional flashes of insight. At the moment he seemed amazed by the awful things adults did to each other.

"Who?" he asked his father.

Rip told him.

"Where'd it happen?"

"Training room in Nimitz Stadium," Rip answered, then reluctantly added, "Apparently he stayed late after yesterday's game to use the whirlpool."

"Wow," Garry repeated. "I wonder if Uncle Ronnie was there." Filming the game.

Michelle's brother, Ronnie Covington, was a cinematographer for NFL Films. We had been with him scarcely two weeks ago on Thanksgiving; and to hear Garry tell it, the day was the high point of his young life.

Chelsea's thoughts had taken another direction. "Premeditated?" she postulated as she sat down at her spot.

Rip raised an eyebrow and squirmed on his seat. "Not necessarily," he answered, clearly hoping to ease his daughter away from such unpleasant speculations.

I sympathized with Rip's desire to shelter our kids. As head of a small K–12 private school, the painfully human problems that crossed his desk on a daily basis were enough to make any father protective. Yet as a mother, I favored a more realistic approach. Information, I felt, served as a coping tool.

"Lots of people carry guns," Garry observed, as if it were the most natural thing in the world. "I bet with the big bucks those players earn, they really need 'em, too."

I wanted to dispute my son's logic; but unfortunately, he was probably right. Instead I went and collected waffles for him and put in some for his sister. Garry and Chelsea attended another private school, not Rip's, and their bus was due soon.

Gretsky, our young Irish setter, wandered in, observed us all with proprietary interest, and concluded that the situation called for a show of solidarity. He would eat breakfast with his pack. The dog's chewing sounded like footsteps across crushed rock.

The distraction gave Rip a chance to lighten up the conversation, and he chose to tell us about the entries he was judging in the contest for a school mascot. In Bryn Derwyn Academy's brief decade and a half of existence, nobody had bothered to name their sports teams. Rip thought the completion of a new gym offered the perfect opportunity to correct the oversight.

"What's in the running?" I asked.

Rip suspended a bit of waffle on its way to his mouth and consulted the ceiling. "Dorks, Druids, Banshees, Baby Elephants . . ." he replied as if seeking heavenly intervention.

"You're kidding," I insisted.

"Nope."

"What else?"

"Dragons, Deer, Dickenses, that by the chair of the English department, of course. The Doldrums, by the faculty at large."

It was that time of year, early December. Christmas vacation never came soon enough at a school.

"Whatever will you choose?"

Rip shrugged.

"Make one up yourself, Dad," Chelsea recommended.

"Wouldn't be kosher," he muttered, although we could see he was tempted to do exactly that.

Soon enough our kids hurried out to their bus, leaving Gretsky to spin out his frustration in the front hall.

Rip and I cleared dishes in a mutual mood of gloom. Then my husband, too, went to get his overcoat. All the while Gretsky stepped delicately around us, a comic parody of concern.

Rip grasped my shoulders and looked me in the eye. "The murder can't possibly have anything to do with Doug or Michelle," he said.

"I know."

He nodded as if he knew I would still worry, but he didn't know what else to say.

The phone rang.

"Hold on," I stalled my husband, reaching around the corner for the kitchen wall phone. At this hour it was probably for him, something related to the school, somebody out sick or with car trouble, something like that. Yet at home I usually buffered him from the occasional verbal ambush.

After a second, I waved that Rip could leave. His eyebrows rose inquiringly, so I covered the mouthpiece and said, "It's my cousin, Ronnie."

Rip groaned. Judging by the few times I functioned as, shall we say, "a concerned citizen," he has determined that I have an overdeveloped interest in police matters, an inclination that, as my husband, he would very much like to curb.

Understandably, a call from Ronnie immediately after reading about a football player's sensational death pushed all of Rip's protective buttons.

"No, no," I said hastily, intending to assure him that his first conclusion was wrong. "It's about Michelle. Something about the baby."

Rip solemnly nodded good-bye and mouthed that I should phone him at work. Then he closed the door tight behind him.

As I settled my backside onto the kitchen counter and the receiver against my ear, the Morton's salt slogan came to mind.

"When it rains, it pours."

It was beginning to sound like our family motto.

TWO

"Is the baby still okay?" I asked anxiously. Ronnie's sister, my cousin Michelle, had previously suffered at least one miscarriage and recurrences were always an unspoken fear.

"So far," he answered. "I think. But it's serious, Gin. Doug is really freaked out."

Growing up, Ronnie had always relentlessly called me Cuz, in spite of—or perhaps because of—my protests. His using my real name now underscored our new, totally adult relationship and emphasized the seriousness of his phone call. With that one-word change, Ronnie's fears for his sister and her baby raced along the wire and burned straight through to my bones.

After a needed breath, I softened my voice. "Exactly what happened?" I asked. "Do they know?"

"All I know is they're keeping her in the hospital a few days. Doug said when she gets out, she'll have to take it really easy."

"What's the prognosis?"

" 'Fraid I can't help you there, Cuz." Ronnie verbally shrugged off the question, tried to make light. A bachelor in his mid-thirties, he was unfamiliar with the grittier details of childbearing and seemed eager to keep it that way. Who could blame him? I've been through it all twice, and I run away screaming from any conversation that starts with "My labor lasted . . ."

"No problem," I said. "So what do you want me to do?"

Ronnie breathed easier. "You always could read me like a book," he said.

"Come on. Out with it," I urged. "You know I'll help if can."

"Glad you haven't changed. Didn't your dad call you Tink, or Tinker, or something because you were always trying to fix things?"

The memory physically hurt. "Briefly," I admitted. "Until some other kids picked up on it." And altered it to mock me—Tinkle Bell, Stinker . . .

"Yeah," he said, remembering. His sympathy came across the line now, giving me a pang. "Good old Tink. I knew I called the right cousin."

It came to me in a warm rush, the realization that I still loved Ronnie and Michelle. Neglect had simply obscured my link to them like a fine dust that time settles over a landscape. If we were to return looking for a familiar landmark, we would probably be disappointed. And most likely, to our loss, we would shrug and accept whatever was left.

Still, now and then somebody tries to resurrect the best of the past. Orchestrated by our Aunt Harriet, Thanksgiving had been such an experimental reunion. As an experience, the day was typically Siddons and therefore uniquely memorable. As a cure for time and distance, the effort probably came up short.

Now as this phone call dug farther and farther into family business, I found myself wishing I really was back in my cousins' lives, rekindling some of our former closeness.

Ronnie got to his point by way of the mulberry bush. "Michelle has friends down there; but it's still their first year in Norfolk, and she doesn't know anybody well enough to ask them to help out.

"And of course Doug's mother is way the hell out in California. Plus she works, and anyway she hasn't really come to grips with Coren's suicide." Yet another tragedy, but farther removed, having occurred on a thinner branch of the family tree. I didn't really know the details, and I certainly couldn't ask.

"It's much too early," I agreed. Two months to adjust to a daughter's death? I doubted that two lifetimes would be enough.

"And Harriet and Cynthia are . . ."

". . . are Harriet and Cynthia," I finished for him. My mother and her sister were endearing eccentrics who "meant well," as they say, and sometimes even did well. But no one would mistake them for practical women. Either one could be counted on to cause Michelle more work and anxiety, not less. Then, too, my mother didn't drive and Aunt Harriet shouldn't.

Obviously, as far as useful relatives on the Siddons side of the family went, that left me and Aunt Harriet's overachieving daughter, Gloria, who holds the World's Busiest Woman title hands down—just ask her.

I began to wonder exactly what I was talking myself into.

"So what do you want me to do, Ronnie? Go down there? Clean the house? Cook a little? What?" During the season did professional football players go home for dinner like regular people? And if so, what did they eat? Roast ox? A pig in a blanket?

"Sure, Gin. That would really be nice. I think just having somebody sensible around will really calm things down, and believe me, after that murder in the stadium, both of them need all the calming down they can get."

"I'll have to make a few arrangements for myself, but I can probably work something out."

"Great. Thanks . . . Cuz."

I laughed a little uncomfortably over the confession I was about to make.

"You know," I began, "the way you quizzed me on Thanksgiving . . . I thought for a second you wanted me to go down there and see what I could find out about the murder."

I laughed again at the folly of such a thought. Armies of police and lab technicians were already on the case. The media was no doubt poised to saturate the news with non-reports of the authorities' non-progress for weeks to come. Experts would be dining out on the lurid event for years. The more I thought about my ridiculous knee-jerk notion, the giddier I got.

Ronnie laughed a little, too, but not quite as heartily as I, so I forced myself to sober up. "All those questions you asked when you were showing us around your office. Must have gone to my head."

My adult self-image has never depended on how quickly my hors d'oeuvres disappeared, and Ronnie's zeroing in on where my pride really lived had brought memories of our childhood closeness into vivid focus. My cousin, the Smart Bomb.

Even still, it should have amused him that my subconscious had tried to volunteer me into what would probably be the most scrutinized murder investigation of the year. It certainly amused me.

"Sorry," I finally apologized into Ronnie's silence. "Tension. Once the cork's out."

"Don't worry about it," my cousin said with the magnanimity of a psychiatrist whose patient had just experienced an episode of inappropriate emotion.

Then he carefully added, "To tell the truth . . ."

"Oh, do tell the truth, Ronnie," I interrupted a bit snippily, all at once embarrassed and defensive.

"To tell the truth," Ronnie resumed, "you're not that far off."

Thunk. The sound of the other shoe falling. I waited for my lungs to reinflate, then I rattled off "Waitaminute, waitaminute, waitaminute" in my cousin's ear. "Back up. Are you saying what I think you're saying?"

"What do you think I'm saying?"

"That Doug and Michelle are more than marginally affected by the, the . . . shooting?"

"Go on . . ."

"I can't. That's as far as you've taken me, Ronnie. Dammit. You go on."

"I told you Michelle was in the hospital because of stress, didn't I?"

Had he? "No. I don't believe you mentioned that. No. I'm sure you did not."

"Well, she is."

"Stress over the murder?"

"Yes. No, not exactly. Well, maybe."

"Ronnie!" I yelled portentously.

"Okay," he said. "Okay. I guess I better explain." He paused to gather his breath. "They're both distressed about the murder, okay?"

"Did Doug have anything to do with it?"

Silence.

"Ronnie. I suggest you tell me absolutely everything you know. I will not, get that, *will not* go down to Norfolk to become an accessory after the fact."

"Whatever that is."

"Right."

"Doug didn't have anything to do with it."

"But . . ."

"But they're both afraid . . . Oh, hell, Gin. Tim Duffy and Doug have a history, okay? I'd rather let Michelle tell you about it. I can only give you the bottom line."

"By all means—go straight to the bottom line." My arms had crossed my chest like the steel bar on a warehouse door, something Ronnie could sense, if not see.

He sighed. "Michelle really is having trouble keeping the baby," he related with weighty resignation, "and she really doesn't need to be worrying about whether her husband might be a suspect in a murder. And Doug is *obviously* in the middle of his very crucial first season with the Tomcats, and he really can't afford to be worrying about his wife. So I figured you've been through more stuff like this than the rest of us, and maybe you could like, reassure them, or something."

"Pat their hands. Tell them not to worry. Stuff like that?" Sounded easy enough, unless Doug actually was a suspect.

"Precisely," my cousin agreed, relaxing audibly. "I gave Michelle the spiel for over an hour last night, and I'm telling you I was good. She should have bought it, Cuz. She should have been able to walk right out of that hospital. But all she said was, 'Nice try, Bro.' "

My own breathing felt a little constricted. "Oh," I said, needing to say something.

"Yeah, 'oh.' I've never been within a mile of a murder, and my sister knows it. But you have. We need you, Gin. If Michelle pushes the panic button one more time, it could be curtains for the baby."

Just what I needed, a life or death responsibility. The trouble was—how could I possibly say no?

"Does Doug have an alibi?"

"He was with Michelle."

I groaned.

"Gin?"

"Yes, Ronnie?"

"Will you go?"

"Yes, Ronnie. I'll go." God save us all.

THREE

Heaping household details on top of the myriad responsibilities Rip already carried would have been unrealistic, not to mention unkind. I phoned my mother.

"Gin, how nice to hear from you," she began as if my call had no other purpose. "I'm just waiting for Gracie."

"Who's Gracie, Mom?" Keeping track of Cynthia's friends was as pointless as it was impossible.

"You remember Gracie. My high school chum who lives in Montclair. Her Ralph died a few years ago, so we've been back in touch. She's coming down for a visit."

My hopes sank. "I guess that answers that," I muttered mostly to myself.

"Answers what, dear?"

"I'm going to Norfolk to help Michelle out for a little while. I was going to ask you to stay here while I'm gone."

"Oh," she exclaimed, "Oh!" as if my one sentence told her everything. "You're going down there to investigate why that terrible man was shot, aren't you?" It was not a question. Mother had made up her mind.

"No, Mom. Nothing like that. And I don't think Tim Duffy was necessarily a bad man."

Too late, I remembered that one grain of sand constituted a beach to Cynthia Struve. If she knew I knew the murdered man's name and something, however nebulous, about him, I must be on the case.

I tried reasoning with her anyway; I always try. "Actually, Mom, Michelle is in the hospital, some sort of scare over the baby—I'm sure Harriet must have told you—so Ronnie asked me to go down there to"—here I had to watch my words—"to cook for Doug and take care of Michelle when she comes home."

Mother's laugh was much less inhibited than the snickers Ronnie had endured from me only minutes before. She bent at the waist and let it go.

I waited long enough for her to find a tissue to wipe her eyes. "Everyone knows you don't cook, dear," she imparted between two last snorts. "You're marvelously intelligent and surprisingly good with a wrench, but"—she paused to giggle—"you can't possibly convince me Ronnie asked you to cook."

I scowled, but it wouldn't hold. "Make food, then," I amended. "Doug's in the middle of the football season, and I suppose he . . ." I couldn't help it. I laughed myself. ". . . eats a lot, and . . ."

"Oh, give it up, Gin," Mother advised.

"Okay, sure," I agreed. "I'm going down there to solve the murder of the year. You want to babysit my family while I'm busy making headlines?"

"Can Gracie stay over, too?"

"Sure. Bring Gracie," whoever she was. "Bring all your friends."

"Now you're just being silly."

Mother and I ironed out the particulars of pickup and delivery, then I rang off and went to work on the details of my own trip. Half an hour later I was booked on the U.S. Airways Monday flight to Norfolk, Virginia, departing 3:40 P.M., arriving 4:37 P.M. A shuttle service would take me directly to the hospital. Apparently, Michelle had driven herself in; so after my visit with her, I could use her car for the duration.

Rip listened to my plans with approval until I got to the Cynthia and Grace what's-er-name part.

"We could have managed," he almost whined. "The kids are okay on their own."

"For a week?" My guesstimate, and probably the longest I dared to stay away. "You're involved with that accreditation stuff, holed up in your office even when you're home . . ."

Periodically PAPAS, the Pennyslvania Association of Private Academic Schools, put the schools they accredit through an exhaustive self-evaluation and brief committee visit. The process was as hated by the faculty as it was essential and ultimately worthwhile. But probably more than anything it was time-consuming.

"Haven't been much fun lately, have I?"

"No complaints here. I just thought you didn't need to add laundry and dog dinners and TV monitoring to your chores."

"You're a wise woman, Gin Barnes."

"Sexy, too," I pointed out.

"So I've heard."

To prove how swamped he was, he delegated my ride to the airport. His assistant, Joanne Henry, whom I once affectionately dubbed "Hank," would drop me off then take the rest of the afternoon off. Joanne was also chronically overworked.

And, as it turned out, grouchy about it today. She threaded her Jetta in and out of the Route 476 traffic while delivering a monologue of complaints.

"Beepers and virtual pets going off in class, teachers never looking at their mailboxes, boys peeking in the girls' locker room, girls peeking in the boys'. And you know that's just the easy stuff." She wagged her head. "It's the evaluation process that's killing us—committee meetings every day. Why does it have to take all year to prepare for a three-day visit?" She clucked over the unfairness of it all.

"But that's only once every five years, right?"

Joanne grunted at my optimism and passed a Volvo.

I scanned the scenery: embankments of winter-gray grass, clumps of tidily arranged bushes on the median strip—presently devoid of leaves—and four to six lanes of cars, depending. "Didn't everybody start calling this the Blue Route because the original proposal for it was drawn in blue?"

Joanne ignored me and floored it up to seventy in the passing lane. Rip's most devoted soldier was footsore, which meant the rest of the army probably needed R and R at least as much or more. The last two weeks before Christmas vacation would be morale hell at Bryn Derwyn Academy. If I made it to the airport intact, I would be sure to warn Rip.

Meanwhile, to finish diffusing Joanne, I cheerily answered my own question. "I think that's right. If they had chosen one of the other possibilities we would be riding on the Red Route or the Yellow Route right now."

"Fascinating," Joanne groused. Her beige hair hadn't budged since we set out. Nor had the scowl lines behind her designer-framed glasses.

"Have a chardonnay for me," I suggested when I leaned down to thank her from the security of the Departures curb. "Have two."

She roused herself just in time to remember her manners. "Nice flight," she wished me.

I thanked her profusely, for she had performed two valuable services. One: She delivered me to the airport unscathed, and two: She almost made me glad I was going.

* * *

The plane rushed off the runway and sliced through a slab of stratus clouds into glaring winter sunlight. There was nothing to see, and I had no concentration for a book. I accepted a Sprite and an envelope of peanuts and stared out the window thinking about dominoes.

Hanging up a sweater you bump heads with a cute fraternity guy, and the next thing you know he's your husband. Or you chat up a single mom at your son's baseball game and suddenly find yourself in another car pool. Or your Aunt Harriet revives the traditional family Thanksgiving dinner, and ten days later your cousin Ronnie recruits you to help out in a crisis. Rows of dominoes tumbling down, one event touching off another.

Watching that bed of clouds move under me I imagined myself to be caught up in just such an accidental progression of events, one possibly begun even before the demise of my mother's oldest sibling.

For Thanksgiving had been Aunt June's holiday— the boiled onions, the oyster stuffing, the corny toasts with the sickening sweet sherry, and the kids prodded to come up with something they were thankful for each year. After June's death six years ago, we none of us could face Thanksgiving—not together—so each family faction had begged ourselves off in other directions until Harriet had wisely tugged on our consciences and gathered us in again.

None of us even considered turning her down this year, and all of us had been glad we went. Even later, after I found out fate's game was really tag, not dominoes, and I was "It," I still remembered the day with fondness, exactly as I viewed it gazing out the window of the plane.

The weather had been overcast this year, somber and contrary to our moods. My mother even got the kids to sing as we headed over the Delaware River and through the woods toward Aunt Harriet and Uncle Stan's modest Moorestown, New Jersey home.

We arrived about one, but in order to help Harriet in the kitchen, Gloria and her husband Bill had already vanned themselves and their two pre-schoolers to the elder Applestones' Robert's Park colonial. Perhaps because of Doug's need to fly back to Norfolk in the morning, Michelle and her quarterback husband were already there, too.

Even before we had time to breathe in the odor of roasting turkey, Chelsea got conscripted into babysitting the two pre-schoolers. The last anyone saw of her until dinner was her eye-roll of resignation. Garry recognized what was coming, peppered the air with, "Hi. Hi. Hi," and scooted under Harriet's arm toward the sound of a TV.

Hugs, kisses. Sniff. Detecting even a whiff of roasting turkey required a hearty intake of air and some imagination. I raised an eyebrow in Gloria's direction, and she moved me out of earshot to explain.

"Harriet forgot to turn the oven on. Dinner will be a little late."

"How late?" I ventured.

"Two, three hours, tops. Know any parlor games?"

"No," I insisted. The only such games I knew had been learned through great embarrassment and were not suitable for children.

Gloria tossed her head, which I noticed included a particularly pointy nose. "Well, you'll have to handle the living room. I've got more than my hands full in the kitchen."

Already my mother was gravitating in that direction arm-in-arm with her sister. Gloria rushed to intervene. Evidently she knew enough about her mother-in-law to know that Harriet's sister wouldn't be much better.

To my right lay a dungeon of mahogany and brocade that smelled of musty lemon oil when it wasn't busy not smelling of turkey. I checked for a window to open but noticed that all the heavy drapes had been drawn, the better to view the football game on TV. Rip had already hopped over a coffee table to claim a spot on the sofa next to Doug and Michelle. Doug rose to shake my hand hello.

"Don't get up," I hastily told my pregnant cousin, whose expression had begged me to say just that.

"Thanks," she sighed.

"Feeling okay?" I asked.

"Oh, sure," she lied.

Her brother Ronnie popped up from a chair to grin and greet me. His side of our mix-and-match family tended toward wavy medium-brown hair and darkly edged light hazel eyes framed with lush curly lashes. Much went on behind Ronnie's particular pair, which he had no qualms about revealing. "Cuz, you look great," he insisted with some amusement. "New haircut?"

I elbowed him in the ribs, reaching up to do it. "You know it isn't, turkey." I had been wearing an acorn-lid style since before my senior year.

"Chicken," he retorted.

"Can't wait to catch up."

"Why? It's obvious you haven't changed."

I threw him a look and turned toward the edge of the dining room where Garry had been skewered by Uncle Stan, Harriet's throwback of a husband. For company he had donned a Bing Crosby cardigan of blah blue. Even six feet away his aftershave lotion competed with the sour lemon oil that had been lavished on the furniture.

"Lookit this," Stan told my son with a twinkle in

his eye. Apparently, he had determined that Garry was just the right age to appreciate his dining-table humor, and he couldn't wait another second to start in. Garry tilted away from my uncle's shoulder while Stan pressed him to admire the reflection of his knuckles on the back of a stuffing spoon. While Garry squinted to see, Stan rubbed his index finger up and down.

"Dolly Parton taking a bath. Get it?"

Garry snorted. "That's totally wild," my son exaggerated politely. "Know any others?"

Meanwhile, Rip seemed to be chatting up Doug, I hoped without any intention of asking him to speak at the dedication of Bryn Derwyn's new gym in January. But role models were scarce, especially in my family.

"Doing anything January sixteenth?" I heard Rip inquire.

"I won't be getting ready for the Super Bowl, if that's what you mean."

Overhead I heard children running; but since they weren't running past the TV, nobody seemed to care.

I pushed through the swinging door into the kitchen, and the world tilted.

"Hello, darling," Mother cooed. "Want to stir the gravy?" She thrust a foil-lined envelope in my direction.

"Ack. No, no, no," Aunt Harriet yipped. "We've got enough cooks." Her hair, a bluer gray than my mother's, had been yanked into spikes of frustration.

I had an impression of pots and pans everywhere, filling the counters left and right, plus the table in between, cluttering even the floor in spots. A gray cat mewed and walked around one.

Gloria stood alone, a slender stalk trembling in the eye of the hurricane. "Harriet's right," she said with lawyerly composure, "we can manage here. Why

don't you just take some pretzels out to the guys.''
She handed me a bag of Bavarian jawbreakers and a
basket.

"Beer?'' I asked hopefully. It threatened to be a
long afternoon.

"I don't . . . Of course,'' she said, realizing her error. She extracted a six-pack of long-necked bottles
from the antique refrigerator and pushed it toward me.
Then she resumed chopping celery on a piece of
waxed paper. As I retreated I imagined her muttering
deliriously, "There's no place like home, there's no
place like home.'' I'm pretty sure it was only my
imagination.

Eventually halftime arrived. Even after a six-year
hiatus, most of the family was sitting mute as mush-
rooms in front of the TV. Stirring us up seemed to
be in order.

"Ronnie,'' I said reflectively, gesturing with my
beer bottle. Unlike Gloria, I did drink the stuff. "Isn't
NFL Films pretty near here?'' I asked hopefully.

"Sure. Ten minutes, give or take.''

"Could you stand to give some of us a tour?
Garry's taking a photography course . . .''

During the football season I knew Fridays and
Thanksgiving to be Ronnie's only guaranteed days
off. Asking him to go to the office today was quite
an imposition, yet it seemed preferable to sitting there
growing spores.

Ronnie called over his shoulder to Garry. "Hey,
kid. You wanna see my office?''

"Yeah!'' Garry almost purred with excitement. As
I said, he was seriously into photography.

"Anybody else?''

Doug accepted, and I very much wanted to go.
However, Stan and Rip preferred to stay to watch the
second half of the game, and Michelle had fallen
asleep against some pillows. Doug removed her

glasses and folded them on the end table before we left.

A voice coinciding with our airplane's touchdown rattled me out of my reverie. "Please remain seated until the plane has come to a complete stop in front of the terminal."

I peeked out the window at tarmac and low clouds. I had arrived in Norfolk.

Yippee.

Four

I liberated my lumpy carry-on bag from the overhead compartment, but it wrestled itself free from my grasp and fell heavily on the arm of an unoccupied seat. Eventually, working hard not to bruise anyone, I deplaned into a long hallway and skirted the usual metal detection station.

Glancing back I noticed a no-nonsense gray sign: NO MACE, NO GUNS, NO WEAPONS, NO JOKES. Another comparable rectangle alerted outgoing passengers to which (foreign) airports the secretary of transportation determined were not maintaining effective aviation security measures.

Along a relatively empty hallway a sign depicting Paul McCartney's smiling face welcomed me to ''. . . Norfolk, World Headquarters of People for the Ethical Treatment of Animals.'' A red six-sided sign that said ''Stop eating animals'' was positioned about where fans might have expected a guitar.

Farther along a picture of an elderly woman in need of a wheelchair scowled at me in black and white. To her right a hand filled out a United Way pledge card beneath the copy ''Fill in the blank . . . Generously.''

Apparently some ill-advised fool had chosen an exceptionally humane city in which to commit murder. I was glad I hadn't bopped anyone with my carry-on luggage.

The lobby was clean, more or less round, and dotted with strips of comfortable, dark-red chairs. At opposite edges the Check-in and Ticketing sign faced the Baggage Claim/Ground Transportation escalators.

Downstairs I collected my other bag and stepped out into the chill. A miniature brown building labeled "Airport Shuttle" resided in between the two driveways. Yes, a driver could take me to the Virginia Beach General Hospital. A limousine, really a white car wearing a rainbow-colored swath that read Groome Transportation, would leave within ten minutes.

Perhaps out of respect for my destination, the driver decided against small talk and entertained himself by drumming his fingers to the tune playing in his head.

At least initially Norfolk seemed to be a many-laned highway lined with low, boxy businesses, so I shut my eyes and daydreamed my way back to our Thanksgiving Day tour of NFL Films. Garry had viewed the place with such wide-eyed thrall that I began to wonder whether immortalizing football games might eventually become his profession. Exactly what, I reflected now, had so captivated my son?

For starters, I guessed probably Ronnie himself. Broad shoulders flexing as he steered his comfortable car, my cousin had appeared to be physically capable of playing the game he recorded on film. Indeed, he told Garry, Doug, and me that one or two of the other cinematographers had played professionally.

"It's very physical work," he remarked as he maneuvered his car to a stop behind a tidy stretch of landscaping. Rising prominently from the bushes was a white "National Football League NFL FILMS" sign complete with the NFL logo. The company was actually owned and operated by the league, which accounted for the use of the logo, also for the comfortable working relationship between them and the teams.

We were all standing in the parking lot huffing steam when Garry gave voice to his confusion. "What's so physical about it?" he asked, causing Ronnie to pause and turn back.

He rubbed his cold hands together then spread them wide. "I guess you've seen me rushing back and forth on the sideline with a camera on my shoulder?"

Garry nodded.

"Well, that camera weighs about thirty-five pounds," Ronnie told him. "But for every game I also have to move six metal cases of equipment in and out of vans, airports, hotels, and stadiums. The cases weigh forty to seventy-five pounds apiece. I've got a cart, but the cart weighs twenty-five pounds all by itself."

Doug contributed his own thought. "Then when you get back here you spend, what? ten, twelve hours a day putting it all together?" He clearly admired his brother-in-law's dedication to his craft.

Ronnie nodded modestly. "Right. So I can use all the stamina I can muster. Usually I lift weights. Tomorrow I'll probably run—especially if I eat what I think I'm going to eat tonight."

I remembered that Fridays were his only days off. Fridays and Thanksgiving.

"I'm really sorry to bring you back here today," I apologized, finally realizing the magnitude of what I had asked.

"I can stand it if you can." He winked at me then headed toward the largest of the two low, pale-brick buildings belonging to the company.

"Do you really have to go to all that trouble?" my son inquired. He hated carrying so much as a book bag.

"We think so," Ronnie answered, casting me a conspirator's smile.

Clearly my eleven-year-old son hadn't given the mechanics of sports coverage a second's thought until that minute, but now that he was here he desperately wanted to find his own path into that world. Fortunately, Ronnie recognized the genuine interest in Garry's perky posture and flashing eyes, and he took each of the boy's questions seriously. Otherwise the kid might have become as annoying as a woodpecker.

"Why?" he asked for the first, but certainly not last, time that afternoon.

"Because we're the historians of professional football," my cousin patiently explained. "Twenty, thirty years from now people will be able to pull out a tape and watch the Miracle in the Meadowlands, or the Immaculate Reception, maybe some Joe Namath or Brett Favre. Pretty wonderful stuff."

Doug shook his head to disagree. "It's a little more than that," he chided his brother-in-law. "You make us look great, man. Larger than life. It's an art form. Admit it."

Ronnie's cheeks pinked up. He pretended that the building's security system required all his concentration.

Doug shrugged off Ronnie's discomfort and finished lecturing me. "To football, they're Ernest Hemingway and Vincent van Gogh all rolled up. They only do highlight films, not TV coverage or print or anything else, and they're the best. You can see ten seconds of an NFL Films' product and know it's their work. Hell, you can *hear* ten seconds . . ."

I smiled my undivided attention, although my cousin-in-law wasn't telling me anything new. Even when Ronnie first landed the job, I understood that he would be turning admiration into art, effectively creating the polar opposite of the commercial hype I hated. Probably neither of us would ever say so, but I think Ronnie's work bridged the years for us, provided an adult basis for some of the rapport we shared as kids.

In an effort to mitigate Ronnie's embarrassment I remarked, "Our politicians should be so lucky," meaning that the American inclination was to lionize entertainers and revile anyone in authority. Childish, really. And also very human.

Since such sentiments didn't really fit into casual conversation, Doug got the short version. He also got the point.

"Yes," he agreed with a slight squint.

"Moving right along . . ." Ronnie squirmed. He ushered us into a short narrow hallway and launched right into his spiel.

"Here's where we drop off our cans of film when we first come back." He gestured toward a shoulder-high section of gray cubbyholes, each marked with the upcoming Sunday's games written on strips of masking tape.

"Cans of film?" Garry asked. "Don't you use videotape?"

"Nope," Ronnie replied. "Videotape looks too harsh, too realistic."

"So?" Garry pressed.

"We're after a softer, more polished effect. True, film is more expensive, more perishable, and less convenient, but we think it's worth it."

"It's a very distinctive look," Doug agreed.

Garry's expression was dubious, pure Iowa, and Ronnie laughed as he led us toward the film processing lab, a darkroom with little to see, but apparently the largest of its kind.

Adjacent to the lab stood some high metal cabinets with glass doors used for drying. Inside, the 16 mm film would be threaded up and down like yarn on a loom. At this point a working print would also be made from the negatives.

Around a corner Ronnie showed us a boxy apparatus with reels. The whole area smelled strongly of chemicals, and my cousin wrinkled his nose with just as much distaste as the rest of us. "Nasty stuff," he remarked. "Every time film is handled, it has to be cleaned."

The editor's room we peeked into had plenty of desk space lining the walls, tall, slatted windows and a few posts with strips of film dangling down. A couple of comfortable chairs and a coffee mug that said "World's Greatest Dad" personalized the place.

The long room outside the storage vault for negatives offered only a slightly more feminine ambience—a candy dish near the phone, and a pink sweater hung on the back of a chair. On the long shelflike desk were what appeared to be winding machines and stacks of flat gray film cans labeled in pastels. Signed pinup posters of male athletes adorned the corkboard on the wall. Ronnie poked irritably at a keypad on the wall at the end of the room. "This door stands open all day, so I don't usually have to deal with the daily password."

"Turkey?" Doug suggested almost innocently.

Ronnie cast his brother-in-law a playful scowl, then brightened. "Got it," he retorted as the door buzzed us in.

He reached around to turn on the light and stood back to let us enter.

"Wow!" Garry breathed. A tall, long room not quite big enough for basketball lay before us. Left and right, floor to ceiling it contained blue metal shelving nearly full of fifteen-inch red, silver and blue cans of film. Miniaturized, it would have looked like poker chips on scaffolding built from an erector set. This time a milder chemical odor permeated the air.

"These are all negatives, everything we shot of every game," he said. "All carefully labeled and pretty easy to find. Only the older stuff, the silver nitrate film, is stored in an old church somewhere."

"Why?" asked my son, the nudge.

"Flammable."

Garry mouthed an O.

"We have the first football game ever filmed, too," Ronnie boasted. "Rutgers versus Princeton. Filmed in 1895 by Thomas Edison himself."

"Who won?" Doug inquired.

"No idea," Ronnie replied.

The quarterback's forehead creased with disapproval. Football should be all winning and losing; any other perspective missed the point. Neither Ronnie nor I bothered to argue with him.

"Shortcut," my cousin confided, leading us through a side door into another lengthy hall illuminated by safety lights. White paint glowed warmly along most of the way, but in the middle, horizontal strips of decorative wood literally sparkled with gold statuettes reposing on individual shelves.

"Here we've got the Emmy wall, the reception area, and the executive offices," Ronnie remarked.

Garry's eyes bulged at the sight of dozens of Emmys, each pair of slender arms holding an open globe aloft.

"How many?" Garry inquired, and we all knew what he meant.

"Sixty-nine the last I checked."

"And counting," Doug added.

"Any of them yours?" my son asked my cousin.

"Garry!" I scolded.

"Two," Ronnie replied proudly. "Want to see which ones?"

The two new soulmates shambled off around a corner, leaving me standing awkwardly with Doug. I took the opportunity to ask how Michelle was doing with her pregnancy.

"Pretty good," her husband answered, "all things considered. She hasn't had it easy."

As a quarterback, Doug was permitted to buck the trend and have a neck and an ordinary hairstyle. Aside from his size, the only thing intimidating about him was the intelligence in his eyes. Yet at my mention of his wife, those ice-water orbs softened into blueberry gelatin.

"When's she due?"

"Ten weeks, give or take a couple weeks." His worry lines told me he feared she wouldn't last that long. Superstitiously, I refrained from asking more.

Doug threw out a verbal lifeline. "Hard to get into that school Rip runs?"

"Not for relatives," I smiled, appreciating his perceptiveness. To return the gesture we would send an application with their baby present, which Michelle and Doug would glance over then throw away. We were each of us just being human, trying to draw together socially.

When Garry and Ronnie returned, we walked through the Tele-Cine #1 room, a curved bank of monitors with a computer keyboard and a big batch of slide switches. Here the film's colors would be enhanced and the edited work print transferred to video tape.

"Hey, Gin," Ronnie whispered as he showed us out the opposite door. "Didn't you sort of solve a murder a month or two ago?"

I stared at him, caught by surprise, wondering how he knew. Then all at once I caught on. Ronnie was a relative, therefore Cynthia had access to him. My mother, The Mouth, had been bragging about me again.

Hoping to head off any mention of certain sleuthing activities I preferred to keep to myself, I answered, "Not exactly."

"But . . ." Ronnie sputtered. "That dog bite thing. I thought . . ."

"No," I lied with conviction. "That wasn't me."

Ronnie scratched behind his ear, causing a clump of medium brown hair to poke out like a hook.

We had arrived outside the room where Ronnie told us the 'lower thirds' were added. "That's the graphics showing the name of a speaker, or the score . . ."

"Next to the picture of the helmets?" Garry was indeed tuned in, absorbing like a high-priced paper towel.

"You didn't . . . ?" my cousin quizzed me out of the side of his mouth.

"No." I had solved the crime, of course, but denial seemed the most expedient way of undoing my mother's damage. If Cynthia had her way, I'd be up on a shelf holding the world in my hands like one of those Emmys.

Ronnie gave an exasperated little sigh and waved his hand at a roomful of NASA-like switches. "We use several different tracks of sound—dialogue, ambient sound, music, narration, sound effects, and so on; and we fade each one in and out however we want."

"You tape the sound separately?" Doug inquired.

"Yes. The camera only has film in it. The soundman carries a DAT—digital audio tape—machine, and I'm sure you've noticed the boom mikes—the fuzzy ones on long poles. Also, we occasionally wire coaches and certain players. That's how we get the calls on the field, the sound of the hits," he turned toward Doug, "things you guys say to each other on the sidelines. Neat stuff."

We came to the end of a hall. "Here's one of the

places we mix the sound . . . using machines from the CMR,'' Ronnie told us, opening yet another door.

CMR stood for Central Machine Room, which was a long rectangle with both side walls filled with boxes with buttons and monitors and wires. ''This is where the final edits really bring the shows together.'' Technicians also worked there with outside customers who were getting ads done.

''What about the Philadelphia Flower Show?'' Ronnie quizzed me while Garry ran his finger along a chest-high table. ''I suppose you had nothing to do with that?''

We both knew he was alluding to the death of my mother's friend, Iffy Bigelow, but the way he phrased his question allowed me to say, ''I had nothing to do with that.'' Of course, I referred to the operation of the show, not the arrest of Iffy's murderer.

Ronnie scrunched up his nose and squinted his eyes. ''You're bullshitting me,'' he whispered, visually checking that Garry wasn't near enough to hear.

''Moi?'' I said with a dainty blink.

My cousin sent me a have-it-your-way glance and knocked his knuckles against a door marked ''Engineering.''

''We repair our own video equipment,'' said Ronnie the Guide. ''In fact we have shops to fix anything we use. Even a wood shop to build sets for our studio.''

We also passed a few rooms containing AVIDs, machines that allowed film editors to cut and paste by way of computer commands. ''Word processing for film,'' Ronnie called it. ''Greatest thing since football.''

After we made our way upstairs, Ronnie opened yet another cubicle marked ''MIDI Room.'' Naturally, Garry asked what that meant.

''Named after the computer program our composers use to write music.'' Inside was a conglomeration of stereo equipment and an abbreviated music keyboard.

''You have your own composers?''

''Sure. Why not?''

Nearby was the TOC, or Transmission Operations Center, where numerous transmissions were received throughout the week and finished videos were sent to the league and networks as needed.

''Garry . . .'' Ronnie shepherded my son aside. ''This part is pretty amazing,'' and he began to explain about the eight fiber optic lines and three satellite dishes used for viewing all the Sunday NFL games as they occurred. Hired TV watchers Ronnie referred to as ''kids'' apparently sat across the front row of a modest-sized theater, each with his own TV.

''It's their job to log the highlights as they happen—okay?''

Garry nodded.

''Then all their selections are edited into a one-minute highlight package, which we transmit right back for showing inside the stadiums.''

''Wow!'' Garry exclaimed, his eyes widening with awe.

At other times the theater would be used to screen the finished products, such as the 35 mm film of the latest Super Bowl to be shown in the Football Hall of Fame.

Ronnie hung back in the doorway. ''Seriously, Gin,'' he whispered. ''You can tell me.''

I glanced pointedly toward my son. ''Not now I can't.''

''Oh. Gotcha. Little pitchers have big ears.''

''What if the electricity goes out?'' the little pitcher piped up.

''We have an uninterrupted power supply, a UPS,'' Ronnie answered patiently.

"What about if it rains or snows real bad on game day?"

"We live for bad weather."

"Why?"

"Because that's when we get our best stuff, like icicles on the goalposts, steam coming off a bald head, or maybe rain pouring down the stadium steps like a waterfall." Visual stories, the pictures that were worth a thousand words.

"You ever get sued for filming somebody who didn't want to be filmed?" I wondered aloud.

Doug emitted a burst of laughter and Ronnie smiled back at him.

"What?" I asked, annoyed that I didn't get the joke.

"Every move we make on the field is fair game," Doug told me. "It's in our contract."

Ronnie nodded. "Even if you scratch your . . . ear."

Doug conceded graciously. "You saw that, did you?"

"Sure. I'm saving it for your personal retrospective. 'Doug Turner's Best Moves.' "

We saw another bar-coded video library used by producers putting together outside projects.

The master vault where several wide white metal shelves stood tightly together like movable walls with but one adjustable gap large enough for a man to walk through.

Ronnie told Garry, "Try turning that." He referred to the shiny black handle protruding from a ten-inch white wheel at the end of the shelf right in front of us.

Garry prepared himself to set to. To his astonishment, the shelf unit, perhaps twenty feet long and loaded with tapes, moved with ease. "Wow!" he exclaimed again.

"One pound of pressure can move nine hundred

pounds of weight,'' my cousin informed us.

Another room stored and duplicated the audio tapes for each game.

Back downstairs we saw the Green Room, which was merely a lounge for the visiting ''talent''—the host and guests from NFL Films' three regular weekly shows during the season, or celebrities there for the industrial or rock videos that were the mainstay of the company during the off season.

Ronnie named a few of the current hit bands he had worked with personally, and Garry's eyes took over his whole face. ''Wait till I tell Chelsea. She'll go bonkers.''

''What's with Elvis?'' I finally asked. The Green Room and its two dressing rooms had been decorated with collages of Elvis Presley photos, as had many of the hallways.

''Steve Sabol,'' my cousin answered. ''His father was founder of the company, and he runs it now. Steve's the big Elvis fan.''

''Why?'' Garry again.

Ronnie shrugged. ''Elvis's favorite sport was football.''

Garry left it at that, but my own imagination connected the dots.

Elvis had possessed an astonishing charisma. He was, and continues to be, a larger-than-life phenomenon. There would never be another icon of popular culture like him. But, I realized, the same could be said of Jim Brown or Walter Peyton. Looking closely at one of the oval decoupaged tributes to Elvis, I realized that it illustrated the wonderfully personal connection between pro football and NFL Films perhaps better than anything else I had yet seen.

Farther along the hallway an in-house 1950s-style diner featuring plenty of chrome over black and white tile advanced the theme.

"Breakfast, lunch, and dinner on Sundays. Breakfast and lunch Mondays, of course. Dinner Tuesdays and Thursdays. We've got beds and lockers available here, too."

Plus their own travel agency and a shipping department that handled five hundred packages a day.

"Overwhelming," I decided.

"Want to see my building?" Ronnie asked.

"There's more?"

We toured Ronnie's video domain politely, but I was on technical overload. Only Garry remained jazzed and wide-eyed.

When Doug's stomach growled audibly, he asked whether Ronnie had caught the noise on tape.

Soon afterward we piled back into Ronnie's Audi and returned to Aunt Harriet's, all of us weary from hunger.

Before we went inside Garry pulled me aside. "I'm going to try it, Mom," he announced earnestly.

"What?" I asked.

"I'm going to film the ultimate Frisbee game they do Sunday mornings at Bryn Derwyn. What do you think?"

"Go for it," I said. The puzzle of what my son would grow up to be would remain unanswered for another decade or more, but this made for a most interesting start.

The inside of Aunt Harriet's house finally passed the sniff test. Turkey and jokes and old family stories would soon circulate around the table.

And later, over coffee in the kitchen, I would tell Ronnie whatever he wanted to know.

"Everybody out," the limousine driver joked, for I was the only passenger he had. Glancing out the window I noticed a bas-relief blue cross next to the words "Virginia Beach General Hospital" on the portico of the building's main entrance. Reading signs usually centered and reassured me, but this trip was too sudden and unexpected. For a second I couldn't believe what I read.

My driver helped me to the curb with my luggage and accepted his fee and a tip with a grunt. I let out a plume of cold breath as the building's doors slid aside for me to enter.

Like all hospitals, the lobby ambience projected a cool sterility. And as usual, I felt as if I were defiling a private sanctuary that welcomed only health care professionals and their patients.

I hefted my travel gear over to the information desk and asked the receptionist the easy question: Where would I find my cousin Michelle?

The answer to the difficult one—what I was really doing there—I would have to work out for myself.

FIVE

Michelle wore a pale-blue hospital gown and a lavender cable-knit cardigan. A stiff white sheet and a flannel blanket covered her bulging lap. When I stepped into her private hospital room, she set her paperback aside and pushed her glasses back in place.

"Gin!" she greeted me with weary cheerfulness. "Pardon me if I don't get up." I noticed then that she was attached to a monitor.

"How you feelin'?" I asked.

"Scared shitless. How about you?"

"Not bad," I replied neutrally. "Actually I'm hungry."

"I'd offer you something, but . . ."

"But you're already eating for two."

A tear slipped down her cheek.

"Hey," I said, sliding my rump onto the bed beside her and stroking her arm with my hand. "Kewpie's going to be fine. So are you." Doug had jokingly named their unborn baby QB, for quarterback, which was his position with the Tomcats. Michelle teased him by slurring the name into Kewpie, as in Kewpie Doll, to remind him the child could also be a girl. My use of her pet name made her laugh, but not for long.

"What does your doctor say?" I asked.

Michelle shrugged. "I'm stabilized now, but, but he's making me stay another day or so just in case.

He thinks I do too much when I'm home.''

"Do you?"

Another shrug. "I never thought so."

With hospital beds costing so dearly these days, my guess was that Michelle's doctor worried about another emergency, enough to keep her near medical help until he believed her crisis to be past.

Yet, if there was any truth to his excuse about her overdoing it, he had provided me with plenty of reason to be there. If I could relieve Michelle in any way that would help her carry the baby longer, my trip would be eminently worthwhile. From my own experience and female common knowledge, I realized that every day a premature birth could be delayed increased the chances of the child's survival and decreased the possibility of any number of frightening complications.

Yet when Ronnie phoned, he had pitched me with other, more pointed arguments. "They need you, Gin," said he. "You're exactly the person for the job. Nobody else in the family has done what you've done."

"I'm sorry, Gin," Michelle protested now. "You have enough to do without coming down here. Ronnie . . ."

"Ronnie knew if he told me what was going on, I wouldn't want to be anywhere else. Besides, you and I just started catching up on Thanksgiving, and now we can do it right."

Ronnie and I had been the tight ones when we were young. Born when we were eight, Michelle was ten when we were eighteen, a staggering difference back then and the reason I didn't know her well. My loss, I realized, a sentiment that she discerned with a flattered smile.

She had a marvelously expressive face, one that invited you to join her every emotion. On Thanksgiving I had noticed Doug flicking his eyes toward her every so often, like someone habitually touching a new wedding ring to make certain it was still there. I realized now he probably had been monitoring how she felt and taking his cue from her.

Deliberately choosing a harmless conversational path, I referred to our Thanksgiving dinner gossip. "I couldn't believe you never heard some of those family stories."

"Grandpop Siddons!" Michelle widened her eyes and nodded. An advance man for the circus, the Siddons' storybook contained many of the old man's escapades. A favorite was that he threw his uncomfortable false teeth into the Grand Canyon and never wore teeth again.

"And Fanny Topliss," I reflected. "That was the first I heard about her." About 8 P.M., nearly sated with dry turkey and wet stuffing, we lingered over our cold, store-bought mince pie listening to my mother. The best of the tales was about a widowed aunt named Fanny Topliss, who lived next to her brother and loved to tease him about his pipe. One day when Fanny was hanging bedclothes out a window, she caught a whiff of tobacco smoke and shouted, "I smell a man!" in a booming voice. By the time she got downstairs all she could see were the heels of a door-to-door salesman sprinting down the road.

"Fanny Topliss," I mused. "You can't make up a name like that."

Michelle turned toward the window, toward the low, tree-softened landscape outside, and I realized that all roads, however rocky or soft, led back to her primary concern. We were talking family, the genesis of life, about the people who took you in when you were down and out, the ones who ran when you called. Even the most friendless mass murderers had relatives, mothers who cared.

"The baby isn't all you're worried about," I stated gently.

Michelle waved her head back and forth. Her long fluffy pale-brown hair touched her cheeks, and she pushed it back with both hands. Then she left the hands behind her head, turned her elbows in protectively.

I waited until she lowered her arms. She eyed the corkboard with its two get-well cards, slid her gaze out the window and back to me.

"I know Doug didn't do anything wrong," I assured her, hoping that was what she needed to hear.

She drew in a ragged breath, smoothed a hand across her abdomen, her baby. When she spoke, she nearly whispered, forcing me to strain forward to hear.

"Innocence isn't always the best defense," she said.

"No," I had to agree.

Our eyes met and made their assessments, their pronouncements. Respect, trust, and affection were exchanged in that moment. Certainly there was more to be said, but the start was right; and if the start was right, usually the rest would come.

"I think Doug's going to be a suspect," Michelle confided, finishing off any hope for getting by with platitudes and hand patting.

I nodded with resignation. "Ronnie thought you might be worried about that. Did something happen during the game?"

"No."

"Before then?"

Michelle looked away. Her lower lip trembled. "I think it had something to do with Coren."

That raised the hairs on the back of my neck.

Doug's sister, Coren, was the one who had very recently committed suicide. Although I couldn't guess at any connection between Coren and Tim Duffy, I didn't like the timing. Not one bit. Especially since Doug's only alibi was Michelle.

"Do you want to tell me about that?"

"I'm not sure I know the whole story. Maybe you better ask Doug."

She lolled her head back on the pillow. Beside her a jagged white line zigzagged across a blue screen. The screen faced the door to the hallway, sheltering her from the second-to-second ups and downs of her physical existence—and her child's.

She had given me a difficult task, pressing a near stranger for details about his motive for murder, but if I was to honor Ronnie's request and relieve Michelle's mind, I needed information about the source of her stress.

Michelle suddenly seemed exhausted, and I did pat her hand. My pass into the hospital world had nearly expired anyway.

"So what does a professional football player eat for dinner?" I asked.

My cousin's eyes widened. "Oh. Oh, my. Doug eats everything you put in front of him."

"Lucky for me."

She appreciated the joke. Apparently my culinary reputation had preceded me to Virginia. "But I'm afraid there isn't much in the house to eat. I was on my way to the grocery store when . . ."

She lifted the arm with the wire attached.

"No problem. Just give me your car keys and directions, and I'm outta here."

Before I left, the mother-to-be became wistful. "Thanks," she said. "Ronnie said you would take care of everything."

I wanted to demur, but Michelle was the most relaxed she had been since I arrived. Wow, I thought. Mission accomplished. Can I go home now?

Of course that was just a little mental jitter, natural considering the tasks ahead. I had never tried to feed a football player before. Neither had I tried to solve a crime of national interest.

"Life is one obstacle after another," Dad liked to remark, often with a lug wrench in his hand. "Just take 'em one at a time, and you'll be fine."

With that comforting thought I concentrated on finding Michelle's red Jeep Grand Cherokee in the hospital parking lot. Small successes build confidence. Any educator's wife could tell you that.

SIX

The early winter night had closed in well before my arrival in the Broad Bay Point Greens section of Virginia Beach. Still, the Jeep's headlights reflected off a couple of low white cart crossing signs advertising the proximity of a golf course. Lawns appeared to be a crazy quilt of brown or some hardy grass that survived frost in this moderate climate. The trees and shrubs I could pick out in the dark offered a settled-in appearance, although the tree heights suggested that this residential area was little more than a decade old.

Doug and Michelle's house offered an individuality of its own, as did each custom-built neighbor; but the preferred appearance was shuttered brick colonial. I parked in my cousin's drive and awkwardly wheeled my belongings up a bumpy brick walk to the white front door, attractively adorned with a leaded window of frosted glass and two matching apertures to the left and right.

Inside I rushed to punch off the security system using the code Michelle had provided. Only then did I stop to catch my breath in the cold artificial light of the center hall.

By now I was light-headed with hunger, so I abandoned my luggage at the bottom of the stairs and rushed the hot food I had picked up into the kitchen. Blessing both Michelle and the anonymous cooks at

Harris Teeter, the grocery store she had recommended, I tucked into some gourmet fried chicken and cole slaw. I also zapped a baking potato for myself. After I washed up both me and the kitchen, I finally felt ready to examine my surroundings.

The Turner home was spacious, tidy and dotted with the empty spaces of a couple who had recently moved in. The formal, oyster-white and pale-blue living room, for example, contained a sofa, two end tables, one coffee table, and one lamp—period. The dining room needed a sideboard or hutch or something. But everything around had been tastefully chosen. My guess was that the relative newlyweds were currently too preoccupied with the football season and Michelle's pregnancy to put too high a priority on furnishings.

"Whatever you bring into your house will soon become home, and you'll never get rid of it," Grandmom Siddons had cautioned me. Today if you sat Doug and Michelle's place next to mine, anybody's grandma could see who had caved in to expedience and who was holding out for the good stuff.

The most completed spot, the family room off the opposite end of the kitchen, lured me in. Full of pine bookshelves and sturdy, comfortable seating, a braided wool rug in brighter colors than my own warmed the space. Prominently situated for viewing was a huge TV and VCR unit with a stack of tapes on the nearest shelf.

Notably absent were any trophies, game balls, or plaques that most athletes of note would display prominently somewhere in their homes. I knew Doug had earned his share, but either he was averse to such preening or he disapproved of living in the past. Refreshing either way.

Even the small home office in the back of the house held only the modern necessities: a computer on a small desk unit, a file cabinet, and a chair.

As it was already well into the evening visiting hours at the hospital, I surmised that Doug had gone directly there. He probably didn't even know I had arrived, and I supposed that Michelle would tell him I was here.

Meanwhile, it seemed that I had nothing to do but amuse myself, so I watched a sitcom until it was time for Monday night football. Yet the television soon faded into background noise. I just didn't have the concentration for it.

I was drawn instead to the pile of newspapers on one of the family room bookshelves. This morning's *Virginian Pilot* offered the local scoop on Tim Duffy's murder, so I microwaved a cup of Earl Grey tea and settled into a cushy chair for a crash course in the Turner household problem.

The information I gleaned was interesting in its sparsity. Tim Duffy had been shot in the whirlpool of the stadium training room soon after the Tomcat's victory over the Houston Hombres. Time of death: between 5:30 and 6:30 P.M., on infamous December 7.

The assumption being forwarded by the Tomcats' spokesperson and seconded by the police was that an enraged fan hid in the stadium until an opportunity arose for him or her to ambush Tim when he was alone.

How that person knew he would be alone was a question that interested me, but not overly much. Since the ambush had obviously succeeded, either the murderer was lucky or patient or knew Tim's habits—it didn't matter much which.

Unfortunately, the police would need even better luck than the assailant. With no eyewitnesses and enough traffic around the crime scene to occupy a forensic team for a month, I couldn't imagine how the law enforcement officials would pin this one on anybody. As so often happened, I suspected they would have to match the case to the evidence after the killer was identified some other way—some clever, creative way.

My curiosity twitched. A large batch of very high profile people were about to be examined under a lens roughly the intensity of the Hubble telescope; and since they were by nature just as human as the rest of us, it seemed likely that very few of them would stand up to the scrutiny. Too bad. Pedestals were pretty hard to climb and damned easy to knock over.

Yet at least initially a fragile grace period would reign while the PR people held back and the police painstakingly garnered their facts.

Perhaps if I could get Doug to confide in me, I could use that same grace period to steer the media mob away from his pedestal. Although I had serious doubts about my chances for success, any efforts I made toward diverting suspicion away from him would surely ease Michelle's mind and possibly help protect their unborn child.

Then, too, I was Cynthia's daughter and a mother myself, like it or lump it. I desperately wanted to help Michelle and Doug through this crisis. As Ronnie correctly surmised, there was nothing anywhere near as important on my slate right now.

Doug's arrival home coincided with the Steelers picking up a Dallas fumble. I stood to greet my cousin's famous husband.

"Gin," he welcomed me while TV announcers rhapsodized in the background. "Nice of you to come."

Filling the hall doorway, jacket hooked over his shoulder, the man impressed me yet again with his Nordic virility, assertive jaw, and just plain hunky charm. Inevitably, there would be swarms of female fans. I wondered whether Michelle ever worried about that.

"Glad to be here," I murmured, but the ebullience behind me momentarily drew me away. I looked back at Doug just in time to catch his wistful reaction to seeing one of his professional opponents score.

The point after was good and the TV immediately broke for a truck commercial, some musical blast with a country-western twang.

"Anyway," I continued, "Ronnie knows how disappointed I am with the Eagles this year, so he thought I should to come down and see a real team."

"Like hell," my host responded to my joke, for the Eagles were on fire and the Tomcats had been tightrope-walking the 500 mark all season.

We continued to smile at each other from a comfortable distance, avoiding the social hug and kiss. We weren't really very well acquainted, and neither were we blood relatives. Plus we were alone in his house. Soon our awkwardness would probably ease into friendship, but we hadn't quite arrived there yet.

"How you doing?" I asked.

In answer he tossed his jacket on a chair and walked over to a bar unit that was part of the bookshelves. "Want something?" he offered.

I shook my head no and sat down again.

Despite the December temperatures, Doug wore casual slacks and a golf shirt. His arms looked much less muttony than a lineman or a tackle, limber and strong, not freaky huge, just in proportion with his big strong frame. The hands getting ice from the miniature freezer, pouring amber fluid from a bottle, seemed nimble and sure. He could have been the same fit college guy he had been so recently, except for his face. His face had aged a decade.

"Michelle had another scare," he told me.

"Oh, no," I gasped.

"It's over. I think. Hell, who knows? But she was okay half an hour ago, and everybody insisted that I come home—doctors, nurses, Michelle—everybody." He looked at his drink and waved his head. "Like they were more concerned with taking care of me than taking care of Michelle and the baby." He scowled at the drink as if it was the whole cockeyed world, then he tossed it down and poured another.

My eyebrows straightened with surprise and mild disapproval. Surely athletes didn't drink during the season. Did they?

Of course they did if they wanted to, just as they came home for dinner and shopped for clothes and played with their dogs. I hastened to remind myself that my father had coached a high school team roughly twenty years before, so many of my inherited preconceptions were bound to be naive and out of date.

Doug lowered himself into the other TV chair, and his eyes scanned the game in the same meaningless, habitual way I always read cereal boxes or warranties or anything in print that fell before my eyes. I pushed the mute button, and my host didn't even blink.

"She's beautiful now, don't you think?" Doug reflected. My presence here underscored Michelle's absence and mandated that we speak almost exclusively about her.

"Yes," I agreed, although nearly all I knew of Michelle at this age was that she looked lovely when she slept, and she had expensive taste in furniture. Consequently, I readily adopted Doug's impressions as my own.

"You met at a party?" I prompted.

"Yeah, Ronnie brought her. I swear when I looked at her my heart stopped." The way clichés rolled off his tongue I surmised that he had not been an English major at the University of Michigan.

"She's the best, Gin," he mused. "I don't know what I'd do without her." Evidently, he would not grab the first groupie he tripped over. I began to like the guy.

"You do seem perfect together," I observed.

"Oh, yeah. She's patient, kind, gentle. She's going to be a fantastic mother. But you know all that." I did now.

"Opposites attract," I teased, and Doug chuckled with me.

Yet, as always, there was truth within the joke. Doug's profession was so stereotypically masculine, he probably needed Michelle's old-fashioned femininity for balance.

"She's worried about you," I hinted, hoping his confidential turn would last in spite of the football game flickering in front of our eyes.

The man sighed back into his chair.

"We've got a heap of expenses right now," he admitted, misinterpreting my change of direction. "The new house, doctor's bills—pshew—the baby . . ."

"You've got a very promising future," I said, taking pity on him. In a few years he would probably be endorsing everything from dental floss to spackle.

"Not as promising as it was yesterday."

That certainly put the conversation on fast-forward. "Because of Tim's death, you mean? I take it you don't think he was killed by a crazed fan."

Doug snorted. "What do you think?"

I shrugged. "You tell me. How likely is that theory?"

Doug waved his head and flicked out his hands. "Not very. Security does a sweep—a check—of all the rest rooms before locking up. I suppose somebody really determined could avoid detection, but the whole idea is pretty farfetched."

"Why do you say that? More than a few of the fans look a little out there, if you ask me." Shaved heads painted like helmets, signs that read "Kill the Raiders"; why couldn't one of the nuts—be nuts?

"Oh, I'm not saying it isn't possible. Not after what happened to Monica Seles," the tennis top seed who was stabbed by someone from the stands, ostensibly to benefit the other contender.

"We all get threats," Doug admitted. "But people rarely carry them out."

"Wait a minute. You *all* get threats? Death threats?"

"Well, yeah, sort of. You can't spend a lot of time worrying about them. It's just part of being famous."

Did that mean the more famous you got, the more threats you received, until some truly insane person concluded that the best way to validate his life was to kill you?

John Lennon's demise suddenly came to mind, giving me the cold sweats and a stomachache.

Doug noticed my horror and tried to mitigate it. "They're almost always hot air, Gin," he assured me.

Almost always, which meant that every once in a while one of the threats was dead serious.

I nodded robotically while another thought tapped me on the shoulder, something important I was overlooking, the very point Doug had been trying to make while I was busy being scandalized.

He did *not* believe the murder of Tim Duffy had been performed by a random maniac.

"Sorry," I said, waving away my digression. "You were trying to tell me you think Tim was murdered by someone who knew him."

"Of course. And pretty soon the police will think so, too—if they haven't figured that out already. Like I said, the looney 'toons rarely act on their anger, but people with rock-solid motives pop off their enemies all the time.''

Doug was right. To kill another person was to put one's own life in acute peril, so nobody whose mental faculties were in working order would go that route without a heap of provocation.

''I guess you know Michelle's scared to death the police will suspect you,'' I stated, hoping the liquor had mellowed him enough to forgive my impertinence. ''She mentioned something about Coren, but she says she doesn't know the whole story.'' Hint, hint.

Doug stood up, stretched, and yawned. ''Steelers are going to lose it,'' he observed, referring to the game on television. ''Good.''

He turned toward the hallway, perhaps intending to go to bed.

''Doug,'' I called after him.

He stiffened as if to brace himself for an onslaught of female concern.

I wanted to offer him reassurances, but the words weren't there. ''There's fried chicken in the refrigerator,'' I told him instead.

SEVEN

The Turner household guest room was equipped with a bed and a phone, an ugly mauve princess job of the type that never breaks; it just stops matching anything. Michelle had probably taken it with her to college. Doug offered me the use of it right after he handed me some towels, and I decided to make myself even more at home and ask whether his computer was on-line and could I please borrow it in the morning?

One blond eyebrow raised, but he recovered quickly. "Sure. If you really need something to do with yourself, I've got a bunch of games in there."

What I really intended was to do some Internet research to try to help him, but I was afraid that much honesty up front might tie his masculine shorts in a knot. After all, this was a guy who sweated and grunted for a living while on the sidelines enthusiastic women with Barbie bodies and short skirts kicked their feet up to their hat brims. Maybe time would prove Doug to be the Alan Alda of the sports world; but until I found that out, best to keep quiet about my prospective sleuthing efforts.

So I lied. "I just like to watch my stocks," I said with an earnest face.

Fortunately, the stock-market ruse proved effective as well as expedient. "Oh," said the professional quarterback with the off-balance respect I like in a man, "in that case..." Doug briefly summarized how I could sign onto his carrier as a guest and access the World Wide Web with the rest of the Whiz Kids.

I thanked him and promised a huge breakfast at whatever hour he preferred. "Rasher of bacon, dozen scrambled eggs?" I offered with an enticing roll of my shoulders.

He winced and said, "Thank you," but a bagel and coffee would be fine until he got to the stadium.

"That's lucky," I realized. There was still no significant food in the house.

We parted company with awkward platitudes, he to the master suite thirty feet down a pale-blue carpet, me to my guest bath of off white and gold and, of course, the mauve princess phone.

Rip answered on the first ring.

"Yo," I said. "You in bed?"

"Who wants to know?"

"Sparkle Plenty," I replied.

My husband settled back on his pillow. "Well, Sparkle. What are you wearing?"

I glanced down at myself. "Gray sweats. I didn't pack very well."

"You didn't have a whole lot of time to think about it."

"I never do. Why is that?"

"Let's not run up your cousin's phone bill on that one."

"I'm pretty sure they can afford it." Despite Doug's financial concerns, even the most pathetic professional football salary would be way beyond what anyone in private education could ever expect. But of course football players had to sweat and grunt for it—and, I reminded myself sternly, take concussions and broken bones and death threats in their stride.

"How's Michelle?" the intrepid educator asked.

I told him she was worried about losing the baby and afraid that her husband would be accused of murder.

"They alibied each other, Rip," I said. "If Doug's got a halfway decent motive, he could be in serious trouble."

"I thought the police were going with the crazy-fan idea."

I related Doug's reasons for discounting that. "Plus the timing bothers me," I thought aloud. "The stadium was such a risky place to do it, you know? Why not somewhere else, anywhere else?"

"Gin," Rip said, to secure my attention.

"What?"

"Don't start."

My enthusiasm sank even as my heart warmed. Rip never could handle me putting myself in harm's way. Hammering nails, installing chandeliers, climbing ladders—even though he says he understands why I love all sorts of challenges, he still twitches and fidgets over some of the things I tackle.

"I'm cool," I said. "Not to worry."

"Yeah, sure," Rip responded. "Next you're going to tell me you're down there to cook."

I opened my mouth then closed it. "What exactly are you saying?" I asked.

"Nothing."

"Nothing?"

"Nothing, as in not anything. You're down there to help, and I trust you to keep your wits about you and stay out of trouble. Besides, I don't see how you could possibly involve yourself in the case. Plenty of police are already working on it, and . . . ."

"Stop right there, bub," I warned him. He sounded headed toward something like "so how could one well-intentioned, female outsider possibly get anywhere?" I did not want to hear anything remotely like that from my husband, even if it was true. After all, I'd kicked many a hat brim for him, so to speak.

"What did Cynthia make for dinner?" I asked, expecting that to be a diverting topic.

"Black-eyed peas and a ham slice with mushroom gravy."

"Humm," I mused. "That doesn't sound so bad."

"The gravy was Campbell's mushroom soup . . ." Of course. ". . . and the peas started out all green." My mother has an almost unbroken record of burning peas, probably due to a flawed attention span. Dad and I learned to eat Cynthia's peas little black dots and all.

"What's this Gracie person like?" I asked.

Rip reflected a moment. "Remember Aunt Bea on the Andy Griffith show? Gracie is smaller and chubbier, and she giggles through her nose."

We went on like that a bit and finally said good night.

For a while I comforted myself by dangling my hand down near the floor, pretending that my husband was no farther away than that stupid, ugly telephone.

Overnight my subconscious must have gnawed at the murder question, because I awoke with a conclusion. That it was an obvious one only served to cement it in my brain.

Tim Duffy had been killed in the stadium almost immediately after a game, so something connected to that day's contest had almost certainly prompted the murder.

Since Doug had explained away the enraged-fan idea, and since the Tomcats had won in front of an adoring hometown crowd, the odds looked best for an intense, game-related motive. Or as a long shot, an unrelated motive involving someone with a highly developed sense of self-preservation—a cold-blooded ex-lover, maybe. Somebody smart enough to realize that the stadium setting would give forensics a fit, yet brave enough to kill in a place that public.

When I got downstairs, bagel crumbs dusted the counter and the fragrance of coffee made my head swim. Nice surprise. Nobody to pamper but me. While I toasted another bagel, I put CNN on the kitchen TV and located the morning's sports page on the chair seat where Doug left it.

The TV news offered nothing factual either regarding Tim Duffy or the Tomcats. Even the newspapers were glaringly short on speculation. I suspected some higher-up someplace of crisis control, and why not? Too many names of note were involved. If silly people could sue Bryn Derwyn Academy just because their son or daughter didn't get into Harvard, imagine what would happen if a beloved wide receiver was erroneously accused of murder! The fallout would probably ripple both our oceans.

Perhaps with that thought in mind, the media confined itself to funeral information and human interest fluff while leap-frogging over anything to do with the homicide investigation. For the moment, that suited me fine.

After breakfast, I padded into Doug's home office in my socks and sweats and played around in cyberspace for a while. NFL.com brought me up to speed on the basics, such as the fourteenth week standings of all the league teams. Houston, the other new expansion team and the Tomcats' opponent the day Tim got killed, continued to struggle to get out of their three and eleven sinkhole. As I had suspected, the win on Sunday put the Tomcats even at seven wins and seven losses.

I found an inventive site done by Ronnie's company showing excellent footage of a touchdown play, lens right on the carrier, moving with him through the crowd—around, up, over, and in—but it took so long to load and so little time to see that my attention glossed over who it was and why it mattered. Doug's computer had been with him awhile.

I read a summary of the week's significant advances but bypassed the plentiful links to information about specific teams and players. No use wasting my whole day filling my head with stuff that might not pertain to the game in question. Michelle could help me focus in, and Doug, too, if he chose to humor me.

Around ten I phoned my cousin at the hospital and learned that she was considered stable enough to come home tomorrow. She imparted a few household do's and don'ts: Don't clean—they had a service. Okay to do laundry. Stuff like that.

During a little lull in the conversation, I cautiously alluded to the source of some of her tension. Although I certainly didn't want to distress her, I needed to know whether I could mention Tim Duffy's death without rushing to dial 911.

"When I visit this afternoon," I opened, "I'd like to get your impressions of the Houston game."

Michelle paused to absorb my implications, but I heard no sharp intake of breath, nothing to suggest that I had set off a panic.

"In what regard?" she asked.

"I just need you to help me understand the dynamics so I won't sound like an idiot when I talk to Doug."

The delicate mother-to-be laughed. "I guess I can do that, although nobody can guarantee that you won't sound like an idiot."

"Oh, ho," I responded sarcastically, while smirking with glee that she had tried to tease me.

Laughter always has been the Siddons family lifeline, and I was thrilled right down to my sweat socks that sober little Michelle was finally reaching out for it.

Already I feared she needed it far more than she knew.

"That Harris Teeter place is amazing," I told her in person as soon as visiting hours began.

After we finished on the phone, I had prettied myself up with brown slacks and a peach-colored sweater. Then I raided the aisles of Michelle's favorite food store as if I could actually afford the place.

"How about those desserts?" she exclaimed.

Beneath her glasses her cheeks were pinker today, and she had twisted her fluffy hair into a topknot that wouldn't make a lump against the pillow.

"There's a raspberry chocolate clam shell waiting for you to get home," I promised. So what if it cost $2.59, she and Kewpie deserved a treat. I had also bought a selection of Dr. Brown's soda (skipping the celery flavor), a couple Italian supreme pizzas, some stuffed grape leaves (always wanted to try them), and a meal's worth of lemon/garlic grilled chicken breast with a side of glazed carrots.

Michelle licked her lips and patted her tummy.

I noticed the newspaper she had set aside at my arrival, and my expression fell.

"Pretty short on substance, aren't they?" my cousin observed.

"Very short on substance," I agreed.

"So what do you want to know about the game?" prompted the quarterback's wife.

I settled onto a chair at the edge of the bed. "Did anything unusual happen?"

Michelle flopped back and turned her head to answer me. "Laneer benched Walker Cross; but you said you saw the game, so you knew that."

A matchup of little interest outside Texas or Virginia, the Hombres/Tomcats game hadn't been offered in our region. Luckily Didi, my best friend, had noticed it in her satellite listing and generously invited all of us Barneses over for the afternoon. The Tomcats' premier receiver had been notably absent from the second quarter on, but at the time I hadn't given it much thought.

"Why?" I asked now.

Michelle shrugged. "You probably remember the Tomcats jumped ahead twenty-one to nothing in the first quarter. So maybe Laneer just wanted to make sure Walker would be healthy for this week's game with the Eagles."

"Reasonable, I guess."

"Yeah, except Walker was pretty peeved."

That, too, seemed natural. Nobody at any level of any sport liked to be benched even for a good reason.

"Anything else?"

"Doug had the wind knocked out of him—twice."

I remembered that well. Doug took tough hits in both the first and fourth quarters and had to step out to recover. Duffy filled in both times, even throwing an exciting final touchdown pass that effectively ended the game.

Just as I was about to ask whether Michelle knew of anyone on the team who hated Tim Duffy, two other visitors arrived. Well-groomed and slender, both were fine examples of what a woman could do for herself given enough time and money. On Philadelphia's Main Line, where I lived (thanks to Rip's occupation), quite a number of women looked like these two, although at home probably half or more didn't dress any better than me. For that reason I reserved judgment on Michelle's new guests; first impressions could be bought and often were a waste of money.

The older white woman exercised her seniority. She lunged ahead of the taller black woman to grasp

Michelle's hand even as her eyes softened over the mound that contained the Turner heir.

"Shelly," she addressed the hospital patient. "You're looking wonderful. The nurse said you're doing great. How do you feel?"

The second woman lingered at the end of the bed with her clutch purse between her hands and a fond smile on her face. Slightly younger than me, she had high cheeks the color of dark chocolate, and her hair had been meticulously straightened and smoothed back into a knot of braids. When I moved back from the bed nearer to where she stood, I noticed that her perfume was Lauren, a fragrance that always reminded me of a florist shop at Easter or Longwood Gardens' solarium right after it had been watered.

"I feel fine, thanks, Barbara. Teal," Michelle addressed the younger woman, "so nice of you to come."

"We've been thinking of you," Teal replied with warmth.

"Let me introduce my cousin from Philadelphia, Ginger Barnes. Gin this is Teal Todd, Morani Todd's wife—Morani is the Cats' biggest and best defensive lineman—and Barbara Laneer. Jack Laneer is the Tomcat head coach, of course. Barbara, Teal and I became friends working on a charity event sponsored by the team."

"Mount Trashmore Three," Barbara concurred with a smile. "Around here we like to turn piles of garbage into playgrounds."

"They're the only sledding hills around," Teal boasted.

"Sounds wonderful. It's a pleasure to meet you both," I responded, nodding to each individual in turn. Both women politely gave me their attention before fussing some more over Michelle.

So the classiness was through and through, not just

show. I settled back to admire the pros doling out sympathy and support, Michelle classing up and warming up in response.

Each day we are all of us chameleons to some extent, different versions of ourselves; but as I listened to the three friends exchange gossip and trivial news, I observed that Michelle appeared more relaxed, more herself, than she had been on Thanksgiving with Ronnie and me.

It struck me now that with an eight-year age difference, she and her brother had probably been more like two only children born to the same parents, no doubt reflecting the evolution their elders had undergone during the years between their births. Ronnie represented feckless youth, Michelle the measured adult.

Barbara Laneer giggled. I didn't hear why, but I giggled along because I was utterly charmed by the woman. She wasn't especially beautiful, not with that crooked pointy nose. Nor was she as perfectly groomed as Teal—a swipe of lipstick was about it. What she was was sincere. One hundred percent real. Artifice never crossed her mind. I fervently hoped I would be just like her when I grew up.

A nurse bustled in on quick, rubber-soled feet. "Excuse me, ladies, the doctor needs a few minutes." She tugged the white privacy curtain along its ceiling track and effectively began to shut us visitors out.

"Buy you two a cup of coffee?" I suggested to Barbara and Teal.

They murmured assent without even looking at their watches. Nice women. Good women. They were exactly perfect for my purposes. I tried not to gloat in the elevator down to the Tidewater Café, Virginia Beach's version of hospital hospitality.

I turned up a palm to usher my two guests in under the dark-green awning with white scalloped edges gracing the entrance. To my right a poster framed in chrome advertised the Colombo frozen yogurt flavors of the day. Tempting, but licking a melting cone like a kid would detract from my interrogation technique.

Barbara passed by the "Salad Garden" housed in immaculate stainless steel and the black "Today's Features" menu hand-printed in blue, pink, and green, offering such things as Broccoli and Cheese Stuffed Potatoes, Vegetable Egg Rolls, and Turkey Pita Wraps. She went straight to the base of the scripted "Drinks" sign and poured herself some coffee.

Teal and I followed her example, and Barbara paid. Part of being a head coach's wife perhaps, or maybe she had simply tired of the overpolite posturing women tend to assume as soon as a check appears.

As we approached the seating area to the left, a lanky teenager with uncombed hair began to leave. His T-shirt depicted the prime-time cartoon character Bart Simpson peeing on the number 22.

"What's that mean?" I questioned Teal.

"We're very serious NASCAR fans around here," she explained. "Twenty-two is the number of a driver."

"Interesting," I thought aloud. Nothing nearly so colorful had been in the morning's sports page.

We settled into seats, and before the conversation could run off in a direction beyond my control I plunged ahead with my agenda.

"Michelle is extremely distressed about what happened to Tim Duffy."

"Of course, we all are."

"Yes, it's horrible. Poor Elise," Barbara lamented. I surmised that Elise was now Tim's widow.

I inquired whether the couple had had children. No. Conversational dead end. I sipped coffee and regrouped.

After an appropriate interval, I addressed Barbara.

"Will the publicity hurt the Tomcats much?" I asked.

We sat on three sides of a square Formica table, and Mrs. Defensive Lineman added her intense second to my question with her eyes, something Mrs. Head Coach discerned at a glance. Careers were at stake here. Very lucrative careers and the lifestyles that accompanied them.

"I guess that depends on what the police find out," Barbara answered, squirming a bit under Teal's intense stare. "The public already thinks Bobby Frye is a flake, in fact they seem to love that about him. But if something sinister gets attributed to anybody on the team, the sympathy could swing the other way faster than . . ."

"Faster than Walker Cross going in for a touchdown," Teal finished kindly.

Robert "Bobby" Frye owned the Tomcats, but that was nearly everything I knew about him except that he had earned millions in the technology field and was rumored to have lost millions as well.

Rather than speculate on what "Bobby" might do if his team took it on the PR chin, I steered my two inside sources more toward the point. "Is it possible that someone on the team had a motive to kill Tim Duffy?" Facially, I confined my questioning eye contact to ingenuous worry on Michelle and Doug's behalf.

Barbara took a panicky gulp of coffee, and Teal snorted.

"No, of course not. The Tomcats are family, isn't that right, Barb? And all families have their squabbles." Her sarcasm was just slight enough to tantalize. Yet to avoid being too heavy-handed I chose to skirt around Teal's hint of dissent for the time being.

Instead, I leaned back and reflected about the pears my mother had been staring at when she heard the news of President Kennedy's assassination on TV. I envisioned sunlight streaming in through her kitchen window making the pears glow almost yellow, heard my mother sobbing into her arms because the announcer's broken voice had set off her own tears.

Reflecting out loud, I said, "I wonder whether this will be another tragedy that always makes you remember what you were doing when you heard the news—like when the Gulf War broke out or John Lennon got shot."

Barbara's immediate answer brought me back, that and Teal's eyes. They had fixed on me with distrust that wouldn't quit.

"Oh, I know what you mean," Barbara reflected. "Jack and I were at the Coastal Grill with our son and his wife when a young man came in from outside. 'Tim Duffy's been shot,' the man announced to his friends at the table right next to us. Well, the whole room just about held its breath, and everybody seemed to look straight at us. It's a fairly small place, and I guess a lot of people had recognized Jack when we came in."

"What did your husband do then?" I prompted.

"He got a dark, intense look on his face. Teal, you know how he gets when it's third and long yardage and the center bobbles the snap?" Teal nodded that she knew. "Then Jack just tapped our son's hand and said, 'John, will you please drive your mother home after dinner? I believe I should be going back to the stadium.'"

During the last of Barbara's exchange Teal had returned to watching me with undisguised hostility. Clearly my veiled "Where were you the night of December seventh?" probing hadn't fooled her.

Now she told me, "I saw it on the eleven o'clock news with my husband—in bed," each word like the wave of a knife.

Barbara sensed something amiss and sat up

straighter. "What?" she asked while her eyes flicked back and forth between Teal and me.

Teal was too preoccupied fixing me with a searing gaze to answer, but I quickly tired of standing my ground. I softened my face and turned to the older woman.

"My cousin almost lost her baby because she's so worried about what will happen to the team," I explained with an abbreviated form of the truth. "I promised her I'd try to assess the damage and, with luck, I'll be able to set her mind at ease before anything worse happens. Losing this child would devastate her."

Teal took a breath, "And just how do you propose to *set her mind at ease*?" Sarcasm still predominated, but the threat was gone.

"How about a baby shower?" The idea had been tickling the back of my mind, but now that Teal forced me to state my intentions out loud, I liked it. Michelle's only friends in Norfolk seemed to be the wives she had met working on the Tomcats' charity event—and who would know better about the inner dynamics of the team than the women who were married to the players? Gathered so soon after the murder they would almost certainly talk about their fears and suspicions.

Teal not only saw through my offensive strategy, she signed on in less time than it takes some people to blink. And why not? Only moments before she had fixated on Barbara's response regarding the murder's impact on the team. Now I seemed to be mirroring her own concern, only from a slightly different angle.

"We'll have it at my house," she told me, leaving no opening for discussion.

"This Saturday?" I queried. Extremely short notice, but Teal appreciated the urgency. In fact she seemed to understand me right down to my soul, something only Grammy Struve had been able to do—until now.

Barbara's mind must have wandered, for her face screwed up when she asked, "Have what Saturday? What's going on?" which erased any notion of me being like her when I grew up. She was genuinely nice, all right, but already it was evident that she was far more comfortably off and sheltered than I had ever been. Not her fault, of course, but worldliness wasn't something you could return like a defective watch.

"Teal wants to help me do a baby shower for Michelle," I answered, as if my exchange with Teal had contained no innuendoes whatsoever. "Not a surprise one, though," I cautioned. Heaven forbid.

"Delightful," Barbara responded, relieved to finally catch on. "We could all use a pleasant distraction. I'm amazed that nobody thought of that before. Please," she begged, "let me bring the dessert. I'm known for my desserts."

And just that quickly it was settled—all except for securing the recipient's cooperation, something I looked forward to with a certain amount of unease.

You see, the most likely reason no one had yet dared to throw a baby shower for Michelle was because of her difficult pregnancy, compounded by her previous miscarriage. More than just superstition, women instinctively knew how—and when—to protect each other from the pain of packing away booties and T-shirts and pastel sleep sacks after the unthinkable has happened. Merely securing Michelle's cooperation for this potentially heartbreaking endeavor would hurt. It hurt me just imagining the conversation.

Yet I believed Michelle would cooperate. More was at stake here than her maternal sensibilities.

Barbara was the one who finally glanced at the

time. "That's decided then," she beamed. "Let's go tell her the good news."

Teal and I hung back for two seconds to finish silently assessing each other, a comprehensive task that included all orientations and opinions, past histories dating back to birth, all applicable statistics, including current checkbook balances and the number of pennies rolling around in the bottoms of our purses—well, my purse, because Teal only carried plastic.

That accomplished, we smiled complacently at each other, then followed Barbara back to the elevator.

EIGHT

Michelle stared at me when Teal told her we wanted to have a baby shower for her on Saturday, so I knew my cousin knew the idea had been mine.

"Be a good chance for everybody to put this Tim Duffy business behind them," I hinted cautiously. "A chance to focus on something positive." Michelle heard that as *Teal and I are working undercover here, I hope you'll back us up*, and, *It'll be good for you and Kewpie, too*—communal optimism, women's magic, old as time.

"Thank you, Barbara, Teal, Ginger," Michelle replied with a last glance toward me. "What a sweet idea."

"We'd like to invite, uh, Wanda Cross and Lyn Smith," Teal improvised, naming a receiver's wife and the wife of the third string quarterback respectively. Then she glanced at me to check that I followed her reasoning; and, as I didn't dare hold her back, I smiled my compliance. If Morani Todd was half as aggressive as his wife, he would probably make the NFL Hall of Fame.

With hands folded on her bulging lap, Michelle pressed her lips together and watched the three of us with a fascinated smile.

"And Pamela Cork, everybody likes her," Barbara bubbled on.

"She doesn't date Roger anymore, Barb," Teal

alerted the older woman. "In fact I'm pretty sure she married somebody else. But you're right. Everybody liked her." To me she said, "Pam used to be with Roger Prindel. He's the Tomcats' offensive coordinator." An eyebrow told me that Pamela might be worth tracking down.

"And Mandy Shifflett," Barbara continued in spirit, if not in sync.

"Certainly," Teal agreed. I had dug out an airline folder with enough blank space to write a list. Teal handed me a pen.

"Phone numbers?"

"Green book in the kitchen drawer by the phone," Michelle told me with lips twitching as if this were the most amusing routine she'd seen in weeks.

"Bo Shifflett's another receiver," Teal clarified for me. We seemed to be leaning toward the wives of offensive players on either the giving or receiving end of the ball, men whose team functions were similar to Tim Duffy's. I could scarcely wait to learn the reasoning behind Teal's guest list, but patience was still a virtue, last I heard.

"Angela Dionne?" Barbara suggested. "She'd probably love an afternoon away from her own kids."

"Sure," Teal agreed with less enthusiasm.

I dredged up the name of the team owner from my earlier research. "Is Robert Frye married?" I inquired.

"Go straight to the horse's wife's mouth?" I added under my breath for Teal.

"Horse's ass would be more like it," she murmured back.

"Bobby Frye?" Barbara giggled in response to her own thoughts. "I don't believe he even has a girlfriend." She laughed outright, and Michelle couldn't help but join her.

Before visiting hours ended, there were five or six

other acquaintances of Michelle's on the list. By then I had no idea whether they had been targeted by Teal or mentioned by Barbara, but one thing was certain: Saturday was going to be an interesting day.

An answering machine message told me Doug intended to pick up his own dinner and go straight to the hospital again, so I heated a few stuffed grape leaves in the microwave and scraped a carrot for myself as an afterthought. I thought the grape leaves tasted pretty grassy, but I liked the stuff inside just fine.

Next I sat down with Michelle's green phone book and set about inviting people to the baby shower. As any telemarketer can tell you, early evening is when you catch people at home.

"You mean one o' them white bread with no crust cucumber sandwich kinda showers? That the kinda thing you mean?" one woman named Luella Hixson inquired.

"Well . . . yeah. I suppose you could put it that way," I admitted.

A hoot of laughter assaulted my ear. "Count me out, sister." Luella snorted. "Lord, you white people slay me, you really do." The connection broke.

"Guess that's a no," I answered for myself.

I had to leave a couple of messages, but the overall response was promising. All I had left to do was pick up a gift somewhere and an assortment of those frou-frou decorations no shower can be without. Wine might have been good for loosening tongues, but Barbara had vetoed the notion. "Not in front of the baby," I believe she put it, and she was right. Michelle couldn't indulge for the duration, so it wouldn't be polite to tempt her.

However, Michelle was not presently home, and I had picked up a bottle of my winter beverage, red wine—one glass at dinner, mostly on weekends. After one evening alone in a huge strange house I felt I deserved any sort of warmth I could muster.

When the phone rang beside my left elbow, I nearly knocked over the whole bottle of hearty burgundy.

"Hello," I barked.

"Uh" came the familiar voice of my daughter. "Mom? Is that you?"

"Sure is. Sorry, but you startled me. I thought you were a salesman."

"Um, Mom?" my daughter began. "How long do you cook frozen pizza in the microwave?"

"Didn't Nana make dinner?"

"Um, yes. But Garry and me, Garry and I, um, we're still hungry."

I told her to read the directions on the box.

"So how's everything going? Is Nana's friend nice?" By then I had surmised that Rip was out at a meeting.

"Gracie? Oh, yeah. She's just like Nana." Not a particularly comforting thought.

"What are they doing?" as in *right now!*

"Oh, they're just watching an old cowboy movie. It has a blond actor in it and a little kid with bad teeth."

"*Shane?*"

"That's the one. It's really boring, Mom, but Nana and Gracie are leaning forward with their hands up at their mouths like they're half ready to cry."

"They *are* half ready to cry. I've seen that movie. Why don't you and Garry take your pizza to your rooms and start your homework?"

"You mean it?" Ordinarily pizza was not allowed past the dining room, not until Garry's neuromuscular synapses finished practicing and Gretsky learned to use a napkin. Chelsea's bedroom carpet was white—

need I say more? But I had drunk a little of the wine and my thirteen-year-old daughter had actually picked up the phone to call me, and . . . and aren't we all allowed to feel mellow from time to time?

"Wow, Mom. Thanks. Do you think when I'm finished my English I can, like, borrow the TV back?"

"Maybe after *Shane*, but say please and try to pick something Nana and Gracie would like, too. They're supposed to be on vacation."

"Oh, they're on vacation," Chelsea told me. "You don't have to worry about that."

So, of course, that was exactly what I worried about, even as I turned on Doug's computer and settled down to learn a bit more about the Tomcats whose wives were invited to Teal's on Saturday.

Pretty much of what I found chugging along on Doug's old computer read like the sports page, just illustrated and in color. Statistics, who went to what college, notable accomplishments this season, injuries. Also, expert predictions for the upcoming week—including point spreads.

I did not kid myself that all of the other people perusing the same material were solely interested in lowering their blood pressure. Football pools circulated among Bryn Derwyn's faculty and throughout just about every other business I'd ever encountered. Risking a few bucks on a media-informed guess helped to make dull games matter and provided water-cooler conversation ad infinitum. A few places even had informal lunchtime "banquets" to award the winners. Some participants might even argue that the pools were a cockeyed sort of public service.

Just not for me, possibly because my watering hole was the kitchen sink.

I did find one old article linked to both Tim Duffy's name and Doug's regarding their previous college rivalry. Whoever did the Tomcat Web site probably kept the piece connected to their home page because of the human interest angle. Both men had come out of the University of Michigan, both were quarterbacks, and both now played for Norfolk's professional team.

Apparently Tim had been red-shirted as a freshman and suffered a knee injury as a fifth-year senior, opening the gate for the precocious first-year quarterback, Doug Turner.

Duffy had been drafted in the sixth round by the Oakland Raiders, played with fair to moderate distinction for three years, and got picked up in the expansion draft by the Tomcats.

The same year, last year, Doug was chosen right out of Michigan in the Tomcats' first shot at the regular draft. Rumor had it that owner Bobby Frye liked the potential press the continuing rivalry would generate, but other sources reported that head coach Jack Laneer was enthusiastic about Turner's prospects and requested him without any regard for their personal history.

Since my cousin was married to Doug, naturally I followed the Tomcats, watching them whenever possible. So I knew that Tim had started for Laneer last year, but Doug took top billing all this season. He was healthier, smarter, and niftier, and from a spectator's viewpoint, just plain more fun to watch. But don't just take my word for it: the Tomcats' first season record was 5–11, and this year's was 7–7 so far.

Before my eyes quit on Doug's glaring monitor, I read up on Willet Smith, the thirty-three-year-old QB the Tomcats acquired for insurance just this year. Smith had hopes of catching such record holders as Joe Montana and Dan Marino before rotator cuff problems slowed him down. But he was still a savvy playmaker and a fan favorite. Also, as yet, neither Duffy nor Turner were pulling in superstar salaries, so Smith's monetary expectations didn't deplete the overall budget too badly. And pretty soon he would be out to pasture anyway.

While I was on-line, I also checked on Robert "Bobby" Frye, learning only that he was a venture capitalist and chairman of the board of Supratech, a holding company for several cutting-edge technology companies. The grainy picture that accompanied the item wasn't much help either.

The sound of the television around the corner in the family room made me jump off the seat of my chair.

"Doug?" I called.

"Oh, hi, Gin," he called back. "Didn't know where you were."

I shut off the computer and joined him. He looked miserable—eyes puffy from fatigue, shoulders slouched, hands hanging between his knees. If I'd have flicked him between the shoulder blades with a forefinger, he'd have toppled to the floor in a heap. Or forechecked me with an elbow, either one.

"Everything okay with Michelle?" I asked, just to be sure.

Doug had put in a homemade tape of Sunday's game with the Hombres; even at low volume I recognized the announcers' voices and the commercials. Doug stared at the set as if listening to a eulogy.

"Michelle?" I prompted. "Everything okay?"

"What? Oh, yeah. She asked me to ask you to pick her up around ten-thirty or eleven tomorrow."

"Wonderful. That's great news."

Doug didn't seem to think so, according to the creases around his eyes and mouth.

"Isn't it?" I asked.

"What? Sure."

"So what's the problem? You look . . . down."

Doug turned toward me and blinked, so I repeated my question.

"The police pulled me out of practice today," he said.

"Only you?"

"No."

"Well, then."

Doug impatiently cut me off. "They got pretty rough, Gin. Especially about my rivalry with Tim. Dammit. There *was* no rivalry. Not on my part, but try to tell that to the cops. Listening to them you'd have thought I hated the guy just because we played the same position."

"Didn't you?"

"Hell, no. Why should I? I beat him out in college, and I beat him out in the pros. Why the hell should I hate him?"

"Because of Coren."

The man reeled, just reeled. And his eyes ignited. I found myself watching his hands, his feet, as if he might lunge at me and grab my throat.

I held up a hand. "That's what Michelle is worried about, Doug. Michelle. Not me."

Doug stood then and moved around a little, trying to calm himself down, probably because he knew what I said was true. Even if they hadn't discussed it out loud, he knew Michelle had been hospitalized largely because of fears regarding him and Tim Duffy's murder.

Keeping myself collected safely on a side chair, I began to work my way into Doug's confidence, asking first whether Michelle would be more scared or less if she knew the whole story.

Doug set his hands on his hips and fixed his eyes on something internal.

"Why don't you run it by me?" I suggested.

The eyes transferred to me. "Better yet, why not

go straight to the D.A.?'' he taunted. *"Douglas Collin Turner, is it true you blamed your sister's suicide on Timothy Duffy?"*

I swallowed my shock, pretended to stay calm.

"Did you?" I pressed.

Doug's fury erupted. "No I did not blame Tim Duffy for my sister's suicide. She was wild all her life, willful and irresponsible." He shook his head as he tried to describe the woman who was gone. "Beautiful, smart." He shook his head some more and leaned an arm against the bookshelves.

"Coren was always one extreme or the other," he said, glancing back at me. "Jell-O," he said with a sigh. "She hated the texture of gelatin, said it made her throw up. So finally it did. That sort of thing." He wagged his head, shaking off tears.

I nodded that I understood.

Doug began to pace off his frustration, talking as he went. "Two years ago she became obsessed with a guy, a nice guy. I thought, 'Great. She's finally going to be okay.' They got engaged, signed up a church, planned a big reception, the whole bit."

"What happened?"

"He dumped her."

When I opened my mouth to say something sympathetic, I discovered that my throat had locked up. In fact, all things considered, I'd probably heard more than enough.

But Doug had finally started, and he needed to tell the rest. So I pulled my knees up and hugged them and told myself if he could live through it, the least I could do was listen.

"Turned out the guy really wanted kids," Doug continued. "I mean *really wanted kids*. Coren couldn't have any."

"But . . ."

"But what does that have to do with Tim?"

I bit my lip and nodded.

Doug stared at the ceiling with disgust before turning to glare at me. "Tim and I were rivals all right. At least he saw it like that, and I guess I couldn't blame him. It was just a stinking shame I couldn't do anything about it."

I rustled in my chair, squirmed really.

Doug left off glaring at me, flipped a hand. "Tim's last year at Michigan, his big chance to show off for the scouts. Along comes little snot-nosed Doug Turner, and guess who steals the spotlight?"

"I thought Tim got hurt."

"He also got better, but by then it was too late."

So far Doug's scenario sounded like an earlier version of their experiences with the Tomcats. Neither story explained why the police would suspect Doug of hating Tim, entirely the reverse.

"So what did your sister have to do with it?"

Doug's breathing tightened. "Coren? She came to visit me at Michigan. I took her on the rounds of the postgame parties, just showing off my big sister, you know? She got loaded, Tim saw an opportunity and went for it."

I swallowed noisily.

"He gave her VD, Gin. Tim Duffy was the reason Coren couldn't have any children."

My hand flew protectively to my throat. "On purpose?" I asked. "I mean, did he know?"

Doug shrugged and waved his head ambiguously. "Gonorrhea and chlamydia are easier to detect in men than women. For one thing, I'm told it hurts like hell to pee. So yes, Tim was most certainly aware that he had those venereal diseases when he . . . met . . . my sister."

This was not sounding good, not good at all.

I murmured something about Tim being a sleaze,

if not worse. "Did he at least warn Coren so she could get treatment?"

Doug shook his head no. "Coren blacked out that night. She wasn't even positive she and Tim had sex."

"How convenient," I thought aloud, causing Doug to scowl at my sarcasm.

"Anyway," he continued, "Coren went back to school and went on behaving like Coren—even laughing when I nagged her about using protection. 'Always,' she insisted. 'Always.' That's why she overlooked her own symptoms so long; she really believed nothing was wrong."

Denial, I decided, probably coupled with the arrogant optimism of youth.

Doug caught my skeptical expression. "I know, but she really did black out that night at Michigan, remember? It wasn't until she landed in the hospital with a rip-roaring case of pelvic inflammatory disease—from the untreated gonorrhea and chlamydia, in case you wondered—that she finally figured out the carrier had to have been Tim."

"What did you do?"

Doug snorted at himself. "Stormed back to school with every intention of beating Tim Duffy to a pulp."

"Did you?"

This time Doug's laugh was directed at himself, and it held more humor. "No," he admitted. "I just couldn't do it," he told me with the memory still in his eyes. "Duffy totally fell apart. He even cried." Which according to Doug's expression was nothing one future professional football player cared to see another one do.

I rubbed my chin and gave rein to some typically cynical thoughts. For instance, I knew far too many people who were adept at summoning up whatever emotional response would get them out of trouble.

Faced with a furious and extremely fit Doug Turner, every last one of them—man or woman—was capable of crying buckets if they thought it would save them from whatever punishment they deserved.

Another thought distracted me. "What did Tim say about the gonorrhea and that other thing?"

"Chlamydia, it's one of our most common sexually transmitted diseases."

"Yeah?" I had never heard of it.

Doug nodded. "Three to five million Americans get it every year, a lot of times in conjunction with gonorrhea."

So now I knew, but I hadn't really been after the sex ed. I needed Doug to return to what Tim said about infecting Coren.

"Tim said he was in the middle of treatment, and he was symptom-free. In other words, he thought he was safe."

I puckered my lips while I weighed the implied "youthful ignorance" excuse. Young people have always believed that sexually transmitted diseases only infected the other guy—also that condoms were much too premeditated and unromantic.

Yet Tim and Coren had been two fairly worldly, sexually active young adults. They should have been way beyond the need for childish delusions.

For my money it was far easier to believe that Tim Duffy had been so jealous of Doug that he couldn't resist hurting him when the opportunity presented itself, that just for spite he maliciously seduced or drugged or just plain overpowered Coren into unprotected sex.

Or I suppose he could have simply "taken advantage" after she blacked out. Date rape, we call that now; and I found myself hating Tim Duffy, wishing there was a way to make him pay for his sins.

Then, of course, I remembered that the guy had

just been shot dead and that my cousin's husband made a very viable suspect.

Returning to how Doug had bought into Tim's remorse, I shook my head. "This was Coren—your sister. Weren't you just a little suspicious that Tim used her just to get back at you?"

Doug grimaced. "Would you think that of somebody you'd known for years?"

In a heartbeat, depending on who it was.

Naturally, my silence gave away the thought, and Doug frowned his pity on me and my poor opinion of mankind.

"Well, I wouldn't," he all but scolded. "Tim told me he was attracted to Coren, and he thought it was mutual. My sister was a beautiful woman—why shouldn't I have believed him?"

Because you were sheltered from reality by talent and intelligence and good looks?

But God forbid I should suggest such a blasphemy, and anyway the generalization was probably unfair.

Furthermore, I did believe Tim's story—up to a point, especially if Coren telegraphed her sexual proclivities the way a woman looking for action usually does.

Regardless, it was simply too coincidental that it was Tim who capitalized on Coren's inclinations rather than anyone else she met that night—and exactly at a time when the encounter happened to do her serious harm. Anyone aware of Tim's grudge against Doug would view that scenario as premeditated, particularly anyone listening to the story from a jury box.

Had any of Tim's subsequent behavior wised Doug up to his rival's intentions? A prosecutor would surely find out and would just as surely use any damning information to skewer Doug.

The quarterback lifted one shoulder and gazed

sadly at his hands. "Both Tim and my sister were stupid and irresponsible that night. Nothing could change that." His eyes shone with emotion, and his voice struggled with the words. "But Tim didn't pour those pills down my sister's throat," he finished. "Coren did that all by herself."

I pictured an attractive young woman, obsessive and flawed, happiness within reach. Suddenly her fiancé confesses that he wants children more than he wants her. Overwhelming guilt. Intolerable despair. No children, no marriage and, to Coren's mind—no hope.

Any D.A. worth the hide on his briefcase would argue that Tim Duffy had indirectly caused Coren Turner's suicide, thereby providing Doug Turner with an excellent motive for murder.

I asked Doug my next question with as much optimism as I could muster, as if a hopeful attitude might get me a better answer.

"Were you and Michelle really alone together when Tim Duffy was shot?"

"Um-humm," he responded honestly. But his eyelids drooped and concern ruined the edges of his smile.

NINE

Watching Tuesday night sitcoms after Doug's dramatic revelation would have offended our sensibilities, and trivial conversation was as out of the question as excusing myself to go read a book. Yet it was only 8:30 P.M., too early for either of us to turn in.

"That a tape of Sunday's game?" I asked. Tomorrow night Michelle would be there to bridge our social chasm. Tonight it was up to me. "Would you mind going back to the beginning?"

More than the pleasure of watching the Tomcats' first few scores, I wanted Doug's take on the subtleties behind what went on. All of them.

Doug hit the remote, his lip curled with amused tolerance. Then when the game restarted, he locked his hands behind his blond, Dick Tracy–square head. At that moment I almost became wallpaper.

"You don't get enough game films at work?" I teased.

Doug turned toward me and the lamp at my side, revealing that he needed a shave. "Oh, yeah. Sure. But the police kept asking me . . . I just wanted to see it again."

"You tape all your games at home?"

He smiled somewhat sadly. "Michelle does, for QB," for their son, or daughter. I suppressed a pang, turned my attention to the first ten plays of the game.

In only six minutes thirty-five seconds a combination of hungry runs and smoothly handled passes resulted in a Tomcats touchdown.

While he watched, my cousin-in-law the quarterback began to develop a mildly internal expression that, if I didn't intervene, would eventually shut me out completely. On my dad, I used to call it his "football face," but eventually I came to recognize it as the concentration necessary for winning a battle.

I hastily asked Doug a question. "Is it true that Laneer scripts his opening series like Bill Walsh?"

That earned me a flick of an eyebrow. "Yes," Doug responded. "Yes, he does."

"May I?" I asked, holding my hand out for the remote.

Out of habit Doug hesitated, but he did relinquish the control.

Gratefully, I hit the "mute" button to shut off the blab, then I backed up the action to the beginning of a second down play with seven yards to the first down and twenty-four to the goal.

"If they're playing eight men in the box," I remarked, "why aren't you using a three-step drop and trying to hit the quick stuff?"

Doug sat up, both eyebrows stretched high and his jaw slack. Yet he earned points for a quick recovery and extra yardage for not asking how I learned what I knew.

"We discussed that in meetings," he answered, "but we still thought we could hit the deep fade."

That itch satisfied, I let the tape roll.

On second and goal from the seven, the Tomcats' tailback bulled his way to the two yard line primarily on will power. Then on third down Doug faked the run so beautifully that his bootleg dump pass to Walker Cross made the touchdown look easy.

"Go 'cats!" I erupted, causing Doug to laugh uncomfortably.

So modesty did explain the absence of the trophies from his home. Nice to finally be reaching the real Doug, the athlete I could endorse for reasons other than his marriage to my cousin. I promised myself not to embarrass him again with my outbursts.

A routine point after touchdown kick gave the Tomcats a quick 7–0 lead.

A comfortable silence continued between Doug and me through two quick changes of possession, each team punting into the hands of the opponent after failed third downs.

As my dad liked to remind Mom and me, football was really pretty simple to understand. Your guys got four chances to move the ball ten yards toward the opponent's goal line. If they didn't get at least that far, they lost their turn.

Dad also insisted that football was remarkably difficult to master, especially when you factored in the number of variables produced by twenty-two men in motion. As a result, fans with every degree of expertise all managed to enjoy the game each in their own way. (My best friend Didi, for example, only went to admire the players' tight pants.) Throw in some fun things like beer, catchy promo songs, and cheerleaders and you've got an entertainment industry valued in the billions.

Billions. The mind boggled.

I went back to my own way of watching the chess pieces run and collide.

We passed the part where Doug got sacked by a human wrecking ball and sat out a couple of plays. During his absence Tim Duffy attempted a third down screen pass to Walker Cross, who was remarkably open; but the receiver stumbled and fell flat on his face reaching for the ball in the sort of graceless flop that makes a runner check his shoelaces.

But the coach's assessment of what went wrong

was all that mattered; Duffy probably faulted Cross for failing to catch the ball, and Cross probably blamed Duffy for a lousy throw and for just plain making him look bad.

Luckily, when the Hombres took over possession, they tried to get their offense going with a flanker reverse but botched the deep exchange. The ball took an unfortunate bounce and Morani Todd, the only Tomcat in sight, grabbed it on the run. Doug laughed when I punched the sound on long enough to hear the crowd cheer Morani into the end zone. Tomcats 13—Hombres 0.

I fast-forwarded through the point after kick and about eight commercials. Doug blinked but otherwise remained motionless as if he was sliding back into that private mental zone. While the quarter changed, I asked him, "What happened next?" mostly to retain a portion of his attention.

"A mixup in the Hombres' secondary gave Smith the chance to zig and go. The fans probably thought it was great coaching on our part, but we were lucky to get the seven points."

The Tomcat wearing the number 86 ran off the field. "Wasn't that Walker Cross going out of the game?" I inquired.

"Yeah, Laneer pulled him."

"It wasn't because of that bellyflop back when Tim was in, was it?" The incompletion Cross no doubt blamed on Duffy's pass.

Doug waved his head. "We were ahead by 21. Jack might have wanted to keep Cross healthy for this week's game with the Eagles." A slight flicker of hesitation suggested there was more behind the decision to bench the Tomcats' best receiver than a desire to save him for a tougher opponent.

I put the tape on pause. "But what?" I pressed.

Doug scowled at his hands. "It's no secret."

Which probably meant whatever it was had been leaked to the press.

"Walker's got an incentive built into his contract, a combination deal. He gains so many yards, catches so many passes, scores so many points, he gets a guaranteed contract for next year."

Not being a reader of the sports page, I hadn't seen the news item. Also, I wasn't sure I understood the implications, so I asked.

"It means he gets $1.7 million next year even if he stinks the joint out and gets replaced right away."

The calculations took about half a minute, but I got there. "So how close was he?" I asked.

"Touch and go. The playing time he missed will really hurt." In other words, losing three quarters of Sunday's game might have cost Cross the opportunity to achieve the yardage or points he needed in order to secure the $1.7 million.

"Subtle," I said, meaning sneaky. If the benching had occurred during a later game, the fans undoubtedly would have taken note and as a result thought less of the Tomcats' management. Three games back they would forget such a move—if they ever noticed in the first place.

"Is Bobby Frye hurting for money?" Ordinarily teams were insured against injuries, but Walker's wage guarantee fell outside of what insurance typically covered. His money would have to come directly out of the Tomcats' budget.

Doug shook my thought away. "Not something a guy on salary like me wants to talk about."

Maybe not, but the wives dependent on the guys dependent on the salaries might talk. In fact, I'd be amazed if they kept quiet.

I restarted the game. The only abnormality in the third quarter was a bungled snap by Tomcats' center, Patrick Dionne, a utility player who rarely drew negative attention to himself. Usually he would simply hand the ball to the quarterback through his legs, but from the shotgun formation the snap really amounted to a small toss. Dionne's third-quarter slipup had been a crooked wobble that forced Doug to step left to grab it, slowing the start of the play and resulting in a sack.

"What was that all about?" I inquired.

"I guess Pat's concentration lapsed for a second," Doug stated flatly.

"With third and fifteen on the Hombres' forty-yard line?"

Doug's face tightened. "It happens."

While I buzzed through another batch of time-out commercials, I went reflective and took aim at the same time. My question spiraled straight into Doug's numbers.

"Does Walker Cross carry a gun?"

The sleepiness my host had been developing disappeared. "How the hell should I know?" He stared at me hard.

"Do any of the guys?"

"Oh, shit, maybe. I don't know. Probably. I told you we get threats."

"Yes, you did."

"Well, I don't know of any one specific guy who carries, if that's what you're asking."

"Fine. The murder weapon hasn't been found anyway, so I guess it doesn't really matter. And of course all the Hombres were flying back to Houston together at the time of death, so none of them is a suspect . . ."

"Suspects? Is that what you're looking for here?"

"Of course. Aren't you?"

"Well, yeah, but . . ."

"But what? Women aren't supposed to bother their pretty little heads over such gritty details?" I hoped to heaven he would have the chance to watch Michelle give birth; it would do them both good.

"I didn't say that."

I treated Doug to my schoolmarm scowl.

"Well, maybe that was what I meant. I forgot this was you. I mean, Ronnie told me about . . . Oh, shit."

"Apology accepted. Now let's run through the fourth quarter. You narrate. And don't leave out any of the good parts."

TEN

For both football drama and murderous potential, the fourth quarter of the Tomcats/Hombres game deserved a four-star rating.

Attempting a punt, the Tomcats' kicker got clocked on his own twenty-seven yard line. The ball caromed back toward the goal, and just before it rolled out of the end zone one of the opponents dove on it for the touchdown.

A fluke, but the TV cameras caught a few Hombres punching the air with the fervor of frustrated egos. "See that?" said the glint in their eyes. "We're better than our record."

Unfortunately the Tomcats' defense missed that message because they softened into a prevent mode and allowed a steady, nine-play drive to result in an Hombres field goal.

"We knew it wasn't over," Doug recalled, referring to the 21–10 score, "but we thought we were still okay."

Reflecting that confidence, the Tomcats' offensive coach chose the conservative route, directing Doug to hand off to the Tomcats' strongest runner three times straight, a decision that netted only four yards and eliminated a mere two minutes from the clock. On the fourth down punt, the Hombres returned the ball to their own forty-four yard line.

"Here's where we switched to a full zone blitz,"

Doug remarked with a shake of his head. The Hombres promptly executed a weak-side screen pass and took the ball fifty-six yards to the touchdown.

Too little, too late, I agreed with Doug, although not critically. The mental calculations kept the game every bit as interesting as the execution and were equally as chancy.

Seemingly content with a potential 21–17 win, the coaches instructed Doug to use up the clock with three more running plays that went nowhere. Riding on momentum, the Hombres took the fourth down punt and pushed forward into excellent field position—again.

"Watch this tackle by Morani," Doug encouraged me. "Pshew. He really saved our bacon."

I stared with awe as the defensive lineman flattened a 295-pound tackle, then broke loose and crushed the ball carrier as well, singlehandedly stalling the Hombres' drive.

With all their timeouts remaining and 4:35 left in the game Houston opted for a three-point field goal to make it 21–20. Why not? If their defense held and they regained possession, they had plenty of time left to kick the field goal they needed to win.

Yet by the two-minute warning the Tomcats had worked their way to the Hombres' twenty-five yard line. Second and five. Another touchdown appeared to be within their reach, or at least a field goal.

Beside me Doug wagged his head mournfully, recalling the ten-yard holding penalty that came next. Then a mixup led to a missed handoff that stranded him with the ball. The tape showed him retreating, scrambling, and finally getting smothered under a pile of Hombres. I noticed Doug rolling his shoulder as he watched himself being escorted off the field for the second time that day with a trainer at his elbow.

"Still bother you?" I asked.

"Eh, no more than usual. Knocked the wind out of me."

The Tomcats now had third and twenty-four on the forty-four-yard line. Tim Duffy consulted with Offensive Coordinator Roger Prindel at the sideline before trotting onto the field to substitute for Doug. I turned the tape's sound back on to hear what the announcers had to say.

"I've never seen Duffy look so intense," the color commentator remarked to himself and a few million viewers. "He really looks hungry."

Duffy's intensity puzzled me, too. The Tomcats were winning by one point, and with time running out, surely Tim's single objective would be to position his team for a field goal—three more points would put the game out of the Hombres' reach.

Yet Duffy took the snap, rolled to his right, and shot off a perfect pass to Shifflett, who had breezed by everybody and was well on his way toward the end zone.

Touchdown. Tim Duffy trotted off the field collecting congratulations—sadly, for the last time.

The kick went through the crossbars. The crowd cheered and danced in the stands. The Hombres frittered away the last fifty-seven seconds, and the game ended. The final score: 28–20, Tomcats.

Doug laughed and wagged his head ironically.

"What?"

"The handicappers. They did it again."

"What do you mean?"

"The spread was seven and a half, and we won by eight." Which meant that all the water-cooler geeks who wagered on the Tomcats won both their bets and that week's bragging rights. Anything less than a seven-and-a-half-point difference and those bettors would have lost.

Doug's remark simply alluded to how often the

spread came close to reflecting the actual outcome of a game.

"That *is* amazing," I agreed.

When I phoned Rip that night at bedtime, I repeated Doug's wry observation. "Don't you think that's quite a coincidence?"

"Not a coincidence so much as a science," my husband disagreed. "The spread is supposed to make a bet for either team equally attractive. That way—theoretically at least—the pot will be even on either side. The losing money covers the winners, and the bookies don't lose their shirts."

"So since Sunday's spread was right on, the bookies—whoever or wherever they are—probably made out fine."

"Ummm, close enough," he equivocated. "They also take their cut up front, remember?"

I supposed that meant none of them had much reason to flip out and shoot a second-string quarterback.

And yet someone had done just that.

I felt guilty picking Rip's brain any more at that hour, especially when that was exactly what everybody else had done to him all day. So instead I asked what the kids had chosen to watch with the grannies after the rerun of *Shane* ended.

"Professional wrestling," Rip moaned, making it clear what he thought of the choice. "Thank goodness they all went to bed." Hint, hint.

After a few endearments, Rip and I said good night; and I turned out the light and snuggled in.

Professional wrestling?

I closed my eyes and tried to picture the facial expressions, Garry and Chelsea on opposite ends of the family room sofa with Mom and Gracie in between, all of them leaning forward, smiling at the TV? laughing? cheering? All of the above?

I shuddered. Then I squeezed my eyes tight to erase the image. Pretty soon I was asleep.

ELEVEN

When I peeked out the window early Wednesday morning, the grass gleamed silver/white with dew. Across the way a neighbor's car windshield displayed a pattern of ice that would melt with the first rays of sun, only minutes away. But for now long, damp shadows stretched away from a backdrop of thin clear blue.

Pants and a sweater, I concluded as if I had a choice.

I took my time in the shower, leaving Doug to his own morning routine. When I finally arrived in the kitchen, he was busy cleaning up what looked to be a breakfast of eggs, toast, yogurt, fruit, and coffee. Practice resumed today. No doubt he needed the fuel.

"Is there a big library near here?" I asked after we mumbled the amenities. As always, the first sip of coffee opened my eyes, and the smell of a toasting bagel promised me a worthwhile day.

"What do you need?" asked my host.

I wrinkled my nose. "Old magazines and newspapers, I think."

He closed the dishwasher door and examined my face. I had forgotten makeup, but that wasn't it. "You're researching suspects," he concluded.

"Um-humm," I replied gently, as if the conversation were Ping-Pong and I was serving to a beginner.

His pale eyes broke contact, and he gave an exasperated sigh. "Why?"

An answer he could understand: "I take my family very seriously." My sense of justice, my perception of my own responsibilities as a human—he wouldn't get any of that without a lengthy study of me, and neither of us wanted or needed to become that close. Besides, explaining myself would have been too much like discussing religion or politics, something I refuse to do with anybody.

Doug read my face again for a few seconds. Then he shook his head and blinked. "I've never met anyone else quite like you." The statement came with a pinch of surprise.

"Likewise, I'm sure," I replied, because technically he was right. We are all unique. "So are you going to give me directions to the library, or what?"

He drew a map on Michelle's grocery-list pad.

"How about a party supply store, too—for Saturday's shower?" He sketched in directions to a strip mall on Virginia Beach Boulevard.

"Anything else?" He meant to be sarcastic. The idea of me helping him and Michelle with anything more difficult than laundry sat hard. His whole upbringing insisted that he feign amusement, just as his self-image required that he transparently fake tolerance of my efforts on his behalf.

More than understanding, I sympathized with him. The odds were I would fail; and if that happened, playing it his way now would make it easier to laugh off later. For both of us.

In the meantime I intended to dig into Norfolk dirt until I was satisfied there was nothing more to be found. At the very least my efforts comforted Michelle, and maybe they really would save her and Doug from unwelcome scrutiny. If I hurried.

"One other thing . . ." I forestalled Doug as he

reached for his jacket. "Mind if I come by the stadium later?"

"You want to watch practice?"

"Not really. Afterward would be better."

That puzzled him.

I lifted a shoulder. "Maybe you could introduce me to some of the guys, maybe as they're leaving?" Although I didn't hold out hope of looking inside the training room, I wanted to get a sense of the scene of the crime.

Doug used a thin-lipped eye roll that was becoming quite familiar. Fortunately, marriage to Michelle had already taught him that humoring a Siddons offspring took much less time than reasoning with one. Stubbornness was our family's predominant trait.

My host returned to the pen and pad on the kitchen counter under the phone, wrote, tore off a sheet. "Security's been beefed up," he said. "This'll get you into the hallway outside the locker room. Then you're on your own."

"Super," I remarked. He deserved a kiss on the cheek, but he still hadn't shaved. "Super Bowl," I teased instead, garnering me another eye roll.

The Virginia Beach Public Library was a low white meringue of paneling and glass set on a base of brick. Tucked into the curve of the front entrance and rising from a low square of clipped hedge, an abstract silver sculpture either reached for the sky or attempted to take off.

At the edge of the right-hand garden next to the variegated brick walk a tiny sign proclaimed "Adopt-a-Spot" and "Princess Anne Women's Club of Virginia Beach." In tiny letters between the others the single word "Litter" reposed in a pristine expanse of white. I thought the message regrettably unclear, especially considering the literate location.

The library-related signs, however, came across crisp and bold. "Entrance" in red and white above the glass and chrome door. "Emergency Exit Only" on blue, "Renewals, Reserve Pickup," and "Check Out" painted on individual long white tubes in a dangling stack hung to the left, and a white "Information" on a rectangle of red tubes above a long central island.

Also, the glassy openness of the place said "head room," and what else does a library need to say?

I zeroed in on the Information counter and secured the aid of a woman wearing black and white—white shirt, black skirt and vest. I was tempted to make her blush, just so I could ask, "What's black and white and read all over?" When Chelsea was five, the answer was either "a newspaper" or "a blushing nun."

For fifteen minutes the woman led me into a maze of resources that might provide background information on Bobby Frye, Supratech, and my choice of Tomcat coaches and players. Then she turned me loose.

My tolerance for technology was stretched thin by the time I finished, but from the *Boston Globe*'s archives, "Take a Peek in Our Old Drawers," I learned that Bobby's original name had been Robert J. Freyerhoffer, shortened to Frye. He had survived a nasty divorce, barely, from a woman named Joline.

Supratech held several technology companies under its corporate umbrella, all of which manufactured or developed complicated equipment that either made other equipment work better or cleaned up after their messes.

I also learned that Jack Laneer had come to the Tomcats' head coaching job directly from a Cinderella college team nobody not in a neighboring Louisiana parish ever heard of. In other words, Jack Laneer sounded like a judiciously chosen bargain.

The New York Times and the *St. Louis Ledger* sports columnists thought the Tomcats' leader made the transition to pro coaching with ease. *The Philadelphia Inquirer* wanted to wait and see, but Philadelphians are like that.

To my astonishment my watch said ten-thirty. I'd been exploring cyberspace so long I was going to be late picking up Michelle. So I hastily patted my computer monitor good-bye and dropped the various materials the reference librarian had selected for me back at her desk with profuse thanks.

Then it was back in the Grand Cherokee and a hasty trip to Virginia Beach General Hospital.

Michelle sat on the edge of her bed swinging an extra-wide red flat on her toe, back and forth, back and forth. She wore a huge blue denim jumper and a pink blouse. I assumed that Doug had selected the outfit in haste.

"You're late," my pregnant cousin pointed out.

"Sorry." Involved as I was with my own agenda, I had forgotten that discharged hospital patients were only slightly less eager to get moving than greyhounds leaving the gate.

"Take you out to lunch to apologize?"

Michelle's tension evaporated, leaving her wilted. She eased her bulk down from the bed and reached for a black overnight bag, but I beat her to it.

"No, thanks. Let's just get home," she replied.

We remained silent while a nurse transported her to the entrance curb in a wheelchair, silent really until we were half a mile from the hospital when Michelle finally exercised her curiosity and asked what had made me late.

"Research at a library."

"Find anything useful?" she inquired in an effort to sound interested, but she wouldn't remember my answer if she heard it at all; she was that exhausted.

"Just some background. Nothing earth-shattering."

That satisfied her for now. Michelle lolled her head against the headrest and shut her eyes.

She brightened as soon as we entered Broad Bay Point Greens and drove past the tasteful cart-crossing signs. When I stopped in her driveway, she unbuckled her seat belt and climbed out of the Jeep before I could turn off the ignition and do the same. Her eyes drank in the sight of the dark shutters against the earthy brick red, the frosted glass design on the door windows, the ornamental grasses rattling in the breeze, the seagull overhead, and the sky beyond.

I handed my cousin her keys, and she entered her home hungrily, without bothering to suppress a silly smile of pride.

"How about some tomato soup and a tuna sandwich?" I suggested.

"Toasted cheese instead of tuna?" she asked hopefully. No arguments on who would cook, I noticed. Convenient, but not necessarily a good sign.

"I can probably do that—in my sleep," I teased, keeping it upbeat, keeping my worries to myself.

We ate, and, as predicted, Michelle could scarcely wait to take a nap.

"Mind if I go out for a while?" I inquired from her bedroom doorway.

"No. No, of course not." She was already under the covers, her denim jumper replaced by a nightgown.

"You be okay until dinner?"

"Fine. Go. Go." She wiggled a few fingers to shoo me out.

I went, but still I worried—about her and Kewpie/QB.

And about the timing of her recent crises, which came so suddenly after the news of Tim Duffy's death. Had it been caused entirely by shock, compounded by her fears regarding her husband?

Or had it been brought on by something even more awful to contemplate—overexertion along with extreme stress?

I shook the thought away, biting my lip to punish my disloyal suspicions. Doug and Michelle had been at home together at the time of the murder. Having dinner. Watching TV.

Doug and Michelle—together. That's what they said, and that was the end of that—for me, anyway. Let the police break their alibi if they could. I had plenty of other pots to stir.

Plenty.

TWELVE

Party City in Collins Square claimed to be "The Discount Party Super Store," and so it was. Two weeks and one day shy of Christmas, the vast seasonal aisle to the right of the entrance almost sighed with fatigue. Or maybe the shopworn disarray had just occurred. Either way, it looked like my friend Didi's closet prior to a big date.

The baby-shower aisle ran perpendicular to the holiday items, just in from the shelves facing the checkout. Pink and blue ribbons and paper storks, "It's a Boy" banners, tissue umbrellas, invitations shaped like Teddy bears, and a thousand other miscellaneous items hung from wire hooks on pegboard, not that you could find the pegboard easily. Every item was frivolous—yes. Silly—yes. Tasteful . . . no.

Panic seemed to rise from my fingertips to my ears as I did the aisle up and back. Luella Hixson's dismissive "You mean one o' them white bread with no crust cucumber sandwich kinda showers?" taunted me, and I developed a low-grade blush trying to imagine what a twenty-four-inch tissue accordion baby bottle would look like in the home of Teal and Morani Todd.

"It's for a good cause; it's for a good cause; it's for a good cause," I chanted as I loaded a plastic basket with my selections. A contraption you were supposed to hang from a chandelier made the cut. It opened into fluffy accordion tissue streamers, four of them that swooped down the sides of your dining table. Pink and blue, of course. Plus a fourteen-inch stork and a couple of balloons for the mailbox. Ordinary air from ordinary lungs would have to do—I refused to return for helium. I thought about little upside-down umbrella candy cups, but in the end I simply couldn't do it, not with Luella's "Lord, you white people slay me" echoing in my ears.

The checkout clerk answered my inquiry about a baby store with a jerk of her thumb. "Babies 'R' Us," she added, straight across the street. Investigating a murder would not get me out of buying a shower gift. Balancing the national budget and curing cancer would not get me out of buying a gift.

So I scooted the car across the busy highway into the Loehmann's Plaza lot. A Calico Corners upholstery fabric store like the one in Devon, PA, made me momentarily homesick while offering a clue to the affluence of the plaza's customers.

Along the strip the entrance arches for Babies "R" Us were sheltered by a short Spanish tile overhang, but inside looked like any spacious baby equipment store I'd ever seen.

As my own kids were now eleven and thirteen, I requested guidance in my selection. Babies might not have changed since Moses's time, but manufacturers of baby-related products were still churning out new fads.

"Prams are extremely popular," oozed the clerk. We had just passed a $339.99 Milano Carriage/Stroller, and she accurately discerned that I would not be springing for it.

"Umbrella strollers are out?" I inquired.

"Um, well . . ." she hedged. "How about a vibrating hammock swing with a lounge chair?"

"How about this bouncer seat?" I countered, framing it with my hands.

"Wrapped?"

"Wrapped," I agreed. "Put a pacifier in the ribbon, okay?"

By the time I paid up, I could scarcely wait to get over to the stadium and spy on murder suspects.

Even after a forty-minute drive into Norfolk, a fifteen-minute search for the stadium area, and a couple spins around the long block to find the entrance Doug recommended, I was still a bit early for ogling exiting Tomcats. A stroll around outside seemed worthwhile. Admire the sights. Get the lay of the land.

Nimitz Stadium, named for Chester W. Nimitz, one of only two five-star admirals from World War II, resided across from Norfolk's Scope Arena and was surrounded by St. Pauls Boulevard, Brambleton Avenue, and Monticello. The lot where I left my car bordered on the latter, so I set out past the phone company's building toward the "newly expanded" Open House Diner. The Greyhound Bus station on the corner of Brambleton looked as overused and undercleaned as every other bus station I'd ever seen.

From the brief lawns gracing the street sides of the sports complexes some unassuming, winter-bare trees waved good-bye to me as I proceeded on Monticello. Walking briskly, I came within sight of a three-story shopping mall named MacArthur Center. All around, parking garages had stepped into the vicinity like big feet into small shoes. Most of them still retained the dove-gray color of new cement.

The impression was lots of people around for lots of different reasons. An escaping murderer could explain himself, or herself, without much difficulty, especially if the killer wasn't personally connected to the victim. What I still couldn't imagine was a crazed fan having poise enough to calm down and slip away unnoticed. The opposite seemed much more likely.

I retreated, then turned right past Scope. The sun hung low at that hour, impatient to drop the temperature on this short December day into the freezing range. Already my face wore a damp frigid mask, and pulling my wool collar up didn't entirely prevent my silver hoop earrings from conducting the cold right through my earlobes.

Scope Arena reminded me of two sugar cookies with chocolate filling sewn together with zigzags of white thread. Nimitz was more baklava, honey-colored layers of wafer cut in the shape of a stop sign. The blimp perspective on TV showed it to be a fragile gold ring with an emerald center, something the Super Bowl jeweler could really work with should the Tomcats ever rise so high.

The guard inside the office entrance Doug suggested rose from his seat behind the curved desk he manned alone. White-haired and lean, he puzzled over Doug's informal permission slip long enough to memorize it. Either he would send it along to the FBI for a fingerprint check, or he would let me in. I couldn't guess which from his expression.

"Douggie's cousin-in-law, eh?" the man remarked after he formed his conclusion. "Know where you're goin'?" The Southern drawl warmed him up considerably. Maybe the sour expression etched into his wrinkles came from too much black coffee.

"I'm new in town."

He gestured that away as he opened a gate at the end of the desk. "Whole bizness only been here two years anyhoo." He chuckled at himself then strode through the lobby toward a hall with elevators and a door at the end.

On the way past I admired the welcoming decor: plush Astroturf-green carpet, two orange sofas bracketed by walls displaying a huge aerial photograph of the stadium's opening day. Opening day because a ceremonial wedge of six twin-tailed F-14's flew overhead. Piloted only by top guns, these "Tomcats" looked a lot like the triangular staples used to secure pictures into a wooden frame. Oceana was presently the only Navy base that flew F-14's, so naming the area's professional football team after them seemed perfectly natural.

The guard led me through the interior door into the lowest walkway that ringed the stadium.

"How is attendance?" I asked as I followed him across a short expanse of cement to a thirty-yard-long ramp that ended with a cattle chute onto the field.

"Depends on which way the wind's blowin'," he replied as he turned to leave. "Locker room's over there. You can't go in," he added, just in case.

The hall had the humidity and smell of a crypt, and a cold blast of witch's breath blew in off the field. I rested my back on the wall and my elbow on a green wire trash can. The halogen lights in the inner walkway did nothing to dispel the eeriness.

Two unmarked doors of gray metal punctuated the northern direction I faced, the locker room door to my right and the training room to its left, according to the news coverage I'd watched after the murder. Inside the two rooms were apparently connected.

I monitored the two doors while pursuing my own thoughts, i.e. all the ways there were to make money from a football franchise: parking, tickets, endorsed souvenirs, concessions, stadium ads, programs and program ads, radio and TV ads and coverage, superbox rentals and catering, and probably other frills I forgot.

Attendance mattered for most all of those categories. Attendance depended on a winning record, and a winning record depended on the men who would soon file out of the two doors in the opposite wall.

"Hey. Whatchu doin' 'ere?" He was twice my size, two-eighty or more, and his confrontation two steps out of the locker room made me think of street gangs and rape.

I told him I was waiting for my cousin.

"Who you cousin?" he inquired none too sweetly. I wondered whether this was his usual personality or whether he secretly worried that I might shoot him.

"Doug Turner."

"Yeah? You want I should tell Douggie you here?" He was calling my bluff, or so he thought.

"Not if he's in the shower," I said. "We're not that kind of cousins."

Two-eighty snorted his disappointment, turned, and walked up the ramp without announcing me to anyone. I hadn't recognized him from my research or from watching the games on TV.

Still, he had offered me a chance to think about exactly who I was poking with my pin of suspicion. Men more than twice my size. Men with super physical prowess and cunning. College graduates almost to a man, for college football was their prep school and their farm team together, the stage from which they were selected for adulation and wealth most of us would never know.

At the Thanksgiving table Aunt Harriet had asked Ronnie what a certain few players were like as people. Before answering Ronnie glanced at Doug with a conspiratorial smile, a smile that telegraphed that the question came frequently and would be answered with harmless, disposable words.

Uncle Stan noticed, too, and cut through Doug's intended cotton candy with a cleaver.

"I'll tell you," he said as if his Bing Crosby sweater had suddenly developed starch. He had been pouting at his teaspoon, dismissing it as a possible

Dolly Parton's bathtub. Now he tossed it aside with a clank and spread his gnarled hands. "Plenty of them bastards are spoiled brats. Present company excepted, of course." He glanced placatingly toward Doug. "They got talents you and I can only dream of— phenomenal talents—twenty-ten vision maybe, superior eye-hand coordination. A competitive streak the size of Canada. Strength, speed, stamina. Size *and* smarts." Stan paused to suppress a small belch, which nobody missed because we were collectively holding our breath.

He waved a hand. "Ever since they was little, everybody's been telling them they was special, treating them special, making them think they stood out from the crowd just because they could knock other guys down and maybe catch a ball." He frowned his parental-style lament. "Their heads get turned, just like happens to movie stars and billionaires."

Ronnie bunched his napkin into a wad and tossed it aside. "You're right, Stan," he admitted. "A lot of them are blessed and pampered and probably even arrogant. But what can you expect? If that many people fussed over you, sooner or later you might think you deserved it, too."

Michelle nodded. "Either that or they go completely the other way and take no credit at all."

"What do you mean?" Harriet asked.

"Lots of the players are very religious," Michelle elaborated. "They think God's responsible for everything good that's ever happened to them."

"Where do you stand?" Harriet asked Doug rather bluntly, even for her.

"Yeah. How come you turned out so normal?" Stan seconded.

Doug's blond complexion glowed crimson under the family's scrutiny. When he finally determined that yes, we truly expected an answer, he bucked up and gave us one.

"I'm just a hired gun," he said. "When I'm out of bullets, they'll get another gun."

Stan interrupted everyone else's silence. "Naw," he said, making us realize how wedded he was to his theory or how deeply he was into his cups.

Generously, Doug helped him out. "Then again, whenever I got cocky, my mother refused to let me have dessert." He lifted a forkful of mincemeat and crust.

Michelle raised her glass of cider. "Here's to your mother," she said, but Doug couldn't hold his smile. His mother was presently out in California alone, struggling to cope with her daughter's death.

As I shivered in the icy hallway outside the Tomcats' locker room, it was Stan's stubborn convictions that led me to think of another comment I had heard. About the time the O. J. Simpson murder trial eclipsed the weather as the conversational topic for strangers, I had taken a camera to a repair shop in Upper Darby, Pennsylvania.

"It's football," the owner reflected as he tinkered with my old Yashika. "Gives players the impression they can get what they want with force."

And another remark by a man in his sixties who still played club football: "You can hit people . . . and it's legal." This on a TV special about the prevalence of the game. The reporter's interview with a little boy in his first peewee year sounded much the same. Both athletes were pleased as punch to have found a behavioral loophole.

Just then a maintenance guy burst around the corner. I squealed. He had been aiming to throw an empty cup in the trash can I was leaning on, but he braked to a halt and gawked at me.

"Waiting for my cousin," I offered in anticipation of another challenge.

"Think I oughta frisk ya?" he inquired. The name on his blue overalls said "Frank."

"You and what army?"

"Me and my little, aw, shucks, you're too easy." He turned on his heel and disappeared, but not before clarifying the point to which Two-eighty had indirectly alluded. Women stood in this hallway regularly, waiting for their husbands or boyfriends; or, if they were fans, hoping for a glimpse of the players.

The point was, it didn't take much strength to pull a trigger.

Soon two men burst from the locker room carrying gym bags. The darker one with a huge diamond stud sparkling from his left ear paused to hammer his finger in the air. "No way, man, Butkus hit much harder than Lambert. Man, that Butkus was a fuckin' truck." Since the speaker was in his late twenties, even younger than I, I understood the discussion to be rhetorical.

When he glanced my way, I straightened up and held my breath. He was Walker Cross, #86, the receiver whose guaranteed contract had been put into jeopardy by losing so much playing time last Sunday. Laneer had benched him shortly after he tripped up reaching for a toss by Tim Duffy. Whether he blamed the murder victim for his benching was anybody's guess; but my own vote was yes.

Gold chains thick enough to provide snow traction for an eighteen-wheeler rested in the V of his open-throated shirt. He wore a baseball hat backward on his shaved head, elaborate gym shoes, a gold nugget ring, and a thick gold watch. Everything about him screamed money enough for style and ego enough to flaunt it.

Dismissing me as insignificant, he resumed his discussion.

Cross's companion happened to be a direct beneficiary of Duffy's death—the fading star, Willet Smith, #17, formerly the Tomcats' third-string quarterback, presently second in the lineup just behind Doug Turner. He wore a quiet, thoughtful expression in response to Cross's powerful personality. Lighter skinned and smooth-walking in his buffed loafers and camelhair sportcoat, he wore his hair like lumps of yarn above a Fu Manchu mustache. His eyes might have been green or hazel, his slacks black wool and perfectly creased.

I was tempted to shadow them back to the lobby but could think of no way to escape should they confront me. Still, each of them had given me a sense of who they were. Enough for now.

Men began to pour from the locker room in groups of three and four, but often singly, too.

Morani Todd proved to be the most imposing. He wore a custom-sized brown leather sportcoat over a darker brown turtleneck and brown wool slacks. His eyes seemed to apologize for his body's bulk, as if the man himself wished he were smaller. Todd's hands, too, worked the delicate gestures of a scholar. The baby shower would be in his home, and I looked forward to seeing his personal surroundings.

Patrick Dionne, the center, carried his muscle under a layer of lard. Or maybe it was all muscle, but either way he was the classic no-neck jock. Walking that Big-Man-on-Campus shoulder swagger, alone, not speaking or glancing my way, I got no sense of him other than his formidable presence.

Bo Shifflett, on the other hand, made me shiver. He wore sweats in the team colors of sky blue and navy, with the jacket zipped up tight to his chin. A reputed clean-freak, he appeared to have scrubbed himself white, down to his fingertips. In profile, Shifflett's honey-blond crewcut and hook nose suggested the flat, uninvolved gaze of a predator—a hawk with huge pupils calculating trajectory from above, or a fanatic in a bell tower watching you through crosshairs. On Thanksgiving Doug had offered Bo Shifflett's name as an example of a God-fearing player. Curiously, that knowledge did nothing to diminish my fear of him.

Late in the exiting process Doug emerged from the locker room in the company of the Tomcats' head coach. The man appeared to be somewhat older than his wife, Barbara, or maybe the blotches and spots on his fair skin testified to too many years out in the open air.

"Oh!" Doug exclaimed. "Sorry, Gin. Forgot you were coming. This is Jack Laneer. Jack, this is my wife's cousin, Ginger Barnes."

I shook the older man's chapped hand, while he paused to finish what he'd been saying to Doug. Something about the Eagles' offense that didn't matter to me.

While they wrapped it up, I debated about whether or not to be obnoxiously blunt. In the end I decided I didn't really care what Jack Laneer thought of me—in five minutes I probably wouldn't even be a memory to the guy.

"So, Jack," I said into my first opening. "How come you benched Walker Cross last Sunday? Inquiring minds want to know." My inquiring mind, anyway.

The man silently appealed to Doug for help by angling his wispy faded eyebrows into a peak of dismay.

Responding well to suggestion, Doug grasped my elbow and guided me toward the exit. "Her husband's a coach," he remarked over his shoulder by way of apology.

"Father," I corrected him, but already we were beyond Laneer's hearing.

"What the hell was that for?" Doug demanded.

I shrugged off his hand and his question. "I wanted to see his reaction."

"Well, you saw it. Now don't ever do that again. Okay?"

"Okay," I agreed. Why would I need to ask Jack Laneer the same question twice anyhow?

When I called home at dinnertime, Chelsea's voice made me homesick. Yet I was quick to remember the rule that all mothers of teenagers learn the hard way. I opened the conversation in neutral.

"What's for dinner?"

"I did spaghetti, salad, and garlic bread. We already ate."

"You burn the garlic bread?"

My daughter's tone became condescending. "No, Mom. You really just have to watch it."

"Easy for you to say."

She snorted.

"So where are Nana and Gracie?"

"They're over at Letty's playing poker. They left a note. That friend Letty met at Kmart is there, too."

So my mother and her buddy were just next door, not too far away for the kids to find in case of an emergency. However, it was already dark, 6 P.M., which meant Letty was probably losing pennies left and right. For an eccentric old woman she was surprisingly competitive.

"I think you should run over and tell your grandmother dinner's ready."

Chelsea mumbled that it was way past ready—it was cold—but Garry grabbed the phone and rescued me from hearing more echoes of my own complaints. "Where's that old tape recorder we used to have?" he inquired.

"Fine. How are you?" I said.

"Hi, Mom. How are you? Do you know where it is? I can't find it anywhere, and I need it for Sunday."

"In that end table next to the sofa toward the patio door. It'll need batteries."

"Thanks, Mom."

Rip came on. "When are you coming home?" he asked.

"Soon," I replied. As soon as possible.

Spaghetti, salad, and garlic bread sounded pretty good about then, so that was what I made for Michelle, Doug, and me. The old hot dog rolls I doctored up for garlic bread let me down, though. I watched them broil for about thirty seconds, then I began thinking about Jack Laneer's non-answer. Did that mean *he* sat Walker Cross down, or that Bobby Frye asked him to? By the time I decided that no answer was no answer, the hot dog rolls wore inedible oval edges as black as shoe polish.

Michelle, Doug, and I watched a little evening TV together, but the mother-to-be was looking especially fragile. When Doug cuddled her in his lap and began kissing her hair, I claimed I was sleepy and went upstairs. Ronnie had given me his itinerary, and it was time I reported in.

He listened without comment to what I'd been doing, grunted a few times over what I'd learned, and finally said, "What's next?"

"Damned if I know. I have high hopes for the baby shower. But honestly, I'm getting ready to go home. Sunday's about the longest I can stay here."

"Please?" Ronnie wheedled. "I promise to get

you a sideline pass for the future game of your choice
if you stick it out.''

''My family . . .''

''Michelle's your family, too.'' And Kewpie. He
forgot to mention Kewpie, but he probably knew the
baby wouldn't be something a softie like me would
forget.

''Nevertheless.'' I explained that I felt I wasn't really getting anywhere.

''You don't know that for sure.''

''The police . . .''

''Puh.''

''You can really get me a sideline pass? Like you
did for Olga?'' The Swedish flavor-of-the-month he
wished his family would forget.

''Pshew. Will you leave the Olga thing alone already? Yes. I can swing you a pass on a one-time
basis. Just you, not the whole girls' volleyball team
from Bryn Derwyn Academy.''

''What about Rip, or the kids?''

''No.'' That sounded like a real no.

''I'm still going home Sunday.''

Ronnie considered that. ''All right. I suppose you
can't stay there forever, but you'll give it your best
shot between now and then. Right?''

''Right.''

My best shot, another sports metaphor and an in-
advertent faux pas. But just then Ronnie probably
hadn't been thinking about Tim Duffy.

THIRTEEN

Thanks to Ronnie's groveling, my subconscious must have been working all night, because I woke up with an idea. I would try to find out whether Bobby Frye was responsible for Walker Cross being benched. After all, he was the one who would save all that money if Cross didn't reach his quotas.

Discovering whether Frye went sneaky cheap on his premier receiver would also help deflate the notion that Cross solely blamed Tim Duffy for his bad day. Sooner or later I'd have to learn whether any sort of competitive animosity actually existed between Duffy and Cross; but frankly, the obstacles between me and Bobby Frye seemed less formidable than the prospect of facing Walker Cross. Bravery wasn't always wise.

So, since I'm not entirely comfortable with lying in the interest of a greater good—Oliver North and salesmen notwithstanding—my first piece of business was to wake up Didi. Stocks didn't figure much into the Barnes family lifestyle, education paying what it does; but Didi's ex-husband was a broker and she had been a quick study.

"Ugh." my best friend since diapers grunted into the phone.

"It's me," I replied.

"Where are you?" She must have called my house recently and learned that I was away.

"Virginia Beach."

"Michelle still having problems?"

"Yes, and not just with the baby."

Didi got it on the first try. "Tim Duffy!" she exclaimed, fully awake now. As I said, she followed pro football mainly because of the tight pants, but she specifically watched the Tomcats because of my relationship to Doug. And, of course, any American who wasn't aware of Tim's murder had been in a sensory deprivation tank since Sunday.

Regardless, the undercurrent of excitement coming across the wire put me on guard. Incurably hooked on dramatic fiction, my best friend was inclined to romanticize my ability to investigate and her ability to help me. For that reason I used Didi's input as one would cayenne pepper—judiciously—because in spite of any precautions I might take, she was capable of overpowering every other spice in the stew.

So when she said, "What do you need?" in a sitting-up-straight, all-business voice I gulped back a small qualm before proceeding. A pinch of salt, a daily dose of risk. Everything in moderation.

"I need two shares of stock in a company held by Supratech."

"Why?"

"To use as a crowbar. I need to get inside Bobby Frye's door." She would know who he was; he was wealthy and divorced.

The pauses between questions stretched. "When?" she asked.

"I should be dressed to go out in about half an hour."

I visualized Didi with her blonde head tilted just so, thumb and forefinger rubbing her forehead.

"So what do I need to do?" I asked. My impatience was probably as predictable to Didi as her "Thinker" position was to me.

"Do you have an account with an on-line discount broker?"

"Would I be calling you if I did?"

"Sorry. Need my coffee. Does Cynthia have a broker for her retirement income?"

I vaguely remembered a doddering man Mom introduced as a genius with money. At the time I made a mental note to ask more about him and then forgot to follow through. I jotted down another note, this time on paper.

"Nobody I can call this morning," I answered.

"Okay. I'll just buy them for you."

"You can do that?"

"Are you going to pay me?"

"Well, sure."

"So what's the problem?"

"Won't somebody be able to check whose name the stock is in?"

"Not this morning they won't. It'll be held at the broker's in street name—lucky for you. If Bobby Frye found out you only owned two shares . . ."

"Right." I would be screwed.

We ironed out the details. Didi would consult Supratech's Web site to learn which companies it held, then she would buy me a couple shares of one of them through her own Internet account. Didi demanded lunch at Pizza Hut next Tuesday as her commission.

Michelle lent me a Black Watch plaid blazer and slacks outfit from her pre-Kewpie collection, and I was just hopping into my second shoe when Didi called back.

"Break a leg," she said after she assured me I was now a stockholder of Kenthaven Electronics, maker of computer cables and various other widgets.

"Bless you and the horse you rode in on," I riposted.

"By the way," she remarked in a casual manner

that made my skin tingle. "Did you know Bobby Frye is being sued by some of his stockholders?"

My throat made a strangled noise.

"I take that as a no," Didi surmised. "Need the details?"

"Yes," I croaked.

"Okay. Bobby is, among other things, president of Goaltech, the Internet provider. So he got the bright idea of buying a company that makes routers, which are used in the comm rooms that are located in every state where Goaltech operates. The comm rooms—communications rooms—are sort of big closets full of fiber wires and rows and rows of blue racks. A router is a little piece of hardware that forwards e-mail, directs your Web inquiries to the right data-banks, stuff like that. In other words, Bobby had Goaltech buy a company that made some of the hardware it uses to physically operate its system. You with me?"

"Yes."

"The problem is that the company he bought makes lousy routers, which the Goaltech people found out the hard way—by using the product themselves."

"Ouch."

"Ouch is right. Tied the whole system into knots. Subscribers bailed left and right. Goaltech's stock took a dive, and the stockholders put together a nasty little class action suit aimed directly at his highness. Bobby's insurance company is fighting it, of course, but it looks like he's already taken a direct hit where it hurts the most—right in his pocket."

"Amazing. How did you find out so much so quick?"

"Phoned Harvey. I wanted to ask him which Supratech holding to buy for you." Didi's ex-husband was still a broker. However, he lived in New Mexico.

"Thanks," I said with sincere gratitude—who

wants to hold even two shares of a rotten stock? "But wasn't it a little early to phone Albuquerque?"

"Harvey did seem a bit snide when he told me about the lawsuit. You think I woke him up, huh?"

A light bulb went on. "Yes, I mean no. I don't think that was what ticked him off," I remarked with the glee of any garden-variety gossip.

"I didn't wake him up?"

"Oh, you woke him up all right. But I'll bet both my assets he was jealous."

"Of Bobby Frye?"

"Divorced and rich, your favorite kind. You said you were in a hurry to buy into one of the guy's companies 'for . . . a . . . friend.' "

"Son of a bitch, you're right. You still owe me fifty-six forty-eight, but Pizza Hut's definitely on me."

I hung up and smiled. A real live investor in the American economy. Me. Interesting feeling. Exhilarating. Scary. I felt simultaneously on the edge and out of my element. At home I would give one of the shares to each of my kids, to let them experience the kick, maybe learn from it.

But only after I used my purchase to meet the owner of the Norfolk Tomcats.

Even with Didi's confidence builder in place, I had more homework to do before presenting myself to Bobby Frye's minions. First I would make certain he was in town, a good bet considering all the problems the shooting must have caused the Tomcats. Then I needed directions to his Virginia Beach office and time enough to drive there.

Phone calls accomplished all but the latter, and by eleven-thirty I was fidgeting from foot to foot in an elevator full of Yuppies.

At first the snuggled-up feeling bothered me, but

as each floor claimed another one or two suits, I found myself wanting to shriek, "Don't go!"

When at last the glossy copper doors deposited me onto Bobby Frye's floor, I alone stepped out into the blue and teak lobby.

"Mr. Frye's office?" I inquired of the receptionist.

"Is he expecting you?" the woman asked with polite neutrality.

"Yes," I said. If not me, someone like me but far more official.

The receptionist gestured down a short hall to another anteroom of steel blue. Even in that short a distance my black flats picked up enough static electricity to friz the lining of Michelle's slacks. I restored the air pockets around my shins, then waited while the Supratech's chairman of the board's assistant finished on the phone. She didn't seem so much petite as shrunken, perhaps from the Amazon size down to something that would fit under a Christmas tree.

"Yes," she said to the caller. "I'll tell him . . . you have to cancel lunch because," she was writing, "because your mother had a heart attack. Oh, Mr. Ingram, I'm so sorry to hear that. Mr. Frye will be, too. Yes, of course, call back and reschedule anytime . . ."

Bobby Frye's desk sentry winced to think of the waste of her employer's precious time, but her sigh seemed to accept that there was nothing to be done. After all, Mr. Ingram's mother must be a real person, albeit an invisible one, and she did have a very real problem. These things happen.

"May I help you?" she asked now that her emotions were back in order.

"I'm here to invite Mr. Frye to lunch," I ad-libbed, quickly adding that I needed his advice on a business matter just in case the woman had something personal going with her boss. After all, he had just gone through an expensive divorce, probably for a very good reason. For all I knew, the reason could have been her.

Both of us jumped when the man himself burst from his inner sanctum. "Sheila," the superexecutive cried, "do you have anything I can use for cuff links? I brought in the wrong kind of shirt."

In keeping with the less-is-more theme, Bobby Frye stood a mere two inches taller than my five foot six. Also, he was small-boned and lean. The Tomcats probably had to resist patting him on the head or bouncing him in the palms of their hands.

Sheila proffered a pair of paper clips and a stapler.

Bobby regarded both choices with seriously pursed lips, finally opting for the stapler. When Sheila pulled his wrist down to her desktop, he squirmed.

"Hurry up," he complained. "I'll be late for my lunch with Ingram." Clomp, clomp.

"No, you won't." Clomp, clomp. "He canceled. Family emergency."

My cue to step forward. "I volunteered to take his place," I said.

Frye furrowed his pale-brown brows together and inquired, "Do I know you?" His subtle black and off-white plaid suit gave off a rich, low-grade sheen; and now that his cuffs were closed, the man projected a certain authority.

Still, I placed his age at no more than thirty-eight or forty. Young to have earned and lost and re-earned a couple of fortunes. Yet I gathered from Didi that it could be like that with technology companies, especially if you pressed the limits.

"I'm a stockholder—and a fan," I replied.

Frye's eyebrows returned to parade-rest. I decided that his smooth cheeks were eminently pinchable. He also had a nice straight nose.

"Oh, the Tomcats. Yes." Personal pride in his

most public possession lifted the corners of his mouth into an impish grin.

"No," I corrected, "of you."

"I beg your pardon?" He stuffed his hands into his pants pockets and blinked at me.

"I'm a fan of yours. I like the Tomcats, of course, but I really admire your other business accomplishments. That's why I'm here."

Sheila eyed me with suspicion, as well she should have. Women can always detect when another of their kind was laying it on thick, something men almost always overlook. However, she was professional enough or curious enough to allow my performance to continue.

For my part, I wasn't so much lying as exaggerating, not flirting so much as taking a shortcut to acceptance. Another man might have used a similar form of flattery with different body language. I didn't feel good about playing games with the guy, and I would establish my unavailability the first chance I got—right after I was sure of my opportunity to ask my questions. But if I had had more time, I would have chosen some other approach.

"I'm afraid I still don't understand." Bobby's tolerance for this was running out. Time to throw my best pitch.

"I own a number of shares of Kenthaven Electronics that I'm intending to give to a certain charity, but I'd like your advice on whether to hold the shares a bit longer. Also, I'm hungry, and I heard that your lunch date fell through."

Bobby Frye pinched his lip and looked me up and down. Then he glanced at Sheila for guidance. She shrugged.

Then before I could manage another breath, Frye's hand was on my back guiding me down the hall toward the elevator.

"We'll go to the Jewish Mother. My treat. Ever been there?"

"No, I'm from out of town."

"Mind if I drive? I've got a new car, and I've been dying to get my hands on it all morning."

"Do you drive as fast as you talk?"

"Not if you don't want me to."

The car turned out to be a red Masarati. Bobby Frye, boy billionaire, held the door and eased my elbow down as I slid inside. That was the first moment I fully appreciated the bravery of the sailors who signed on with Columbus, the ones who didn't really believe the world was round.

"We've all got to go some way," they must have figured, "and between here and the edge of the earth, a meal is still a meal."

FOURTEEN

The Masarati purred on straightaways and growled around corners. Judging by his expression, the Tomcats' owner seemed to be evaluating the sound, listening for flaws.

We passed an elegant old brick-and-stone structure with "Cavalier" written in some sort of plant life across the sloping front lawn, probably a survivor from Virginia Beach's younger days.

"Out of town, eh?" Bobby Frye finally stirred himself to ask. "Where from?"

"Philadelphia."

"Yeah? Eagles are good this year. They'll give the 'cats a run for my money." I tried to smile appreciatively at his humor.

He drove efficiently, quickly but not frighteningly so. "This rides like a dream," I commented.

"You want to try it later?"

"Oh, no. I'm nervous enough right here."

Frye laughed. "I'm not surprised. You're awfully married to be picking up strangers."

My lungs decided it was okay to breathe. "You noticed."

"Oh, yeah."

"Do you mind?"

"Oh, hell no. Makes for a change. Unless you're selling something. It's usually one thing or the other."

I reiterated the stock donation spiel. Frye didn't answer, just steered the powerful car east then south onto a wider avenue along the beach. Left and right were tidy low hotels and other businesses rooted into much paving.

Frye pulled into a lot at 30th Street, nosed the sports car to the curb facing the ocean. The nearest landscape was a bit of grass, an asphalt bike path, then a strip of tall white lamp posts stretching out of sight in each direction. A cement "boardwalk" supported trash cans, two telephone kiosks, and several wooden benches. Beyond that the long, winter-blown beach was stroked by blue, brown, and slate-gray water broken into ragged strips of foam.

Frye opened a window. Sharp winter air spiced with salt water opened my eyes and cleared my head. I couldn't shake my nervousness, though, couldn't forget that despite all his wealth and power, this man probably should be regarded as a murder suspect.

Frye turned toward me, his arm draped behind his bucket seat. "You need the deduction this calendar year?" he asked. He had decided to play my game, answer my question—whether he believed my ploy or not.

I said, "No," because saying "Yes" would have exposed me as a liar. This close to the end of the tax year, if I had even theoretically needed the write-off, I simply would have made the donation and been done with it.

"Then why don't you hold your shares until this time next year?" Bobby recommended. "Our last dividends are posted on December fifteenth. I think you can be fairly confident that the stock will rise in value between now and then, and the appreciation will give you a larger deduction. Your charity will gain greater benefits, too."

"Thank you."

I suddenly felt awful for insinuating myself into this man's life . . . although . . . I quickly reconsidered. He hadn't taken long to agree to lunch with me, and evidently it wasn't because he believed I was available.

Maybe he was just another lonely divorced person, made even lonelier by his success. Regular people scarcely ever invited their bosses out for so much as a drink, and with good reason—too little to be gained, too many pitfalls to avoid—on either side.

"So tell me about this Jewish Mother restaurant," I suggested brightly. "It sounds like fun."

Frye broke off his contemplation of the ocean and scowled as he threw the car into reverse. "Why don't I just show you?"

Had he become slightly peeved with me, or disappointed? I thought I knew how to fix either one, but first we needed to back off, regroup, reconsider.

Not many blocks along and inland to Pacific Avenue an unassuming building squatted at the edge of the sidewalk. Green window squares had been unprofessionally painted with Hanukkah symbols. ?

Frye parked in a far corner of the adjacent lot and helped me out. Then he hustled through the cold breeze to open the restaurant door for me.

Inside to the left lay a long case of baked goods with potholders and mugs hanging above. A ceramic cookie jar of an older woman with round glasses seemed to offer a brown bag of goodies from The Jewish Mother. To the right and straight ahead lavender and aqua cubbyholes with black edges displayed bottled beverages of all sorts. Farther in to the right lay a bar, and beyond that was a stage backed by a wall of photos and a sign that said "Budweiser presents Rumble Fish." For evenings, no doubt.

Everywhere else booths or round tables with bentwood chairs had been scribbled with crayons or markers until what had been graffiti crossed over into a decor.

We found a booth on a far wall and Bobby greeted a smiling waiter, William "Clint" Carter by name.

"Yo, Mr. Frye, what'll it be today?" Clint slapped napkins and flatware onto the scarred table.

"My guest here needs a minute with the menu," Bobby said, "but in the meantime, something to drink?" he asked me with a raised eyebrow.

"Red wine?" I had to lose this edginess somehow.

The waiter listed their offerings, and I chose. My host, however, went with a German beer called Maisel's Weisse.

The menu consisted of four pages of newsprint, which little visitors could color with crayons from a styrofoam cup provided on each table. Cartoons of the bespectacled "mother" graced every page. Food items went by such names as "Gemiste Salad," "Mother's Grandson Frank (a hot dog)" or "Mother's Sister Adele (hot corned beef, cole slaw, and Russian dressing)." I chose "Mother's Mother," a chicken salad sandwich with apples, raisins, nuts, avocado, and Muenster cheese. My host ordered the Jewish Mother Club.

"Pleasant as this is," Bobby Frye remarked after the drinks arrived, "why are we really here?"

I had prepared for this, but I squirmed nonetheless. "Partly the donation"—I hesitated—"and partly I wanted to know if you thought the value of my stock would go down because of the . . . the murder."

"You must have one hell of a lot of stock," Bobby thought aloud. "What is it? A thousand shares? Two?"

I waved the question away. "So what do you think?"

"A little dip, if anything." His face had gone a bit gray, I imagined because he was thinking of the stockholders' lawsuit, which was much more likely to hurt my hypothetical shares than Tim Duffy's murder.

We perused each other for a moment, and I decided I had better address the other difficulty, too. To ignore it would make me appear ignorant.

"We won't even mention the other, uh, problem," I remarked kindly. "You're obviously a superb manager, and I'm sure your lawyers will have no trouble proving that in court." Frye grunted. "A little dip, if anything," I quoted him, again referring to the value of his company's stock.

He huffed out a small laugh.

Mercifully, the food arrived; and I asked Clint to bring me a Diet Sprite to go with it. The wine had been a bad idea—or maybe not, since it was gone.

Alone again, I was faced with a conversational crisis, for Frye had withdrawn into his own dour speculations. I devised a question calculated to make any venture capitalist grin. "Are you developing anything interesting?"

The corporate genius took a bite of his sandwich, marveled at the taste, then allowed some enthusiasm to seep into his eyes.

"Always," he answered. "That's the best part of being in business, taking an idea and running with it."

While we ate, Frye described an intercomputer communication glitch that meant nothing to me, telling me in detail how his engineers had worked for months on the problem and were finally close to fixing it.

"I love solving problems, all sorts of problems," he confessed.

"Me, too!" The words burst forth in an uninhibited gush.

"Like what?" he asked.

I wiped my mouth with a napkin. "Take this mayonnaise, for example," I hoisted my sandwich to illustrate. "The factory makes the stuff, puts it in a bottle. The bottle gets put into a box. The box is moved to a loading platform and lifted into a truck." Bobby had stopped chewing to listen, giving me a buzz from the attention.

"Next the truck drives miles and miles to a store where it's unloaded and the boxes are stacked somewhere. Sooner or later somebody puts the mayonnaise bottles on a shelf."

I pointed at myself. "Then I go into the store, put one of the bottles in a cart, drive it around the store, and eventually transfer it to the checkout conveyor.

"The clerk stuffs it in a bag. I put the bag in the car, drive home, take the bag out of the car and into the house. I finally lift the mayonnaise out of the bag and put it in my pantry. Before anybody even uses the stuff it's been handled and moved dozens of times. There ought to be a better way."

"I never thought of that before," Frye admitted. "But it does sound pretty inefficient now that you mention it."

"Your turn."

"Okay. The earth's full of water, water's full of hydrogen, and hydrogen's full of energy. The trouble is it costs much too much to separate the hydrogen from the oxygen to use it for power." He shrugged.

"There must be a way."

"Maybe there is."

We smiled over our mutual silliness. At least I thought it was silliness. For all I knew Bobby Frye would be on the phone the minute we got back to his office talking with one of his scientists about how inefficient grocery shopping was, and how could Supratech improve upon it?

Time was running out, so out of the blue I asked,

"Why'd you bench Walker Cross last Sunday?" I sounded melancholy when I said it, and perhaps I was.

Frye waved his head in response to the question. "Who says I did?"

I pushed away my plate. "Nobody else cared one way or the other whether Cross could make his quota."

"Football is big business, Ms. Barnes."

I told him to call me Gin.

"Okay, Gin. If you play your stocks the way I think you do, you're no dope when it comes to money. So tell me. Is there a businessman alive who wouldn't cut one point seven million dollars off his budget if it didn't make any difference to the rest of his enterprise?"

Instead of agreeing to the obvious, I answered a different question. "So Walker Cross really couldn't blame Tim Duffy for his loss of playing time."

"No. What's your point?"

"No point," I equivocated, for I had finally realized something else.

Nobody had to pay Tim Duffy anything now that he was dead.

FIFTEEN

When the check came, Bobby Frye examined it and quickly called our waiter back. "Clint," the electronics magnate scolded, "you put Ms. Barnes's Diet Sprite on the bill, but you never delivered it."

"Oh, sorry, man. It's been a zoo here today. Sorry, Ms. Barnes."

He hustled off to correct the total. I noticed that Frye left an exceedingly large tip, so it must have been that never-pay-for-nothing principle, a concept that did little toward eliminating him from my list of suspects.

We parted at the office's parking lot, shaking hands like two people who would never do it again. Next week I would write him a thank-you note—which the diminutive Sheila might or might not bother to show him—and that would most likely be that.

Later in the afternoon Michelle sat on the floor of what would be the nursery, back against the wall, legs splayed like a play-weary doll. She looked fragile and worried again, with her eyes darting every which way and her hands plucking at her favorite denim jumper. From watching her, I caught myself developing the same nervous symptoms.

Putting the crib together had been my suggestion, a maneuver calculated to promote a nice healthy optimism in my beleaguered cousin. Also, I was selfishly glad to be doing something that came with instructions.

Until a few minutes ago Michelle had been playing around with baby names; but the fun of that had wound down. When I glanced over from screwing part C into part D, she said, "I'd like to pay a condolence call on Elise Duffy."

"Okay," I agreed cautiously.

"Would you mind getting the phone—please?" Michelle begged. "I can't move."

I brought her the portable from her bedroom and tinkered with a crossbar while she spoke to the murder victim's widow.

"That's strange," she said after she hung up.

"What?"

"She says she's leaving tomorrow afternoon, but I could stop over in the morning if I really wanted to."

"And you said . . ."

"You heard me. I said I really wanted to."

"Because she was acting strange?"

"Yes. You don't think . . . ?"

"That's the trouble with situations like this," I cautioned my cousin. "Everybody seems guilty."

"I guess." Michelle shook her head cynically.

"Some more than others," I conceded.

The door chimes ruined my provocative pause. I rose to go see who was there; Michelle still didn't look ready to move.

Two gentlemen waited politely on the stoop. One wore an obsequious manner with his baggy black pseudo–London Fog, the other the air of an apprentice.

"We're from the Norfolk police, ma'am. Are you by any chance Mrs. Turner?"

"May I see some identification, please?"

"Certainly."

Shields in nice black leather wallets were produced for my inspection.

"Is it really necessary to speak with Mrs. Turner?" I asked sternly. "She was just released from the hospital yesterday."

"I'm afraid so," the fake London Fog lamented. "We promise not to keep her long."

His name was Lieutenant Glenn, his sidekick Detective Markowitz. Markowitz looked about twenty-six, possibly because he had the transparent freckled skin of a carrot-colored redhead. I'd been lucky in that department. My nutmeg-red hair came with dark-brown eyes and skin that would suntan if I was careful.

Glenn's freckles were confined to the top of his head, above a skirt of black hair that tickled his ears and collar. Naturally, he completed the circle of fringe with a mustache—they always do. Glenn's made him look as if Kilroy was there.

We waited each other out for a while; but since I was bound to lose, I capitulated gracefully and went to fetch Michelle.

Introductions made, the four of us settled into the Turners' sparse living room. The dining chair I brought in for myself made me look and feel like Michelle's guardian, which suited me fine.

"Detective Markowitz and I are conducting the investigation regarding the death of Timothy Duffy, Mrs. Turner," Glenn explained.

He had removed the ponderous black trench coat and looked only scarcely cheerier in brown houndstooth plaid. To speak to Michelle he had to swivel toward her on the sofa. She faced forward and glanced at him only when it was absolutely necessary. She was terrified, but I was at a loss to intervene.

"Yes," she replied. "What has that got to do with me?"

"You knew the Duffys, I presume."

"Yes."

"You know you don't have to talk about this if you don't want to," I interrupted, speaking to my cousin as if the police were not there.

Michelle turned to the right to look at my face. "I'm assuming that the quicker I answer these gentlemen, the quicker they will leave," she said reasonably.

"That's right," Glenn agreed with sparkling eyes. Clearly, his interest had been piqued by my warning.

To dissipate that, I pointed out that his interviewee had gone into premature labor earlier in the week. "I'm sure you wouldn't want that to happen again."

"Of course not."

A flicker of interest passed over Glenn's face regarding the timing of Michelle's problem, and now his left eyebrow twisted into a quizzical curve.

This was not good, not in any way. Not when my efforts to protect Michelle only made matters worse.

"Your husband and Mr. Duffy were rivals of sorts, were they not?"

I glared at the man but held my tongue.

"Before my time," Michelle answered.

"I was referring to the present," Glenn corrected.

Michelle slowly looked at him. "What's your point, Lieutenant?"

"Your husband said you were together at the time of Mr. Duffy's death."

"We were," Michelle answered with a fair amount of pluck.

"Really, Lieutenant. Aren't you being a little rude? What exactly do you want from Mrs. Turner?"

To me, the confidence behind the aggressive question telegraphed that Doug was a favorite suspect and Glenn was after anything he could get that would lead to hard evidence. Since Michelle could not be compelled to testify against her husband, I also surmised that Glenn was desperate, driven to take risks by the tremendous pressure regenerated by the entire media industry each and every day.

Glenn's ruthlessness, which would have endangered most cases, scared me witless. Michelle plucked at her dress and darted her eyes like a woman on death row.

"I'm sorry," Glenn apologized insincerely. "But I had to ask."

"No, you didn't," I challenged. The Kilroy eyes glared at me, wished me in hell or perhaps somewhere less pleasant.

He took a breath and started over. "Tell me about your family, Mrs. Turner. Do you have any brothers or sisters?"

Michelle imitated Glenn's go-to-hell look, while Doug let himself in the front door with his key.

Instantly, the professional quarterback read what was going on and responded.

"Get out," he commanded the intruders. "Get out of my house."

"We have every right to be here," Glenn remarked mildly.

"Not if you're bothering my wife, you don't." Whether Doug was technically correct didn't matter; his implied threat was supported by ample muscle and more than enough fury to see it through. Glenn and his apprentice did not dare to stay.

"This doesn't look good, you know," the police lieutenant remarked as he collected his coat. "Not at all."

"Get out," Doug repeated, and they went.

On impulse I watched through the window until they were gone. The homicide lieutenant drove a long, dark-green Buick with a black top, ugly and drab as the man himself.

When I turned back, Michelle was crying into Doug's shoulder while he absently stroked her back and stared into his own hell.

I left them alone as long as I could, until dinner, when we all made a transparent effort to be cheerful. We even laughed a little, but it didn't last. Faces fell, sentences trailed off.

The damage had been done, and we were all of us helpless to erase it.

SIXTEEN

Friday morning found civilization sandwiched between two unyielding rocks—hard, dark granite below; flat, marble-gray sky above. Nursing our separate emotional hangovers, Doug, Michelle, and I all dressed in neutrals, as if the austere winter light suited our souls.

The night had passed without any emergency dashes to the hospital, but none of us seemed to trust the day. We breakfasted in silence as if even the atmosphere of the house were fragile. Doug soon went off to practice, and not much later Michelle and I set out to console a widow.

A colorless fishing pier cluttered a mirror-like inlet just opposite the Duffy's Alanton home. Motionless tall grasses bordered the banks.

I insisted on holding my cousin's elbow as we approached the Duffy house, for the last of a lingering mist wafted off the water, and I feared the cobblestone driveway might be slippery.

Sheltered by an entryway arch, Michelle worked the brass knocker on the white wood and glass door. Around us the apparently new stucco house offered blank arched windows everywhere, Spanish tile roof above. The overcast sky had reduced its white paint to a cool, forbidding gray.

Michelle needed to sit down soon. Her lips were pressed hard with discomfort, and her breath came in short puffy clouds. I watched her warily and knocked a bit more insistently on the door.

Last night I tried to convince my cousin that she should beg off from this visit. She felt strongly that Elise's flight so soon after the funeral warranted investigation. And, since I wouldn't get so much as a hello from the Widow Duffy without my cousin's introduction, here we were. I vowed to make our visit brief.

And brief it was.

Elise Duffy opened the door breathlessly, her young round face exhibiting several emotions at once—anger, frustration, and sorrow perhaps the most predominant. Her dark hair had been secured with a high clip but wanted to fall back to her shoulders. The sweatshirt she wore was red and torn, the loafers old and coming unstitched. Tear tracks ran from her eyes to her jawbone.

"Come in," she said.

"Michelle really ought to sit down," I hinted as soon as introductions had been made.

"Oh, certainly. Come upstairs with me. There's a slipper chair in my bedroom that's pretty comfortable."

We followed Tim Duffy's widow across a vast expanse of floor to a staircase curving upward. Each tread had been carpeted in pale taupe top and bottom and appeared to be suspended in air.

"Where will you go?" Michelle asked. Suitcases were opened all over the bedroom, four of them on the bed alone.

Elise dumped a drawer of sweaters on the floor and began refolding them before she answered. "Florida, I think. My mother's down there. After that, somewhere alone, preferably a place without football."

"What a shame to leave this beautiful house," I said. "You can't have been here very long."

"We haven't, thank goodness. Otherwise, I might feel obligated to stay."

Uninvited, Michelle shrugged out of her wool car coat. "Was the funeral nice?" she asked. "I'm sorry I couldn't get there."

"Yeah, peachy. Just me, Tim's family, and a few hundred of our friends from the network news."

Bitterness had come so prematurely to this widow that I wondered whether she had been angry with Tim even before his demise.

"Didn't you like football?" I asked innocently.

"Like it?" She threw a black turtleneck into a wastebasket. "The most insecure profession in the world? What was there to like? Tim worked his ass off. When he was home he was usually exhausted, and he was always struggling through at least one injury. But could he take it easy until he felt better? Oh, no. He was in there pumping iron and pushing himself as soon as he could move."

"What about during the off season? Wasn't that better?"

"Oh, he was off all right. Off with his adoring public. Golf tournaments, promotional trips—and the gym, always the gym."

"He was loved," Michelle said, trying to follow her own agenda.

"Yeah, loved," Elise repeated with scorn. "It's hard to imagine why anyone would want to shoot him."

I couldn't quite read how Tim's widow meant that, but it was an opening—probably the only one I would get.

"Do you have someone in mind?" I asked.

Elise paused to look at me while her left hand strangled something made of pink cashmere. The woman was a cloud full of lightning, and I was beginning to look like a tall tree.

"I know this sounds callous," she said, "but no. I don't know who shot Tim, and I don't care."

Noticing that I had suddenly become a target, Michelle intervened. "Have the police been bothering you?" she inquired, one of the questions I had prepped her to ask, especially after her own interrogation yesterday afternoon.

Elise's animosity temporarily shifted off me while she answered Michelle. "I haven't been arrested, if that's what you mean . . ." Her ire came back in full force. ". . . so I guess that means I have an alibi."

I allowed my face to appear injured and misunderstood. Then I repeated that I was sorry she had to leave her home as if I hoped that by starting over I might fix what went wrong with our conversation. It was a futile hope, considering her mood, but it was the natural thing to try.

"You want to know the truth?" she challenged, as if one of us had asked. "I'll tell you the truth. Since Sunday I can't even bear to touch Tim's clothes. Everything in this whole place makes me sick. I'm probably going to have to hire somebody to pack it all off to an auctioneer, because I can't stand to be here." Fresh tears dripped onto the red sweatshirt as she glanced from Michelle to me to Michelle again.

"Tim isn't ever coming back," she told us, "so neither am I."

Down at the front doorway, Elise and my cousin embraced.

"Good luck, sweetie," Michelle said into her acquaintance's ear.

"You, too," Elise murmured back.

Intuition warned me to keep quiet, so I nodded my farewell. Elise's narrow-eyed nod in return confirmed that my instinct had been correct.

The slightest friction and the tree would burn.

SEVENTEEN

"**D**INKs," Michelle remarked on Saturday as I drove us into the section of Norfolk called Ghent. Late-morning traffic had been casual but steady. An occasional snowflake danced around the windshield; but we were toasty inside the Jeep Cherokee, protected from the weather and the harsh lifestyle of the housing projects we had just skirted by American automotive skill and foresight.

"Excuse me?"

"DINKs live here," she said. "Double income, no kids." Ghent seemed to be an enviable enclave of curved streets and individualized homes. Small yards supported sycamores, hollies, dogwoods, and lots of some towering tree with eucalyptus-type leaves but no eucalyptus stink.

Teal and Morani Todd's place was within walking distance of the Chrysler Museum, a dignified stone-block edifice with the obligatory horse-and-man statue out front, except this time the man on horseback was reaching down to help somebody off the ground. Unlike the museum patrons, the Todds had to detour a few steps out of their way to view the Hague River.

"Does Teal work?" I asked.

"Now that you mention it—no."

For several blocks in either direction the homes huddled together like Yuppies on an airport shuttle, everybody dressed up but with different places to go. The Todds' was of the tan brick variety with off-white cubes running up the corners like stitching and arches around the porch to match.

"Break a leg," Michelle told me as we waited at the door.

Teal ushered us into an entrance hall with a center table sporting fresh flowers from somewhere tropical. Our heels clicked loudly on imported tile, reminding me not to drag my feet. The fragrance of baking chicken and cheese alerted my stomach to the midday hour.

Michelle rated a kiss hello from our hostess. I garnered a businesslike nod.

After Teal closeted our coats, she fussed Michelle into the sunken living room to the right where lots of cushy seating had been slipcovered in thick brocades. The colors—dark tan, sea green, and maroon—perfectly complimented the patterned rug, which showed nicely through the glass-topped coffee table. Quiet lamplight warmed the winter shadows, and a gas fire flickered behind a transparent screen. The room summoned up thoughts of Rip, stockinged feet, and a really good glass of wine.

I placed my awkwardly wrapped baby present over by a lacquered sideboard that already held a couple of packages wrapped in silver foil—early gifts that must have been sent by women who couldn't come in person. The inference should have been that today's guests would all be kind and nurturing, eager to support a fellow football wife. But I didn't believe it—not considering that one of them, or one of their spouses, may have murdered a man six days ago.

"You want me to put out the decorations?" I checked with Teal.

"Go right ahead," our hostess encouraged. She wore a brown knit two-piece dress today, some shoes

I admired with interesting straps; and, as I had noticed when we met in the hospital, her grooming was impeccable.

She chattered to Michelle about the guest list while I assembled the fourteen-inch stork and defiled her glass coffee table with it.

Then I proceeded to insult her gleaming mahogany dining table with pink and blue accordion streamers hung from her crystal chandelier. The chairs, all twelve of them, had been removed for today's casual buffet.

The door chimes rang, and Teal hurried to answer it.

Barbara Laneer bearing dessert. "Hello, hello," she hooted, and kept right on going. Teal followed, leaving Michelle and me alone.

"No houseplants?" I teased, gesturing to encompass the artful decor. Michelle giggled, but I realized my hands were clammy and shaking with stagefright, the pressure of sorting through so many suspicions.

More women were coming than I cared about, so to focus myself, I reviewed the interesting ones in my mind.

Wanda Cross, whose husband Walker was being finessed out of a guaranteed contract by Bobby Frye. Either Wanda or her husband might have erroneously blamed the benching on an incomplete pass thrown by Tim Duffy.

Lyn Smith, wife of the third-string quarterback whose fading prospects had considerably brightened since Duffy's death.

Amanda Shifflett, because Bo Shifflett was a wide receiver and I didn't like his looks.

Only one other possible source of information would be missing—Pamela something, the former girlfriend of Roger Prindel, the Tomcats' offensive coordinator. Ex-girlfriends were usually pretty eager to share anything nasty they knew about their former lovers, and I was curious about him because he was directly responsible for the quarterbacks' activities on the field.

Of course, Elise Duffy would be in Florida by now; but since the police had permitted her to go, she probably did have an alibi.

By twelve-thirty the living room was filled with women. Each had been supplied with coffee or tea. Some had helped themselves to the chicken/broccoli casserole and tossed salad. Croissants crumbled on their laps and on the carpet.

I discreetly eavesdropped on some of the women politely waiting for the initial rush on the table to clear. One of them was Amanda Shifflett, a plump steel magnolia with eyes like melting ice.

"Whatever was Patrick thinking when he bungled that snap last Sunday?" she asked a taller blonde who had been identified as Angela Dionne. Although the question had been launched with a chortle, it drove home with a barb. "Did you two have big plans for the evening?"

Angela Dionne blushed instantly and completely, right up to the dark roots of her white-bleached haystack of hair. She struck me as the former bimbo type, the fun-loving, wild thing that a college jock of the same order would cultivate and often even marry. In the company of more refined women Angela's clothing missed miserably, and her worried expression said that she knew it.

The barb referred to the three Dionne children, born in the most recent successive years. Unprepared and impractical as she once must have been, Angela had her hands full coping with her kids and her husband's instant fame. She did not need to be teased by a callous creampuff from Louisiana.

"Be nice now," Barbara Laneer scolded. "Bo's dropped a pass or two in his time."

"Not when they were well thrown," Amanda declared, her chest swelling with indignation.

"How is Calvin's hamstring, dear?" Barbara changed the subject, inadvertently addressing someone occupied with a mouthful of food. While Barbara's intended diversion mumbled something unintelligible, Teal followed suit by asking Michelle about Doug's well-being. Doug, of course, had had "his bell rung" twice during the previous game, giving Tim Duffy his two opportunities to play.

"He's fine," Michelle assured the room.

Lyn Smith paid particular interest to that answer. A white woman married to a black man, she thwarted definition. At times throughout the afternoon I would peg her as calculating, distrustful, and horrifically insecure, yet any of those observations could have been wrong. She held herself too closely, watched the others with too much hunger and resentment. I saw her as the squirming kid in the Halloween costume, the one who telegraphed her identity but then went about proving that nobody really knew her at all.

"Delicious," she said of Teal's food, not meaning it. "Isn't that cute," of a bib embroidered with unimaginative balloons.

When most everyone was quietly eating, I was able to ask the room in general, "How *do* you deal with the injuries?"

The whole room seemed to groan. "They're constant."

"They're a nightmare."

"They're a constant nightmare."

"You can't think about it," Teal disagreed firmly. "You have to believe that if your husband's in good enough shape, he won't get hurt."

"Unless it's a fluke."

"And flukes happen all the time."

"Injuries are inevitable, and some of them have lifelong consequences."

Wanda Cross shook her dark head and black braids slapped like whips against her elevated chin. "They're the cost of doing business," she maintained. "No pain, no gain."

Clearly, she referred to the profitability of professional football rather than the discomforts of training. But perhaps a $1.7 million incentive made you a bit more philosophical on your husband's behalf.

"I still hate it," Angela Dionne confessed. "But Patrick just laughs at me."

"Some men do love the risk," Barbara Laneer sympathized. "It can be enormously stimulating. Why else would anybody work on Wall Street?"

Nobody said "for the money." Nobody had to.

While we ate, the conversation centered around babies and giving birth. Mercifully, the remarks were far less disturbing and graphic than what I heard at my own shower before Chelsea was born. Then my young and foolish friends had clamored all over each other trying to top one horrible story with another. I would have gladly forgotten the whole idea of motherhood if it hadn't been way too late.

Today, however, sensitivity prevailed. The stories were warm or comical, the underlying message always upbeat. Everyone seemed to be aware that Michelle already harbored her own horrors, and like good sisters the women instinctively rallied around her. If nothing else came of the afternoon, my cousin would come away with the sense that she had potential friends in Norfolk, not just acquaintances.

Yet those same guests had been selected by Teal to offer me a superb brain-picking opportunity, if only I could steer the conversation in the right direction. I felt myself lying languidly in wait, a cat lulling her prey into complacency. *Nothing* said my face. *Beware* said my pulse.

The childbirth topic segued into even more typical girl-talk, i.e. complaining about men.

"He doesn't close doors," said one of her mate.

"Or drawers," lamented another.

"And don't give him the TV remote unless you want your head to spin."

"Those awful whiskers in the sink."

"At least your husband doesn't shave his head."

"Lucky we're so perfect." Giggles all around.

"Michael refuses to take his socks off right-side out," said a woman with a button nose. "I even sat him down one day and taught him how. You know, pinch between the toes and pull. He doesn't care. I could have been talking to a brick wall." I had seen her husband play football; she *was* talking to a brick wall.

"Hey!" Michelle said, waving her hand. "I could be having a boy, you know." She had declined the opportunity to learn her child's gender in advance.

"Snakes and snails and puppy dog tails."

"Are you sure about the snakes?"

"Oh, yeah, girl. Remember my first husband?"

"What's a husband supposed to do?" I asked Wanda Cross to prolong the topic. The perceived roles of men and women have always fascinated me, especially because I don't entirely believe in them.

"Provide for me and our future kids" was the surprise reply.

The other women made protesting noises.

"Well, I'm only being honest. A man's got to take care of his woman if he wants her to take care of him."

"Amanda doesn't seem to agree," I pushed.

"I believe a man should be God-fearing and honest," the plump blonde drawled in Southern oratory style. "Like my Bo. He has always put his faith in the Lord."

"That's okay, baby," Wanda agreed. "But you can't tell me you're sorry when he brings home the bacon."

"Don't you put words in my mouth." Clearly, she wanted to add something like *you little money-grubber.* "My Bo is as perfect as I want him to be, and I won't have you smearing his name—or mine—with your blasphemy."

"Hooee." Wanda laughed. "Got a little fire and brimstone going here to-day."

Teal rose to begin collecting dishes.

While the static from the outburst cleared, I mouthed "Pamela what's-er-name" to Michelle, who nodded that she got the message.

"Say, does anybody here remember Pamela Cork, the woman who used to date Roger Prindel? I'd like to get in touch with her; but after she and Roger split up, I lost touch."

"Oh, yeah, Pamela," everybody agreed. "Nice girl. Big help with our fundraiser."

"I heard she got married," Teal remarked. She had been wearing an intense expression all day that I identified as suspicion fueled by concern over the future of the Tomcats' franchise—the reason she had volunteered her house for this party.

"To a horse trainer, I think," Amanda offered.

"What's her new name?"

"What *is* her name?"

The silence lasted only a few seconds, but it felt like five minutes.

"She's Pamela Wilkinson now, and she lives on Princess Anne Road in Pungo. If you want her number, I've got it in my purse." Lyn Smith was the surprise provider of this information, which Michelle accepted with remarkable aplomb.

"Thanks," she said. "That'd be great."

Teal and Barbara began to gather the gifts and set them in front of Michelle's chair.

"Too bad Elise Duffy couldn't be here," the kicker's wife, Debbie Quinlan, thought aloud. This was the closest reference to the murder so far, and it stifled the movement in the room like a lid over a steaming pot.

"At least the Lord gave Tim a good final day," Amanda offered.

"What do you mean?" Barbara Laneer asked. Like her, I, too, wondered what could possibly be perceived as good about the day Tim died.

"He threw for a touchdown," Michelle answered with understanding, if not agreement.

The rest of us glanced back to Amanda to check her sincerity. Bo had caught the referred-to touchdown, which iced the game and also covered the point spread.

"Do the players actually think about the point spread?" I asked.

"They're aware of it," Teal admitted.

"How could they not be?" Wanda remarked. "The press is really into that stuff."

Teal became thoughtful. "Morani gets annoyed when the media underestimates the Tomcats' chances," she said, "but I think he looks at it as just part of the talk."

Barbara spoke with the authority of a head coach's wife. "It makes a certain amount of sense to care about what the public cares about, but I don't think either Jack or Roger can afford to worry about something like that during the heat of a game." I remembered that Roger was the offensive coordinator. "Surely they wouldn't take an unnecessary risk just to satisfy somebody's idle speculation."

I wasn't quite so positive, and perhaps my skepticism showed.

Debbie Quinlan stirred from a reverie and secured everyone's attention. "Roger certainly wasn't thinking about the spread last week," the kicker's wife affirmed. "You know at the end, when Tim went in for Doug? Charlie heard Roger send in a running play."

"You sure?" I asked.

"Oh, yeah. Charlie was furious because he wanted to kick another field goal, and a call like that probably wouldn't have given him the chance to try." She wagged her head. "I guess Tim must have changed the play in the huddle, because, you know, he threw for that touchdown."

The women shrugged off the coach's miscalculation, perhaps extending Roger the benefit of a doubt. They quickly moved on to other topics.

I busied myself rubbing down the prickles on my arms and the back of my neck.

EIGHTEEN

"Sunday," I told Ronnie via the mauve princess phone. "I'm going home Sunday."

When I went upstairs to change clothes after the baby shower, I had checked in with my family; and what Chelsea described had convinced me irrevocably that it was time to get myself back there. Or maybe I just wanted to go.

A few minutes later Ronnie's call from his hotel room in Green Bay, Wisconsin, caught me in a sweater and slip.

"Look, Cuz," he said into my ear. "You're doing great. You've learned all sorts of things. Stick it out a little longer . . . please?"

"I don't know squat," I insisted stubbornly. "I've got more questions than answers, and frankly I'm totally confused."

"No sale."

"What?"

"I said 'No sale.' I don't believe you."

"You're calling me a liar?" Memories of our childhood arguments returned. I could almost sniff the mowed grass of my backyard, almost feel the cool of a wading pool on my toes. Probably I shouldn't have taken off my stockings.

"Naw. I'm just saying you're full of it."

"I beg your pardon?"

"Don't give me that girlie, all-insulted shit. This

is your cousin Ronnie you're talking to. You have a mind like a vise. You never let go of a fact. You're smart, for chrissake, Gin. So don't give me that crap about being confused. I don't buy it.''

Despite his choice of words, I was flattered. And I realized I had gone a bit girlie on him. However, my afternoon had been spent at a baby shower, which was about as female as an activity could get.

"Tell me what you've been finding out," he suggested. I could hear him sipping beer from a bottle, and the pure ordinariness of that brought me back to myself.

"You know that touchdown pass Tim Duffy threw at the end of the game? He changed the play in the huddle from a run to a pass.''

"Good. That's good information. What do you think it means?"

"Probably just that he wanted to throw instead of run.''

Ronnie did not laugh. "Why?" he asked as if he were poking me on my collarbone.

"I have no idea."

"Sure you do."

"Ronnie!"

"Well, don't you?"

"Okay. Ego. He was jealous of Doug's starting status and wanted to show off his arm, try to win Doug's job. Or else he just thought running was a terrible idea, and he was covering for Roger Prindel."

"That's possible. Go on."

"Patrick Dionne muffed a snap."

"And that means?"

"He was distracted? His hand slipped? How should I know?"

"Go on."

I stopped to think. "I don't like Bo Shifflett's wife.''

"Why?"

"She's one of those religious people with blinders on."

"Explain, please."

"Narrow vision. Can't see anybody else's viewpoint. That much rigidity always scares me."

"Fanatical."

"Maybe."

"Holier than thou?"

"Not quite. Egotistical is closer. Like she's dead sure she's right and everybody else is wrong, so she justifies anything she wants to do by pretending that God wants her to do it for our own good."

"Capable of murder?"

"All those people who started religious wars seemed pretty sure of themselves."

Ronnie clunked the beer bottle on the night table—or a desk, depending on where he was sitting. "Go on."

"Wanda Cross is mercenary as all get-out."

"Yes . . ."

"So I can maybe see her flipping out over Walker's benching last week."

"Enough to do bodily harm?"

"Maybe, if she thought Tim was to blame. She's not exactly a benchwarmer herself, if you know what I mean."

"I've never heard a woman described quite like that before."

"Too locker-room for you?"

"You really were Daddy's little girl, weren't you?"

"Watch it, fella. We're not tomboys anymore; we're liberated."

"Yeah, yeah, yeah. So this Wanda Cross woman is assertive, the type to take matters into her own hands. Is that what you mean?"

"Yes. She's aggressive as hell and has strong opinions about how a man should provide for his wife."

"Who else?"

"The owner of the team is curiously frugal—for a billionaire. If he is a billionaire."

"And you know this because . . . ?"

"We did lunch."

"My God, Gin. How did you wrangle that?"

"Don't ask. But if Tim Duffy told Bobby Frye he was going to go to the press with the real reason Walker Cross was benched last Sunday, maybe to sort of blackmail Frye into moving him ahead of Doug in the lineup . . ."

"Bang. I see where you're going, but what was the real reason Cross was taken out?"

"One point seven million dollars—guaranteed."

"Wow." Ronnie took a moment to digest the magnitude of that. Then he moved on. "What about Tim's widow?" he asked.

"Alibi."

"Jack Laneer or his wife?"

"Alibis. They were seen at a restaurant."

"Other players or coaches?"

"I don't know. Willet Smith, his wife Lyn maybe."

"Because Smith is backup QB now?"

"Yes. I couldn't get a handle on Lyn, which made me suspicious, you know? She seemed fidgety, almost sneaky. Or maybe she's just uncomfortable around the other wives. They're intimidating if you're not used to women like that."

"Liberated women, you mean?"

"Touché."

However, he had asked a good question. What was today's common denominator? I thought aloud, trying to answer.

"They had a certain level of polish, most of them.

Maybe from being noticed by the public." Yet even as I said it, I knew I wasn't getting the description quite right. Despite the furtiveness, Lyn Smith essentially had been a mouse. Angela Dionne seemed in way over her head, and Debbie Quinlan actually struck me as quite well adjusted.

"Forget that," I amended. "Never good to generalize."

Ronnie was thinking, rattling the beer bottle on the table. "You don't have it yet, do you?"

"No. That's what I was trying to say when you jumped all over me."

"Never crossed my mind. I'm not that kind of cousin."

I groaned at his lousy joke.

After that we were quiet awhile, just sitting in our respective rooms miles and miles from our homes and thinking. Ronnie was probably staring at a bland hotel watercolor. I spent the time rubbing my hand across the pattern of Michelle's guest room bedspread.

"Do you think Doug's guilty?" my cousin asked with unnerving seriousness.

I sighed and switched the phone to the other ear, stalling. "Not really."

"He's looking good for it though, isn't he?"

"Something happened on the sideline," I mused. "Something we haven't figured out yet."

"If you say so."

"I'm still going home, but can you do me a favor?"

"Anything."

"Were you serious about getting me a sideline pass?"

"Sure. Just you. No kids . . ."

"I know, I know. No volleyball team. Just me—tomorrow. I want to go to the Tomcats/Eagles game."

"Pshew. You sure?"

"It's the only thing I can think of to do." Look around. Watch what goes on. See whether anything suggests itself.

"Okay, Cuz. I'll call the office, find out who's doing the game. You'll have to introduce yourself to the crew, work out some story why you're there."

"Simple. You owe me a big favor."

"That I do. That I do."

To be polite I asked what kind of weather was expected for the Green Bay game tomorrow.

"Rainy," the cameraman replied with surprising cheer. "I should get some great shots."

Artistes. Go figure.

Before I changed into jeans to go downstairs and fix dinner, I called home one more time.

Chelsea answered. "What are they doing now?" I asked.

"Dancing. The jitterbug, I think. You're a genius, Mom."

The first time I had called, Gracie and my mother were toasting the defunct Valley Forge Music Fair with sherry.

"They're sniffling and everything, Mom," my daughter had reported with helpless bewilderment. "You'd think a fancy church got knocked down or something."

In a sense, one had; but Chelsea would never understand that.

"They just found out today?" I inquired.

The local concert hall had been down for quite a while, much to my own sorrow. Not a bad seat in the house, and it had brought big-name entertainers to within ten minutes of our home. True, the most recent musicians had mostly appealed to an aging crowd—such as Cynthia and Gracie.

"Dad drove them over there to that big grocery

store, and the grannies haven't talked about anything else all day. What should I do?''

Not exactly a crisis, this was nevertheless what motherhood was all about. I dug deep.

''Why don't you get that old Fats Domino tape out of my car and put it on?'' I advised. Fats always made me smile—every time, which was why I kept his music in my car. The only other person in the family who could stand his old-fashioned New Orleans rock 'n' roll was my mom.

Chelsea warbled ''Gotta go'' before I could tell her I was coming home. Oh, well. I would surprise everybody.

A genius. My thirteen-year-old daughter called me a genius!

Maybe I should leave home more often.

NINETEEN

Back in my comfortable clothes, I went downstairs to make dinner for two. Doug was already in Philadelphia for tomorrow's game. I told Michelle I was headed there, too.

"You're doing fine now, and I just can't get a handle on this . . . this problem you have, so Ronnie's going to get me on the sideline of tomorrow's game. Maybe that will suggest something."

"Oh. Oh, okay." A crease of worry marred my cousin's brow, but she didn't tense up too badly and the crease soon disappeared. The sudden stress over the murder that put her in the hospital seemed to have dropped to a manageable level.

I tapped my fingers on the door jamb, wrinkled my own brow. "There's one more thing I could do before I go—if you're up for it."

Michelle had been watching television in a pair of green lounging pajamas. Now she leaned forward in her straight-backed chair until her tummy seemed to reach her knees. She pushed her glasses back up her nose. "What's that?"

"Speak to Pamela Wilkinson, Roger Prindel's old girlfriend."

"Oh, right. We've got that number Lyn Smith gave me. What should I say?"

"The truth'll do. Tell her we need some information about Roger for a very important reason, and ask

160

if we can stop by early tomorrow morning before my flight.''

As it was now Saturday night, Michelle had to leave a message on Pamela's machine. Wisely, she refrained from mentioning Roger's name in case the woman's husband heard the message, saying merely that she needed to speak with her about something important.

The teaser probably worked better than making the request in one dose of honesty. Pamela called back an hour later. Michelle sketched out what we needed then explained about my late-morning flight.

''We're up at dawn tending the horses, anyway,'' Michelle's old acquaintance told her. ''If you can be here by eight, I'll put the coffee on.''

Michelle and I were dressed and eager to go early the next morning. The daylight was thin at that hour but growing stronger. The chill, however, seemed determined to stay. I would probably freeze on the Tomcats' sideline later on, but I truly believed it would be worth it. An experience for the mental scrapbook, if nothing else.

Pamela's directions led us from the homey confines of Virginia Beach into the countryside along Princess Anne Road. Only twenty minutes out of the city, it was a different place altogether, both familiar and foreign to me.

While the rolling farmland along the Pennsylvania turnpike beyond my hometown reposed in confident serenity, these Virginia homesteads seemed to cringe at encroaching urbanism as if the land itself knew its lifestyle was endangered. Already black-shuttered white colonials beneath rugged old trees dotted the roadside in among the horse farms. Telephone poles strung with cable TV and other modern necessities rose above the criss-crossed fences.

Yet a simple elegance and tranquility coexisted with the swift but sparse Sunday traffic. Dirt and gravel driveways met the asphalt. Gutter weeds gave way to dormant pastures glistening with frost. Here and there I noticed pockets of snow left over from yesterday's dusting. Rows of whitewashed stables trimmed with red hinted at affluence and priorities the cityfolk wouldn't understand, surprising me again with the realization that some animals lived much better than some humans.

Marking the entrance to a lengthy lane defined by sculpted pines, the Wilkinsons' mailbox was decorated with a weatherproof red bow, a reminder that Christmas was eleven days away—another reason for me to hurry home. Tomorrow would make a week I had stayed in Virginia. Too long emotionally. Not quite long enough to consider the trip a success.

Closure was an essential to me. "Finish your plate." "Finish the season." Finish knitting that sweater, or fixing the drain, or whatever you set out to do—another of the codes my father lived by and my mother admired. Daddy's little girl.

As much as I longed to make certain that Doug's name would never be tarnished by a connection to Tim Duffy's murder, the goal no longer appeared to be realistic. My plane left in three hours.

So it was with a less than optimistic attitude that I followed Michelle into Pamela Wilkinson's toasty kitchen. Muddy rubber boots dried on a mat below the row of jackets by the door. The fragrance of coffee made my head swoon.

We had interrupted Pamela eating a piece of coffee cake. She brushed crumbs off her lips with her wrist before kissing Michelle from the side.

"Sorry I'm such a mess," she apologized. "Just finished with the horses, and I was starved. Come in." She gestured for us to take seats at the end of the long room where a cluster of softly worn furniture draped with ratty quilts bellied up to a wall of windows. The view was of fields falling away to the south. In the near distance four thoroughbreds with thick winter coats stood at leisure huffing plumes of breath into the cold sunny air.

"Is your husband home?" Michelle inquired in a way that alluded to the sensitive topic we had come to discuss.

"Nope. Kevin does an early church service. Your timing is perfect."

Pamela shooed a spaniel with black curly hair off the centermost seat. She wore a sweatshirt adorned with chickadees on a snowy pine branch, close-fitting jeans, and ragg wool socks pulled high over their hem, no shoes. Her face was young, her hair dark, curly, and short.

"Would you like some coffee and cake?" she offered.

Michelle and I eagerly agreed, and minutes later we were settled and comfortably supplied with sustenance.

Michelle had filled the interim with small talk, catching up with her lapsed friend; but when that ran out, Pamela waved her mug of coffee, smiled, and said, "What's this all about?"

Michelle returned a piece of coffee cake to her plate and folded her hands across the top of the baby. "I'm worried that Doug will be accused of killing Tim Duffy," she said outright, not elaborating about the rivalry, not needing to. "Gin's trying to steer the police in the right direction before they even think of Doug."

"And you think Roger makes a more likely suspect?" Her eyes traveled between my cousin and me, asking us both.

"We don't know," I interjected. "That's why we're here. To ask your opinion."

Pamela laced her fingers together and leaned forward on her elbows. Behind her expression of concern resided a cheerful temperament and a trusting nature. She did not, for example, even begin to doubt Doug's innocence. Nor did she take offense that we preferred her ex-boyfriend as a suspect.

"I don't know what I can tell you."

"What's Roger like?" I prompted.

"Sweet," she said hastily. "And very generous when he had money. Trouble was, he never had much, and what he got he blew."

"How do you mean?"

"He'd give me a gold bracelet one week and eat franks and beans all the next."

A prickle started somewhere in my psyche. "How was his self-image?" I inquired as calmly as I could.

"He saw himself as Mr. Bountiful, but there were long stretches when he was disappointed in himself, almost depressed because he couldn't treat me, or his friends, the way he wanted to. I tried to convince him that I didn't need things, just his attention. Of course, during the season he couldn't even give me that."

"Did he ever gamble?" I asked. The prickle had spread, and I could scarcely keep a quaver out of my voice.

Pamela's body jerked. "How did you know that?"

"Some material I read," I told her.

The reason for the reading I preferred to keep to myself. Back in college, before Rip, I thought I was in love with a guy whose father was a "horse degenerate," an inveterate gambler who behaved exactly the way Pamela described. I had wanted to know what I would be in for if I stayed with the boyfriend, what sort of father-in-law I might be saddled with, so to speak. So I researched problem gamblers and learned that a chronically poor self-image reinforced by the gambling losses sometimes escalated to the proportions of a full-blown personality disorder. The profligate spending after a win masqueraded as a feel-good fix but actually represented the quickest road back to misery.

Pamela's face had colored, and her hands wound tight together. "I promised not to tell," she said.

"What's the difference?" Michelle remarked. "He doesn't bet on football, does he?"

Pamela's head jerked. "No. No, of course not. Horses mainly, and other sports. Never football. He'd be banned from the league, and there is only one league."

"So he's discreet," I suggested.

"Yes. Mostly his brother bets for him. Roger doesn't want even the slightest appearance of wrong-doing. He says reporters are like vultures these days. Too many of them and too little news. The hungriest ones go after anything."

I thought of the surplus of print photographers I'd seen on the sideline of an Eagles game. If they had suited up, they could have formed another whole team—there were that many of them.

"Is there something there?" Michelle asked me.

"If there is, I don't know what," I told my cousin truthfully. *Yet,* I might have added.

Pamela chatted more about Michelle's impending motherhood while I finished my coffee and day-dreamed out the window.

The nearest horse was perhaps forty yards away, a bay gelding with twitching ears and a regal bearing. He seemed to be staring back at me, teasing that he knew something I didn't know. "Tell me," I begged him telepathically.

The horse fine-tuned his ears once more, hopped

forward just to make me blink, then turned tail and waddled away.

Gretsky, our aggressive and perceptive dog, never would have stood for such a challenge, so neither did I.

"I'll get it," I told the horse, asserting myself with a strong mental signal. "If it's there, I'll get it."

About then the curly-haired dog stole the last of my coffee cake and put an end to the baby conversation.

"Ack, Poochie, get away," Pamela scolded.

"We better get moving," I told Michelle, and she immediately rose to go.

"Thank you, Pam," she said, extending her hand. "It's been lovely seeing you again."

"I don't think I was much help, but I enjoyed seeing you, too." Another friendship back on firmer footing. Michelle all but floated back to the car.

Soon we were riding northeast along Princess Anne Road trying to evaluate what we had learned.

"What if Roger did bet on the Tomcats—hypothetically," I added for tact. "As offensive coordinator, would he be able to control the outcome of a game?"

Michelle snorted. "Not really. The NFL monitors for that at least as carefully as the FBI watches for leaks."

I scowled with frustration. Here was another person with another flaw, one that had potential as a motive.

"Once?" I inquired.

"Pretty unlikely, Gin. Too many safeguards."

I emphatically reminded myself that the Tomcats had won last week's game, beat the spread, made everybody happy. They had been favored, too, so no surprise there.

I didn't like it, but I had to admit that even if Roger

Prindel did have a gambling disorder, that didn't necessarily mean he had anything to with Tim Duffy's death.

Too bad, I groused. I was running out of ideas.

"Gin," Michelle said, touching my arm to draw my attention from my thoughts.

"Yes?"

"Could we please find a phone?"

"Sure." I realized it was nearly time to call the airline to check on my flight. Maybe Michelle was secretly glad I was going home.

That wasn't it.

"We need to call my doctor," my cousin informed me. "My water just broke."

TWENTY

"Car phone?" I asked hopefully.

"Forgot it," Michelle said through clenched teeth. "Drive."

I drove. Ten-thirty Sunday morning. The infrequent houses appeared locked up tight, people either sleeping in or out to church. Odds were that stopping at one of them would waste our time, so I drove. The expectant mother gripped the sides of her seat, scrunched up her eyes, and sweated from fear.

Never mind that it was too early, Michelle's announcement meant the baby was on its way. Even if labor could be medically halted, the infant would be safer out in the world than remaining in utero and risking infection. So as urgently as I wanted to get Michelle to the hospital, it was even more critical that her baby get immediate attention—literally a matter of life or death.

I worked up a good sweat myself worrying about that. My stomach even developed a sympathy cramp.

Up ahead on the right stood a lone commercial establishment, a roughly painted white clapboard affair with a parking lot—a country store, so it said. No cars. No people. Closed.

I pulled into the lot anyway, braking with consideration for the mother-to-be wincing in the passenger seat.

Throwing open my door, I stumbled out and raced

onto a porch with two picture windows facing front. Hands shadowing my eyes, I peered inside at gas cans, fish nets, laundry soap, and hair spray beckoning from low, no-nonsense shelves. Not a phone was in sight.

Moaning a protest, I dropped my hands and turned in a circle, slapped the top of a picnic table beneath the nearest window.

The sign was obvious after you saw it, a dark-blue rectangle edged in white. A picture of a telephone handset and the word "Phone" indicated the instrument's existence at the far end of the porch.

I clattered down the steps and back to the car for my purse. "What number?" I asked Michelle.

"555-7981," she said. "Dr. Mobly."

Sheltered by more porch roof, the telephone was around the corner, housed in a red box. I dialed, got an emergency number from a machine, called that and got a human, a pleasant-voiced woman who assured me Dr. Mobly would meet Michelle at Virginia Beach General Hospital as quickly as possible.

Which didn't sound nearly fast enough. "Thank you," I muttered through clenched teeth.

"Drive carefully," the doctor's wife advised.

A solid woman of forty-five wearing green scrubs and a concerned smile greeted me from behind the emergency room reception window.

"My cousin's having a baby," I babbled breathlessly. "She's in the car. Premature. Dr. Mobly's coming."

"Okay. We'll take over now. Don't you worry." She came out of her cubicle at a brisk walk and collected a wheelchair.

When Michelle rolled by me, I squeezed her hand and told her I'd be there. My words sounded insubstantial, useless. My cousin offered me an affectionate smile that said much more.

By the time I parked the Jeep, answered some admission questions as best I could, and allowed the nurse to direct me to the second-floor maternity, Michelle was settled in a birthing room with Dr. Mobly in attendance.

A nurse allowed me to peek inside for a moment, no doubt to assure me that all was well, perhaps to forestall a frantic, dithering relative from stirring up the other patients' frantic, dithering relatives.

My glimpse showed me a single hospital bed surrounded by patterned, smoky-blue wallpaper on three walls. The paper above a blue chair rail behind the bed displayed pink and blue flowers on a field of white. A gold-framed impressionist print of a mother and child, perhaps originally by Mary Cassatt, hung directly above the headboard. At the moment only the doctor and nurse could actually see the prettiest wall, but I recognized that thought as ungrateful. My living room should look so nice.

To the right of the bed—monitors, computer-style, and miscellaneous boxes, all working. Plus IVs and a wood cabinet full of supplies. I wiggled my fingers at Michelle. Without her glasses she nodded vaguely in my direction.

"We're going to be awhile, Mrs. Barnes," Dr. Mobly told me. "Might as well make yourself at home."

I told him thanks, wiggled more fingers at Michelle, and receded toward the waiting room; I wasn't Doug or Michelle's mother, or even Ronnie. The riskiness of the birth discouraged me from remaining anyway. If things went horribly wrong, I doubted whether I could handle being there. In fact, I knew I could not.

I hesitated just outside the Mother Baby Unit waiting area. The area contained a round magazine table, a brass lamp, and a ficus tree that needed summer. From one of the chairs a man stared at the tall plywood stork that welcomed visitors. Obviously a father-to-be, his eyes bulged with emotion, and even from several feet away they looked wet. The guy twitched so often I knew he would pop up like a Jack-in-the-box if anyone in scrubs appeared. I didn't feel ready to join him.

By tacit agreement neither Michelle nor I had mentioned calling her husband. For one thing, the Tomcats/Eagles game was scheduled for 1 P.M. Doug couldn't possibly get back in time even if Laneer would have excused him, which no NFL coach would have done. Game day was war, and soldiers were not permitted to go home to their wives until the war was over.

Common sense told me, and most people with their sanity still intact, that the life—and possibly death—struggle of childbirth was infinitely more important; but realities other than time and distance kept me from even trying to notify Doug about Michelle's labor.

''I'm just a hired gun,'' Doug had described himself on Thanksgiving. ''When I'm out of bullets, they'll get another gun.'' As an athlete whose career depended entirely on his performance on game day, he could not afford to be absent for any reason. The opportunities to perform well were far too scarce and eager replacements far too plentiful.

If Michelle was able to understand and accept Doug's absence in that context, I should not—and would not—interfere.

But should he at least be made aware of what was happening? That was the question.

According to Michelle's silence, no. She could have asked me to call, but she had not. The message seemed to be ''Let him do his job. He doesn't need worry or regret or even joy messing with his mind." Generous, and mature. I admired my cousin's good sense.

Yet I still needed a public phone, and I found one nearby.

My first call was to the airline to tell them I wouldn't be on my flight. No, I didn't want to re-schedule just yet, maybe later.

Missing my chance to watch a Tomcats game from the sideline both frustrated and saddened me, partly because I now doubted that I would ever do it. Some opportunities tempt you for one moment then pass from your mind. And about then my adventurous im-pulses craved a good long rest.

Next I dialed the house on Beech Tree Lane.

"Gin!" Rip answered with enthusiasm, and my heart did that little clenching thing it does when my husband sounds happy. "When are you coming home?"

I explained what was going on. ". . . so I really can't say. Soon. As soon as I can."

Garry's voice came through. "That Mom? Hey, let me talk to her." Then directly to me: "Hey, Mom. I filmed that game today. It was awesome, way differ-ent from being in the stands. You could hear what the guys said to each other, like you almost knew what they were thinking. It was way cool. You shoulda been there."

Game. Sunday. Sunday morning? Had to be ulti-mate Frisbee on Bryn Derwyn's field. Garry was their eleven-year-old wannabe player, a groupie, almost the only spectator the ragtag college-age participants ever drew except for tolerant girlfriends, and them only on sunny days.

"I'd love to see your film," I told him.

"Good deal," he concluded. "Bye."

My husband came back on. "Everything else all right?" I asked.

"We miss you."

"Me, too."

Rip and I didn't say much more. There wasn't any need.

The prospective father in the waiting area twitched and fidgeted until I could scarcely sit still myself. To give myself a break, I went down to the Tidewater Café, had a turkey sandwich and lemonade, and tried to figure out how to avoid staring at a plywood stork for any longer than necessary.

A plan emerged. I would ask for directions to a waiting room with a television. On Sunday afternoon it was bound to be tuned to the Tomcats/Eagles game. I'd alert one of those marvelously helpful volunteer liaisons to my whereabouts so that when there was any news regarding Michelle and the baby, they could come get me.

The plan worked. Before the kickoff I had installed myself in a sturdily padded chair with wooden arms. A television offering the Tomcats game without sound hung overhead in a corner. Surrounding me were more chairs, wrinkled magazines and newspapers, crumbs, and one old man.

He and I greeted each other with a nodding glance, using the moment to calculate the degree of consideration we needed to show toward the other's emotional state.

"Sister broke her hip," he remarked for clarification.

"Cousin's having a baby. Premature," I added. "Her husband plays for the Tomcats."

That earned me the man's complete sympathy, which he delivered with a warm, crooked smile. Once a tall man, his stature had visibly dwindled. Once, too, his skin must have been smooth and unmarred by discoloration and liver spots, and the hair across his narrow head must have been a healthy blond or brown, unlike the remaining fine silver threads. I noticed that he wore gum-soled shoes, a plaid shirt, and a tan jacket that was too thin for outdoors and too warm for the room.

"Nice win last week," I remarked.

The man sniffed as if offended. "Houston's corner really screwed up covering Smith. Killed their spirit."

"You're referring to the Tomcats' third touchdown?"

My companion flinched with surprise. "You noticed that?"

"Sure," I told him. "If the guy had eyes in the back of his head, maybe he'd have seen he wasn't going to get any help. But he didn't, so Smith just zigged and ran."

We beamed at each other like insiders are wont to do.

"Fred Wyznicki," he told me offering a dry hand.

"Gin Barnes," I responded.

"Most people probably thanked the Tomcats' coaching for that one," my new buddy remarked. "How do you know the game so well?"

I explained about my father. "How about you?"

"Played."

It occurred to me to quiz this knowledgeable observer. "Listen," I opened, hoping to secure his attention. "All week I've been thinking something went on during that game, something odd. What do you think?"

"Odd like how?"

"Odd enough to get Tim Duffy killed."

"Pshew. So much happened. Laneer pulled Cross out. Dionne screwed up. Turner got the wind knocked outta him—twice." Fred shook his head.

I told him I heard that Duffy changed that last touchdown play from a run to a pass.

Fred shook his head. "Good thing, wouldn't you say?"

I would, but would everybody? Tim Duffy had looked unusually intense going into that play, and I still wanted to find out why.

I decided what I really needed to do was watch the game film again—preferably with Ronnie. He had been on the sideline, after all. Maybe with a little prompting he would remember something that fit in with the information I'd gathered during the week. Or maybe the answer would simply leap out at me.

A nurse soon called my waiting room companion in to see his sister. He wished me luck as he left, and I wished him the same.

For another lengthy hour, mostly by myself, I watched the Eagles annihilate the Tomcats' defense and thwart Doug's best efforts to orchestrate a score. Although I scanned the sideline every chance I got, I was disappointed to notice how seldom the TV camera panned the off-field activity.

With luck, the footage Ronnie and his crew shot last week would offer a little more. As historians of the game, they made an effort to record the whole drama, not just the action on the field. Surely, if there had been an interesting emotional response, they would have caught it. That is, if something better hadn't been going on, if they had been facing the right direction, if, if, if . . .

Desperate hope, but all I had.

The Tomcats were losing 28–7 in the fourth quarter when the volunteer found me slouched in my chair with my eyes half closed.

I jumped out of my seat as if I'd been bit. "What?" I asked rudely. "What happened?"

"Your cousin had a little girl," the woman told

me warily. "Everybody's fine," she added. "But they've got the baby in NICU just to be sure."

"Thank you," I told her. Thank you and God and everybody on earth. I could scarcely refrain from kissing the passing visitors as I bounded my way back upstairs to maternity.

TWENTY-ONE

The plywood stork and I kept company a few minutes while Michelle was settled into her room. I had time to notice that the stork's jacket and hat were blue and that he wore a slightly surprised expression, but I tried not to read too much into either.

Again, Michelle's accommodations were private and nicely appointed with a maple dresser, a small round table and chairs, a chintz-covered sofa, and more Mary Cassatt on the textured walls. The new mother sat up in bed, looking alert and pleased.

"Congratulations," I told her, squeezing her hand rather than opting for a hug. We were still sharing grins, and I didn't want to break that off.

"Thanks," said Michelle, her whole being exuding happiness in spite of her exhaustion.

"Welcome to motherhood," I remarked, meaning it in only the way another mother could. The battle scars, the fatigue, the litany of anxieties—none of them could ever fully overshadow the lifelong baseline of joy, not unless something went drastically, drastically wrong. Given a choice, I doubted that even the women who endured the worst of motherhood would say they'd have preferred not to have been a mother at all.

"You've seen her?" I asked to give my cousin the opening she craved.

Michelle nodded and beamed. "She's a miracle,

Gin, the most beautiful baby girl in the whole world."

Afraid to even think about the infant's chances, I asked about her name instead.

"Probably Jody," Michelle responded dreamily, "but I'm going to let Doug decide when he sees her. Who's winning the game, by the way?"

"What game?"

"Tomcats." She laughed.

I hit my head with a palm, chastising myself for temporarily forgetting why Doug wasn't there. "Eagles were winning twenty-eight to seven ten minutes ago."

"Poor Doug."

"I wouldn't say that. Not today."

"You're right," Michelle agreed, smiling again.

"Am I allowed to go see her?" I asked.

"Of course. Come right back though, okay?"

Michelle wasn't quite finished sharing her joy; and I wasn't quite finished basking in it. No matter what else happened, I would always thank Ronnie for this day—December 14, the day his niece was born and his little sister and I became genuinely close.

An overhead sign that read "NICU/Pediatric Acute Care" directed me to turn right just short of the birthing center past the regular nursery. The hall along the way wore more fresh wallpaper in a pattern that looked like painted strings. Wide maple handrails probably aided anyone with unsteady legs while also protecting the decor from being nicked by gurneys.

The Pediatric Acute Care's double wooden door displayed a plastic-encased blue sign that read "Important! Radio frequency ventilator in use. PLEASE No call phones or two-way radios beyond this point! Thank you."

On the right a sign told me to press a button and look into the camera lens fixed into a shoulder-high box. A nurse wearing magenta scrubs showed me in.

"The Turner baby?" I asked hopefully.

"Right this way," she replied. She was pleasant-faced and contagiously calm, perfect for her job. Two units down a row she stopped and waved a hand. "Here she is."

I noted the low-sided, hip-high bed covered with a pink blanket and a loose diaper. On it front and center lay Baby Jody, a tiny, red/brown wiggling newborn with little hair and many wrinkles. A small clear plastic oxygen tent on a thin metal frame covered her tiny head. Barely more than a handful, the child seemed loaded down with tubes and wires. Frightening not to know what they meant.

"What does she weigh?" I asked the nurse, who joined me in admiring the newborn.

"Three and a half pounds, not bad for thirty-two weeks. Could've been worse."

Beside us an alarm went off, a cross between a buzzer and a whistle. I jumped and stared at the boy next door. The nurse laughed.

"He's fine. Just look at him. Those alarms go off all the time. We have to teach the mothers not to panic just because one of the babies wiggled."

I realized then that the room was full of noise, mostly mechanical in nature.

"So if the baby looks okay she probably is?"

"Right."

I breathed easier. "What is all that stuff?" I finally asked.

"Okay. See the wire taped to her abdomen?"

I looked until I identified the attachment she meant.

"That's a control for the radiant warmer—a thermostat for the bed, in other words. Warmth is especially important for a preemie, so we dry them off as quickly as we can. That stimulates their circulation, too. You see, it's critical that they start circulating on their own, independent of their mother, and if they're cold, some of them don't make that transition. The radiant warmer adjusts for whatever the baby needs.''

"Looks like the thermostat in my oven."

"That's pretty much the idea."

"What about the white things on her chest?" Three white patches held wires in place. The wires seemed to lead to a computer-type monitor.

"Heart rate and respiration." The nurse tapped the large blue screen with its lines and blips. "The Band-Aid sort of thing around her ankle is for the Pulseox, this other monitor. That gives us a reading on the percentage of oxygen she's getting so we can regulate that."

"How about the belly button one?" An IV cord seemed to go from the baby's umbilical stub to a drip bag over on a hook.

"We don't feed the babies right away, so that's for fluids—and antibiotics if she needs them."

I had been holding my breath again, worried how to ask the critical question, afraid not to know.

"What are her chances?" There. I said it.

The nurse looked me in the eye. Hers were soft and blue, sincere, authoritative. "She's doing great," the woman told me. "It may take awhile, but I think she's going to be fine."

"How do you know?" I asked bluntly.

The nurse blinked at me then looked back at Michelle and Doug's child. "None of the stuff you're looking at is unusual for a preemie. Plus she's a little girl. Girls have better statistics than little boys."

"Why?"

The nurse looked hard at me and shrugged. "We don't know. They just do. Little black girls fare the best; little white boys do the worst."

She started to wander off.

"Thank you," I called after her, but she was already reading another chart, reaching for a diaper.

Don't read too much into those last observations either, I advised myself. And for sure don't mention them to Doug. The man spent the majority of every day trying to beat tough odds; he didn't need to hear that little baby girls were born better at it than him.

With Michelle's fluffy hair and peaceful smile, she could have posed for one of the impressionist pictures favored by Virginia Beach General Hospital's maternity ward.

Although the atmosphere was probably about as welcoming and comfortable as such a place could get, I questioned whether my cousin would recall anything about her stay save for her own emotions. All that remained of my own two experiences were memories of holding my children for the first time and the expression on my husband's face. Euphoria was quite a potent drug.

Because the nurse's remarks had been so reassuring, I related them to Michelle. The new mother was in her own zone, about to fall asleep, but her expression thanked me for the information, even though it wasn't news. Hearing that your child was most likely going to be fine was like hearing "I love you." A thousand repetitions would never become redundant.

I could not say the same for myself. "Michelle," I awkwardly began to change the subject. "Doug's going to be here tonight . . ."

"Yes, I called the stadium just now. He's going to come straight here."

"That's great," I said, "so you really don't need me here anymore."

Doug's mother, Rene, would surely come east to help Michelle when the baby went home, neighbors would rally, the women from the shower were nearby and willing. Cynthia and Harriet would visit later.

"I think I'd like to catch a plane back to Philly.

There's something I need to go over with your brother.''

Michelle reached her hand toward mine. "You've been great, Gin. But I'm sure you'd like to get home to your family. Go ahead. Do whatever you need to do.''

I certainly did miss my family, but more than ever I hoped to find a way to finish helping Doug and Michelle. Some vengeful little demon wouldn't let me overlook that the added stress from the unpleasant visit from the Norfolk homicide department had been at least partially responsible for their baby's premature birth. If medical science and luck hadn't prevented a tragic disaster, I would have laid quite a heap of guilt right at those cops' big flat feet.

Even now, I feared and distrusted Lieutenant Glenn and his partner for their insensitivity and closed minds. Until the real murderer was caught, those attitudes continued to endanger Doug's reputation and threatened to cause his mother much more undeserved pain. My chances of finding the truth before they discovered and revealed the background of Coren's suicide were slim, but I still intended to try. Reviewing Ronnie's game film was the only viable idea I had left.

Thinking of Michelle's brother, I said, "Since I hope to see Ronnie at his office tonight, would you mind if I told him about the baby?"

"In person? That would be fabulous. I wish I could be there to see his face. Promise you'll tell me all about it.''

"I'm sure he'll call you.''

"Not until morning, I hope. He'll get in awfully late from Green Bay.''

"That's a deal.''

We parted with sentimental hugs and kisses, and I found my way back to the telephone cubbyhole near the waiting room. There I made my flight reservation and arranged for the airport shuttle to pick me up back at Michelle's house. I also called home.

Garry answered.

"It didn't work," he complained as if our last conversation had never ended.

"What didn't?" I asked while scrambling to catch up with his thoughts.

"The audio. I thought I could mix the sound with the movie like Uncle Ronnie does, but you need more than one tape recorder. So I'm gonna just play music for the whole thing. It's pretty cool, but not as cool as it would have been." My son's dejection came through clearly in spite of his optimistic spin.

"Sorry, Gar," I commiserated, although my mind was mostly focused elsewhere. "Is Dad home?"

"Picking up Chelsea. You wanna talk to the grannies?"

No, I did not; Garry took better messages.

"Listen," I said, "I've got to catch a plane, but..." I told him about Michelle's baby, "way cool," and that I'd probably be home tomorrow. Tonight I was staying in New Jersey either with my cousin or Aunt Harriet. "Got that?"

"Yup. You'll be home tomorrow night, so you can see my movie then."

"Uh, right." Maybe I should have insisted that he write everything down.

TWENTY-TWO

Back in Broad Bay Point Greens I stowed Michelle's Jeep in the garage. I was already packed, so I dumped everything by the front door. Then I paced back and forth in the hallway eating a sandwich while I waited for the airport shuttle.

Quite an assortment of emotions jazzed my nerves. Naturally, I was both elated and concerned over the baby. But I remained quite concerned over Doug's precarious status with the police.

I was further frustrated by the inconclusiveness of this morning's meeting with Pamela Wilkinson. It seemed I knew far too much about the problem and scarcely anything that pointed toward a solution.

Although I was eager to see my family, even that anticipation was dampened by a sense of defeat, possibly because I doubted that I would find anything helpful in a game film I had already seen.

Traveling always unnerved me, too, no matter what the reason for the trip. At home familiar door jambs and tables and chairs guided me when it got dark. I knew where to buy Chelsea's favorite jeans and the back way from King of Prussia to Ludwig. Gretsky softly nuzzled me awake every morning. Rip was near. I knew where I was.

Norfolk made me feel blindfolded. For all I knew, any step forward might have been off the edge of a cliff. Maybe if I plugged into my home outlet for a day or two, recharged, regrouped. Maybe then I could shake off this sense of failure and try again.

The limousine arrived, and I rode in strained companionship with an elderly couple just finished a visit with their serviceman son. With them they carried their own gamut of emotions, world tensions being what they always were.

At the airport I insulated myself against strangers and watched twilight become night outside the walls of glass.

Once on the plane I slept, and seemingly soon we landed in Philadelphia with whistling, roaring jets and the thump and squeak of wheels. Like everyone else, I struggled to look nonchalant while straining to burst from my confinement.

The comparatively fresh jetway air both chilled and revived, but the lobby smelled of old cigarettes and French fries. I bought an exorbitant candy bar then didn't have the hands free to eat it until after I collected my big suitcase.

A lone woman in a large airport at night, I felt vulnerable, as if every move exposed me to another risk. Yet I allowed a gentle older man wearing a tan uniform to persuade me to use his taxi to Mt. Laurel. If he had been younger and dressed otherwise, I'd have refused him.

We set off through a cold drizzle along highways lined with closed industry. Sunday night. Some football games persisted. Others were over. Probably there had been crews of NFL camera and sound men in the airport, and I wondered if perhaps I should have tried to meet up with them, explain my situation, throw myself on the mercy of Ronnie's coworkers.

Yet my initial instinct was probably best. Arriving unannounced would be awkward, but the miserable weather upped my chances of getting inside the office to wait for Ronnie. At least I hoped so.

The cabbie dropped me out in the rain on the NFL Films driveway, and after I paid him he eyed me with concern. "You sure this is the right place?"

"Yes," I told him. "I'm meeting my cousin here."

Water sizzled off the tires as the elderly vehicle slid down the street. When its headlights were gone, only a few damp balloons of misty lamplight remained.

I slung my carry-on over my shoulder and hunched into my coat collar. Rolling my large bag across macadam in the now-steady rain, I worried what my reception would be.

The man who answered my knock on the door of Ronnie's building didn't bother with tact. "What are you doing here?" he demanded to know, his face aghast.

Already my teeth chattered from the cold, and my whole body shivered for emphasis. "I'm Ronnie Covington's cousin, Gin Barnes," I explained. "His sister just had a baby—premature—in Norfolk. I just came from there, and I'd like to wait for Ronnie—if I may."

The man put a hand on my shoulder and ushered me in out of the rain. Then he reached outside for my heavy bag.

"Jeez, you took a chance coming here," he said. "What if Ronnie'd come and gone already?"

"He's been in Green Bay. I thought I'd catch him."

"Yeah, but . . ."

"I'm sorry. It's crazy, I know. But it's been that kind of day."

"Come on, come on. Get out of that wet coat. Ya want some coffee?"

"That would be heavenly."

"Mark," he called to another somewhat younger

fellow dressed in olive drab. "Do you know how to make coffee in that thing?"

My benefactor finished delegating the kindness, then he showed me into one of the empty sound offices, guiding me into a tweed armchair. I must have looked awful to be treated with such deference.

"Is Ronnie's sister all right?" the man asked. He was muscular and weather-worn, with short, thinning black hair and plenty of stubble. He called himself Bob.

"Yes," I answered.

"The baby?" he asked with a wince. Ronnie must have mentioned last week's scare to his co-workers, and this man apparently knew enough about premature babies to fear the worst.

"She's fine," I said with a smile. "So far. But you'll let me tell Ronnie myself, won't you?"

"Sure. Sure. Trouble is, you can't stay here without somebody around, you know?" We had passed through an area loaded with electronic equipment, stacks of videotape in blue cases. An adjacent room housed another library, this time shelves full of videotapes.

From his weighty expression, I realized that Bob planned to leave momentarily himself; and if a succession of returning film crews didn't pass me to the next crew like a relay baton, I was back out in the rain.

"Would you like to see some I.D.?" I asked, hastily pulling out my wallet and flipping it open to my driver's license.

"That ain't it," Bob replied gloomily, waving off my wallet after a cursory glance.

He meant that my identity didn't matter. And it didn't, really. What mattered was that he was responsible for me being in there, and he couldn't take the chance of leaving me alone—no matter what I said.

I didn't blame him. On the contrary, I trusted him and liked him for his caution.

Bob waited until his buddy brought me a mug of black coffee. Then he said, "Tell ya what. I might as well stick around a little while." *But not too long* hung in the air unspoken. With the twelve or more hours a day I knew these men put in at the beginning of each week, simple words like "Thank you" didn't begin to describe my gratitude.

So with strain in the air Bob puttered around, and I finished one mug of coffee and started on another.

At one point I wandered over to a doorway where the most Sunday night activity seemed to be taking place. Weary men who never removed their casual outdoor garb rolled in handtrucks loaded with cases of equipment, stored everything in metal cages marked with their names, then headed for home. My watchdog looked after them longingly.

"Could I wait in Ronnie's car?" I asked at one point.

"It'll be at the airport," Bob lamented.

More crews came and went, a straggling of rain-soaked confederates speaking to each other in the familiar way men do when women aren't around—in-jokes, a little profanity, remarks about the games they'd done that day. I thought they sounded closer than most co-workers, perhaps like the members of a privileged club. My presence shocked more than a few of them into silence.

"Ronnie's cousin," Bob explained each time, but the short version wasn't enough.

About eleven forty-five Bob looked at me and shrugged.

"You've got to go home," I said for him, rising from my chair.

"Yeah, sorry. Drop you somewhere?"

"Hey! Gin, baby," Ronnie's welcoming voice

called from across the broad main room.

Bob and I sighed in unison. Then I kissed the kind cameraman on the cheek and told him, "Thanks, you're a prince." He was gone within the minute.

Ronnie's face blanched as he absorbed the meaning of my presence. "Michelle?" he asked.

"Fine. She had a little girl—Jody probably—and she's doing well, too."

"Wow!" Muddy down jacket and all, my cousin sank into a chair across from the one I'd used so long, his dark-edged eyes sparkling as he absorbed the information. While I related the rest of the details—weight, what the baby looked like, what the nurse said—his grin twitched with delight, and his hands flexed as if they needed to slap a shoulder or grab someone to tell.

But as I had anticipated, his expression soon altered. Delight became concern edged with confusion. He raked through his brown wavy hair and stated, "You didn't come up here just to tell me about the baby."

"No," I admitted. "Not entirely. "I also need your help."

Someone was headed our way carrying a boom mike, so I concluded quickly. "I'd like to watch last week's Tomcats game again."

Astonishment wiped away Ronnie's fatigue. He popped up and nodded to the approaching crew member, whom he introduced as his soundman, Dave. Then he hustled me around the corner out of Dave's way and out of his earshot.

"Have you got something?" The man was bursting his seams, but I put him off.

"Why don't you finish up here, and then we'll talk." By then the place would be even emptier, and maybe Ronnie could set me up with the film.

"Right, right," he agreed, instinctively appreciating my desire for privacy.

"Dave," he called to the younger man. "Look after my cousin here a minute. I'm gonna deliver my film to the lab."

Dave cracked his gum and said "Sure" as a matter of course.

But then neither of them realized what Ronnie had asked.

TWENTY-THREE

Fifteen minutes later the video services department's coffee pot lay washed and overturned on a paper towel, suggesting that my grace period of tolerant hospitality had expired and then some. Dave, the soundman from Ronnie's crew, shrugged back into a cracked brown leather jacket that had seen much service. Then he donned a blue knit watch cap, all without taking his eyes off me. Suggestive. Hopeful. Moderately concerned.

More than enough time had elapsed for my cousin to drop his film off for processing over at the main building. The dropoff slots were right inside the door.

Rest stop? I wondered. Putting something in his car? Ronnie's routine after returning from a game was too unfamiliar to me to form any sort of guess, but Dave's expression confirmed that Ronnie had been gone way too long.

"I guess you want to lock up."

"Yeah."

"Maybe I could just go over and find Ronnie myself," I suggested. "Then you could get out of here."

Dave's already young face lost a couple years. "I'll have to let you in," he thought aloud.

So I put on my coat, grabbed my purse, and left my luggage for later.

Together Ronnie's soundman and I trotted through the rain to where my cousin would have entered the main building. Barring my view, he poked a password into a security pad and soon held the door open for me. Concern covered his face.

"Ronnie's probably in the men's room or something," I reassured my cousin's co-worker. "I'll just holler."

"Yeah," Dave agreed with a laugh. He wiped a drop of rain from his eye. But he lingered just the same.

"Really," I said. "Ronnie's got to be here. You go ahead." The kid was falling asleep on his feet.

"Yeah," he agreed again. "Tell Ronnie he's a pain in the ass."

"Tell him yourself tomorrow." With a dismissive wave the young soundman loped across the dimly lighted lot toward a cheap bachelor car, the sort I recognized from my dating days. It would smell like hamburgers, sweat, and maybe even mold from sitting under a tree in the damp all weekend.

Meanwhile, the metal door was pressing heavily against my hand, struggling against its compressor. Rain had at me as long as I stood half exposed like that, so I stepped back and allowed the door to close with a jailhouse thunk. Chills from more than the weather danced up my spine.

The short hallway ended in a T. To my right were the gray wooden cubbyholes Ronnie had pointed out on our Thanksgiving day tour, each marked with this week's matchups written on masking tape. Some slots were empty, some full, probably depending on when and where the games were played. The one marked Green Bay/Miami had film cans in it, so apparently Ronnie had been here and gone.

So where was he now?

"Ronnie!" I called into the half darkness as I eased my way farther into the building. Only safety lights over exits kept me from walking into the walls.

Nobody answered my shout. I tried again as I turned left at the T. "Ronnie?"

Nothing.

Intermittently shouting my cousin's name, I felt my way along first one hall and then another.

Soon I found myself near the Emmy wall and the lobby flanked by executive offices. The shadows fell like holes in the floor, misshapen invitations to doom. The building had sounds, too—like hot breath or impatient tapping, strange whistles and the thrumming of distant rain.

"Ronnie?" I called, my throat tight and painful. Damp air pervaded the relatively cold building, swallowing my voice, muffling my footsteps, and making me feel as if I were free-floating in a vacuum.

I passed the anteroom to the film vault. Maybe because this area felt warmer, I imagined that Ronnie had been here. Sometimes I trusted such instinctive information, often not—the internal debate continued. Yet one sensation I accepted without question—Ronnie was not here now. Nobody was.

Still, I felt warned.

Call out again?

A sixth sense said no. Fear governed my decisions now, and being quiet felt safest. I slung my purse across my chest to prevent it from knocking against anything—my legs, furniture, the wall. I rolled from toe to heel on my sneakers, grateful they were dry enough not to squeak on the shiny tile.

Where to go next? Up? Down? Circle around? How to decide? I stood quivering in the middle of a large building late at night, alone. Any information received by the usual means—eyes, ears, touch—came under the category of "suspect."

So instinct won the debate by default, moved me along a dark patch of wall, past a doorknob locked tight, past an unusually shaped Elvis bas-relief collage I remembered from the tour.

On the level above came a crash and clatter followed by a heavier thud.

"Ronnie!" I shouted again, almost screamed.

I bounded up some nearby stairs two at a time. "Ronnie, where the hell are you? Answer me, dammit. This isn't funny."

My shouting seemed to fill the building, obscuring everything else. I worried whether I should have kept quiet. But maybe it didn't matter. Maybe I was fried anyway.

I paused under the light that marked the top of the staircase, the only light on the second floor. There I concentrated intensely on what Ronnie said on our tour, what? only two weeks or so ago, but I couldn't remember which rooms were around me—the music department? The main library?

Garry would have known, he'd been that tuned in, plus he was blessed with the flawless recall of youth. Me? By the time we reached the second floor I'd been easing toward technical overload, noting only the odd facts that interested me and dismissing the nuts and bolts. Too bad, because now I couldn't begin to guess where a threat might be lurking.

My skin alerted me to the man before my eyes picked out his form. He stood twenty yards away, a tall, darkly dressed figure looking my way. His arms were partially raised, his knees flexed. Not Ronnie. Definitely not Ronnie.

I flattened against the wall and screamed, shutting my eyes the better to stretch my mouth.

When I looked again, the man was yanking at a far door. The next thing I heard was feet hammering down distant stairs.

Pumping blood absorbed all my concentration. My lungs needed reminding. Muscles that had liquefied with fear took their time firming up. My skin felt slimy.

Fueled by adrenaline, my imagination spun me a probable background scenario, beginning with Ronnie hearing a noise and going off to investigate. Right now he was probably in the room the intruder just left, hurt maybe or worse. I had to go see.

Steadying myself with the wall, I tested a step toward the closed door, then another and another until soon enough I was safely there. The building breathed and squeaked as before, but I heard no additional human sound. The unlocked doorknob released its catch with a satisfying *kachunk*.

I felt for a light switch and found one, flipped it on, recoiled from the brightness. This was the master vault, filled with various-size containers of D-3 digital tape, the masters used to make all of the shows. A narrow work area lay before the perpendicular rows of movable white metal shelving I remembered from the tour.

Surrounded by litter, Ronnie lay sandwiched on his side between the rolling shelves, the soles of his boots toward me and several inches in from the edge. I moved close enough to watch the folds of his jacket sleeve shift with each slow breath.

"Ronnie?" I asked tentatively. He did not respond, just breathed lightly as if asleep.

My first impulse was to release him from the confinement of the shelves, but this was the scene of a crime, possibly an attempted murder. Before I touched anything, I knew I should try to piece together what happened, or at least notice what was where.

From the way Ronnie fell, the intruder must have ambushed him from behind, probably hit him on the head then pushed him forward. If the intention had been to crush the only witness to whatever crime was in progress, something must have interfered—probably not an attack of conscience.

My reasoning was simple. NFL Films was in the business of supplying game videos to anyone who needed them. So with copies abundantly available, why would anyone skulk around the archives at night? The thief had to be looking for incriminating material in order to destroy it. It followed that Ronnie's attacker almost certainly shot Tim Duffy!

I looked to see if maybe the debris from the shelves had gotten in the way and saved my cousin's life, but most of the videotapes had fallen into the aisle to his left. After he was hit, it appeared that he dove onto a shelf and pushed its contents onto the floor—a very heads-up idea, considering. If he could have kept his whole body on the shelf, his attacker would have been unable to crush him. Unfortunately, Ronnie must have blacked out and fallen back into the gap.

"Nine hundred pounds moved by one pound of pressure," he had boasted to Doug, Garry, and me, showing off another NFL Films flirtation with the latest technology. I shuddered to think how easily my son had turned one of those handles.

Yet Ronnie was alive and, from what I could tell, pretty much intact. Only one explanation made sense: My frantic yelling as I bounded up the stairs must have spooked the intruder.

Humph, I congratulated myself. In the future I would have to give instinct much more credit.

Mindful of fingerprints, I pulled a cuff over my hand and, without touching the crank handle, widened the space where my cousin lay. He moaned from the discomfort of rolling onto the back of his head.

"Ronnie," I said, "It's Gin."

"Ooh," he complained. "My head."

"Don't try to sit up."

"Okay," he agreed, relaxing back onto the floor. He had reached up to touch a tender spot, and his hand came away bloody.

"I'll call the police," I began, but just then an alarm went off and obliterated my words.

The intruder again, making his escape.

TWENTY-FOUR

While the NFL Films burglar alarm battered our ears with intermittent blasts of noise, I tried to ask Ronnie a couple of urgent questions. The police would arrive any minute, and who knew what would happen then?

"Did you see who hit you?" I shouted.

"No." He winced when he tried to move his head, which was still resting on the floor between the movable shelves. His hands covered his ears while his fingers pillowed the bump on his head.

"Why'd you come up here?" He didn't get my question the first time so I yelled it again.

"To borrow last week's master tape." For me, sweet guy. "Police have the three-quarter-inch copy," he finished during the next break of blessed silence.

"Was it there?" Confusion. "The tape. Was it there?"

"Never got that far."

"Do you remember diving onto the shelf?"

"Diving? Not really."

No? He had to have been awake and thinking at that point, but if he didn't remember . . .

"Well, I thought you were brilliant . . . and lucky."

"Lucky?"

His surprise at my remark surprised me. Then suddenly I got it. One of the mercies Mother Nature occasionally offered was a spot of amnesia to blot out a painful accident. So maybe Ronnie really didn't remember. And maybe, just maybe he would never piece together the rest—the part where he almost became lunchmeat.

Never mind that my cousin's eyebrows peaked with puzzlement, I chose not to elaborate. He worked here. For him, passing the master vault would be difficult enough without a worse outcome to contemplate.

"You be okay while I let the police in?" I shouted over the alarm in order to evade any more questions.

He nodded, winced, and said, "Sure."

I patted his knee and departed with my hands over my ears, telling myself as I found my way back downstairs that there was a certain amount of safety in the painful noise; no intelligent intruder would stick around and let his ears take such a pounding. Victims, unfortunately, didn't seem to have much of a choice.

At least the dimly lighted halls no longer held any horror. I didn't even get lost. I just wished I knew what I had to smash to disable that deafening alarm.

When the police car roared up to the front entrance, I rushed out to greet them.

"My cousin was attacked by an intruder. He's hurt," I shouted at the two officers as soon as they opened their doors.

The first man slid back into the patrol car to radio for paramedics, additional plainclothesmen, and a forensics unit. The driver hurried inside to shut off the alarm and restore heavenly silence. I wanted to kiss him.

Several minutes later, about the time my ears stopped buzzing, a fatherly type in a tweed overcoat named Detective Schwartz arrived and took over. A jowly sour-looking man, he ignored me and questioned Ronnie in a manner reminiscent of a junior high math teacher I had hated. "Did you see the assailant?" "Any idea what he was after?" Ronnie seemed to get the answers wrong every time. Fortunately, the paramedics arrived and rescued my cousin from Schwartz's critical scrutiny.

Although my potentially concussed kin was up on his feet and feeling pretty decent by that time, an intent young woman in a no-nonsense uniform insisted that he ride along over to South Jersey Hospital for a more thorough examination. Her partner concurred, but Ronnie went macho on them and balked.

"Ex jock," I explained to the woman, and she rolled her eyes with disgust but certainly not defeat. In fact, she drew herself up to about five foot four, swaggered to within eighteen inches of Ronnie's face, and scolded him sternly.

"Listen." She punctuated with a phony finger poke. "You need X rays, and I need to get back on the road. So deal with it." She wore a long French braid of brown laced with blonde, and she looked pretty cute when she was mad.

Ronnie gave her his slow, John Wayne smile then made a show of digging into his pocket for his car keys, which he tossed to me with a wink.

"Guess I gotta go," he told Schwartz, and the cop snorted.

"I'll be along in a minute," I told my cousin's retreating back.

He and his caretakers had scarcely departed before a uniformed officer bounded into the upstairs hall from the stairwell. "Looks like somebody broke into a storage area downstairs," he told the man in charge.

"Show me," Schwartz ordered, puffing his chest with authority.

Trying not to attract anyone's attention, I followed along after him.

The officer led us into the anteroom to the film vault. With the light on we could see that the windowed door to the vault had been broken, circumventing the security keypad with simple force.

Brave bastard was my first thought. Ronnie's attacker hadn't set off the alarm as he was leaving; he set it off smashing this door—with me and Ronnie upstairs!

Subsequently it occurred to me that the intruder had been in at least two of the four storage areas I remembered. Possibly he had been in all four. But why?

And then I knew.

"Wonder what's in here?" Detective Schwartz mused.

"The original negatives," I said, my voice startling him as if he hadn't realized I was there.

"All the original film," I elaborated, including the parts that didn't make it into the specials—the highlight tapes.

"Oh?" Schwartz seemed amused that I knew this. "And why do you suppose anyone would want to break in here?"

"Not just anyone. Tim Duffy's murderer."

Schwartz breathed deeply and let it out slow. "Whooee, you sure do have an imagination."

I scowled and set my hands on my hips. "Think about it, Detective," I all but ordered the man. "Duffy was shot at Nimitz Stadium right after the Tomcats/Hombres game. Doesn't that suggest that something happened during the game that set off the killer?"

Schwartz waved his head slowly, causing his jowls to wiggle. "Not necessarily," he replied with professorial condescension.

I sighed. "You do at least agree it had to be somebody who was in the stadium?"

"Of course. One of the thirty-five or forty thousand fans, if you ask me. You ever seen those nuts on TV?"

Make something of that said his face, which took on the mule-stubborn expression of every man who ever thought he was going to avoid an argument by pretending he had already won.

I slipped into the ingenuous mode Schwartz was bound to misread as easily as if I was slipping into silk pajamas.

I waved a hand nonchalantly toward the broken door. "Do you mind if I check to see whether last week's cans are still here?"

Schwartz exchanged glances with the officer who found the smashed window, a tall lanky sort with sleepy eyes that I found annoying.

"Sure." Schwartz smirked. "You think you can find them in two minutes or less?"

I cast him a nasty look, which made him smile again.

Sleepy Eyes lent me a flashlight because the light switch inside the film vault hadn't been dusted for prints.

"Don't touch anything," the detective advised, his expression now superior—and fretful. The possible connection to America's current high-profile murder case must have triggered his curiosity. Why else allow me to contaminate a crime scene?

Unless he found the temptation to mock my theory, and me, all but irresistible.

Luckily the long room full of tall metal shelves had been labeled clearly down the center aisle. Out of the hundreds of silver, red, and blue film cans I found the ones from the current year and month in thirty seconds, located the correct week in twenty, and noted that the Tomcats/Hombres canisters were missing in scarcely fifteen more. However, I took a few extra seconds to check twice.

"Not here," I reported back, thinking, "Not good. Not good at all." Beating Schwartz might be child's play, but the killer was way, way ahead of us both.

"Okay, get out of there," the detective snapped. "And give Officer Winthorpe here a sample of your hair." Said as if he longed to pull it out himself.

"So now do you believe me?" I inquired without much optimism.

"Believe what?"

"That Ronnie surprised Tim Duffy's killer, who was in here stealing some film he thinks will incriminate him?"

Schwartz wagged his head to indicate that his patience was running out. "I believe your cousin interrupted a robbery and got his head bashed for being in the way . . ."

"But you do agree it was the film of last week's Tomcats game the thief was after?" My own patience had also thinned.

"Mebbee. They *would* be valuable, what with being Duffy's last game and all."

"No." No, no, no. "I mean, yes, the film would be valuable, but don't you think the killer probably wanted it because it incriminates him?"

Schwartz lifted his chin the better to peer at me through the lower part of his glasses, an elder sage humoring the silly young thing. "And who exactly are we accusing of doing all this?" he inquired.

Despite the sensation of someone prodding me along a cattle chute to my own doom, I told him I had a few people in mind.

"Walker Cross got benched during that game, so gaining the yardage or catches or whatever he needs to get a guaranteed one point seven million next year became almost unattainable.''

''So?''

''So he might have blamed Tim Duffy for his benching.''

''Blamed the quarterback for the coach taking him out of the game? Hummm.'' Schwartz played with his jowls thoughtfully.

''Yes. Cross missed a simple pass in the first quarter.'' More accurately, he bellyflopped to the ground like a clumsy oaf, but my listeners were already too eager to be amused, so I skipped to my next suspect.

''Or Willet Smith,'' I told them. ''Before Duffy's death he was the Tomcats' third-string quarterback. Now he's second in line.'' Failing skills, overblown pride—for some these were the ingredients of desperation.

''Um-humm,'' Schwartz mused like a third-rate Sherlock Holmes.

Trying not to make a bad habit sound like a slanderous accusation, I worded what Pamela Wilkinson said about Roger Prindel very cautiously.

''Also, I was told the offensive coordinator likes to gamble—but not on football.''

''You don't say.''

''Yes. And for a billionaire, Bobby Frye is very careful with his money.''

''And you know this because . . . ?''

''I had lunch with him last week. He wouldn't pay for a soda I ordered because the waiter didn't bring it.''

''You had lunch with Bobby Frye.'' Schwartz had been leaning on the hallway wall, but now he stood up and paced reflectively. ''Are you friends then?''

''No. I just met him that day.''

''And he invited you to lunch, just like that.''

''No. I invited him first.''

"Begging your pardon, of course, but why do you think he agreed to go?"

I sighed, not at all happy with Schwartz's attitude, but convinced he should hear all this anyway. He was the one investigating the break-in, after all.

"I'm a stockholder," I explained, grateful once again that it was the truth, "but that's not the point. The point is he's cheap, especially for a billionaire. If he is a billionaire. He's being sued, you know."

"Why was that again?"

"Mismanagement. Alleged mismanagement of one of his holding company's companies."

"No," Schwartz corrected me. "Why did you say he was cheap?"

Repeating the undelivered soda example was bound to make me sound stupid, which no doubt was the detective's intention.

"Because Frye doesn't like to pay for nothing," I answered instead.

Schwartz and Winthorpe exchanged a look similar to the one that asked whose turn it was to pick up the check.

"Can't say I blame the guy," Winthorpe remarked.

"Well, no," I agreed, although I was disappointed to think that wealthy people still worried about every penny. "But Frye admitted he doesn't want to pay Walker Cross's salary if he doesn't have to, and maybe Duffy was going to tell the press that Frye benched Cross just to save the money. With two games left in the season Frye didn't expect the public to pick up on the monetary reason for that."

Schwartz laughed. Out loud. And on cue big, sleepy-eyed Winthorpe snickered along, just scrunched his eyes into slits and chortled.

"What'd you and Frye have for lunch?" Schwartz asked when he was able. "Filet mignon?"

I huffed with frustration. "No. As a matter of fact I had chicken salad and he had the Jewish Mother's Club."

The detective doubled over on that, and his sidekick let go an unbecoming bark.

"Well, then," Schwartz said through quivering lips. "That proves he's our man."

I folded my arms hard across my chest and pressed my mouth tight. I only asked the question because I had to. "Why?"

The detective's nose crinkled as if tickled by carbonation. Yet he managed to meet my eye, perhaps in anticipation of more pleasure at my expense. "Because everybody knows guilt *is* a Jewish mother's club."

The laughter broke loose and leaped onto Winthorpe, riding the big man's back like a rodeo cowboy.

I endured that a minute, then I asked Schwartz another question—just for fun.

"If I looked like him," meaning big bad Winthorpe, "would you still be laughing?"

"Yes. Oh, yes," Schwartz decided.

Then he went back to the fatherly condescension. "Go home, Mrs. Barnes," he told me. "We have work to do here."

I narrowed my eyes, squinting into the shadows for my lost dignity. "Just don't forget to dust those shelf handles real well." Even without the "please," my parting punch glanced off Schwartz like rain off an umbrella.

But I had said it, and I felt better.

"Good-bye, Mrs. Barnes," Detective Schwartz dismissed me, once again the world-weary cop.

TWENTY-FIVE

I used the phone in the receptionists' cubicle of NFL Films to call the hospital where the paramedics had taken my cousin. Not only did I get succinct directions from my location to theirs, I also learned that Ronnie was still being observed in the ER.

Outside I found his Acura and got going. The rain had finally quit, and the anonymous twenty-minute drive through the nighttime streets became a welcome respite. At that hour even the inside of the emergency area seemed hushed, as if the whole world had been socked in by fog.

A nurse showed me where my cousin was sleeping and answered my few questions. Apparently, the doctor was worried about a concussion and wanted Ronnie to remain until morning. Later morning, that is, because it was already after 2 A.M.

I couldn't quite bring myself to nudge Ronnie awake, so I waited, and in a few minutes one of the nurses came in and did it for me.

"Mr. Covington. Hi, there. You okay? How many fingers am I holding up?"

"How many am I?" he replied. Fortunately, the woman was not a prude.

"Don't stay long. He needs his rest," the nurse shot over her shoulder to me.

"Ha," the patient called after her.

I noticed that he winced when he faced straight

207

forward, so I eased farther to his side so he wouldn't be lying on his sore spot while we talked.

"Nobody should be so cheery at this hour," I remarked.

"No kidding," Ronnie retorted. Finding the push button that operated his bed, he raised himself until we were more or less eye to eye.

"How goes it?" he asked, concern showing through the light camouflage.

"Not good," I all but whispered. The cubicle was bracketed by two walls and two curtains that rendered privacy a thin illusion. "It looks as if our guy got his hands on last week's negatives."

Ronnie scowled. The negatives were sacred, the genesis of everything the company did. After they had been developed and printed, they were scarcely touched.

"Would the outtakes from the film still be around somewhere?" I asked.

The highlights had already been made available to anyone and everyone who wanted to see them. In other words, those prints were too plentiful for the killer to retrieve. The fact that Tim's killer took a considerable risk to steal the negatives meant he was worried about something that never made it into the special.

And that meant our best and perhaps only chance of identifying the murderer lay buried in the outtakes—if they still existed outside of the film cans that had been stolen.

"Dennis might still have the print he worked on," Ronnie thought aloud.

"Who's Dennis?"

"The guy who edited that game."

"Can we call him?"

"Right now?"

"I'm not going to sleep until I know who has those outtakes. Are you?"

Ronnie blinked himself a little more awake. "Hand me the phone." A nice serviceable instrument of communication sat right there on the food tray at Ronnie's elbow, for informing relatives of your sudden indisposition, arranging for babysitters, alerting the media. Whatever. I was mighty glad it was there.

Ronnie dialed and waited for his co-worker to wake up.

"Dennis," he said after the groggy answer. "It's Ronnie. Listen, I'm in the hospital emergency room . . . Nah, just a bump on the head . . . but I have to ask you something important . . . Do you still have the Tomcats/Hombres print from last week?"

My cousin's dark eyes gaped. "You do?" Both our faces widened into foolish grins.

"That's a huge relief," Ronnie told the editor. "But now I've got to ask a big favor. First thing tomorrow do you think you can set my cousin up to look at it? . . . Yeah, Duffy's murder. Gin's . . . she's just onto something, okay?" More listening before the men said good-bye.

"Sorry," Ronnie apologized. "I just didn't know how to explain you."

I was bouncing in my chair. "Never mind. What did he say?"

"He said he used the AVID to edit last week's game, which means he erased the outtakes at the end of the day, but he held onto the print because he expected the cops to ask for it. You know, figuring there might be something there. But he also said in all the times he viewed that footage, he didn't notice anything unusual."

I thought I understood. The AVID allowed a film to be edited the way a computer processed words. You typed in commands and the sophisticated machine cut and pasted without actually using scissors or glue. The good stuff got saved while the unwanted footage was simply deleted. Owing to Dennis's foresight, his working print was still safely locked in his office. Otherwise the killer might have found and destroyed it.

"Is he really going to let me watch it?" I pressed. "On a Monday?" The busiest day of their week.

"Sure. He owes me a favor or two. Of course if I don't get there tomorrow, the shoe'll be on the other foot."

I smiled at his work ethic, one of the main ingredients to his success and a stringent job requirement at NFL Films.

A couple minutes later Ronnie told me how to find his apartment, and I kissed his forehead by way of good-bye. We were both wired at the prospect of thwarting Tim's killer and terrified that something else would go wrong before I could view the outtakes. Yet there was only so much a person could hope to accomplish running on adrenaline. I needed real rest to clear my head for the chore, and there was only one way I knew to accomplish that.

So I slogged out into the post-rain mist and drove my cousin's car to my cousin's bed and treated myself to a solid six hours of sleep. The broadminded nurse had doubted that Ronnie was really suffering from a concussion and quite probably could be picked up at ten.

I did not want to be late.

Immediately after I ransomed Ronnie out of the hospital, we drove straight back to NFL Films. We proceeded directly to Dennis the editor's office where a studious, clear-eyed man unlocked a drawer and extracted two beautiful fifteen-inch film canisters in a nice serviceable gray.

A SCORE TO SETTLE

"Do you know what you're looking for?" the film editor asked with a flat mixture of amusement and curiosity. About forty years old, Dennis's fair complexion seemed reddened by an inner heat that dictated short sleeves even on December 15.

"Know it when I see it," I replied.

With a philosophical tilt of his head Dennis began to set the first reel onto his old flatbed apparatus, which was still the alternate to editing with the more advanced AVID. The flatbed was a four-foot-wide, three-foot-deep tabletop supporting what looked like six record turntables, three left and three right. It had a viewing screen at the center of the back and control knobs for forward, backward, and slow motion that even I could operate. After Dennis threaded the first reel of last week's print through pulleys, he leaned on his hands, the better to look me up and down.

"You sure you'll be okay here?" he asked. This was the one and only remaining print of all the shots by Ronnie and his partner. If it accidentally got damaged—by me—a potentially critical piece of evidence might be ruined.

I forced my eyes to hold steady for my reply.

"Just leave me with some coffee and I'm good for hours," I said, as if that answered Dennis's question.

He gave me half a frown and a nod then departed to his waiting AVID and this week's work. When I ran out of film, I was to find him so he could thread the second reel onto the flatbed for me. This was crunch time at NFL Films after all; and doing it himself was faster than teaching me how.

Ronnie, however, felt obligated to review the operation of the flatbed a couple more times.

"Enough already," I finally scolded. "You're making me a nervous wreck."

"It's just . . ."

"I know. The only print."

"No," Ronnie said, causing me to look at his face. What I saw frayed my nerves even further. His concern had not been for the film at all; it had been for Doug and Michelle and their baby. My palms began to sweat, my heart raced, my eyes blinked and darted from Ronnie to the controls to the screen in front of me.

"Go get a shower or something, will you?" I finally dismissed him. "Or pull your game, or catch some sleep. Just get out of here. Okay?"

When Ronnie drew himself up, he winced at the stress on his adhesive bandage. "Yeah, yeah, yeah," he grumbled. But he stroked my hair and trailed his fingers across my shoulder before he left. Afterward, I breathed again and wiped my eyes and blew my nose.

Then I settled down to watch football with a concentration I had never afforded the game ever before, not even when my dad's team played for the state championship.

Maybe it was because of Doug and Michelle and Jody, maybe it was because Ronnie had almost been killed, but the avenues to my senses were wide open, treating me to nuances and impressions that normally would have passed across my consciousness without making any impression whatsoever.

I began to recognize which of Ronnie's shots were planned and which had capitalized on the luck of the moment—ground shots up past a wreath of huddled helmets to thin blue sky, or huffing runners twisting just out of an opponent's reach for another three precious yards. I seemed to be inside Ronnie's head, doing his job.

With a flick of his eyes I saw Patrick Dionne's concentration lapse just before his muffed snap back to Doug.

A SCORE TO SETTLE

The first time Doug took a helmet in the ribs I cried "Oof" out loud.

When Tim Duffy took over that first brief time, his posture telegraphed his joy and selfish intentions directly to me. His frustration, his pride, his aggressiveness were transparent, his mental calculations words in my ears.

But silent words, for neither Dennis nor Ronnie had thought to provide me with sound, probably because it was too impractical. Since the audio and video were recorded separately, I remembered Ronnie explaining that they had to be coordinated manually. This was facilitated by a "bloop lite" that marked both tapes with a beep and a flash, the modern version of the striped clapboard of old "Take one," "Take two" days. Luckily, the quiet seemed to aid my concentration.

I read volumes into the shot of Bobby Frye leaning his elbows on the edge of the owner's balcony box. Like a perplexed boy watching others enjoy his birthday party, he appeared to observe the fans with a mixture of happiness and dismay. Their pleasure reflected on him and therefore pleased him, but he seemed incapable of enjoying the day without analyzing it to bits.

This version of the game included Walker Cross on the sideline right after his benching, his face both grave and haughty. He glared only at the ground, clearly angry, but at whom or what I could not tell even though I reran the shot three times.

Shortly after that, Tim Duffy crossed the camera's path during an Hombres' possession, but I noticed no exchange of any sort between the second quarterback and the receiver.

Plenty of shots showed Jack Laneer narrowing his eyes, shouting, folding his arms to await the outcome of a play. He may have been the general overseeing the battle, but I viewed him as a helpless schemer, unable to block or tackle or pass for his players. Like a parent whose children had grown up, he could offer stern advice, but quite often his recommendations were either misunderstood or misapplied.

For three and a half solid hours I studied the marriage of athleticism and art. "You guys make us look great," Doug had remarked of Ronnie and the other NFL cinematographers, and he was right. Even without the refinements of slow motion and music, color enhancements, or the dramatic juxtaposition of fan response—or player response—or the coach's hollering, my appreciation for what Ronnie and his company did for professional football multiplied.

Unfortunately, I just couldn't see anything wrong.

Around two when Ronnie came in carrying a paper tray of hamburgers and Cokes, my head throbbed and my eyes stung.

"How do you do this?" I asked. "It's hard work."

Ronnie modestly ignored me. "You find anything?"

I showed him my notes.

"Frye, candy store window?" he read with scorn. "What the hell does that mean?"

"Damned if I know."

"You got squat."

"I got squat," I admitted.

"Maybe in the second reel."

I sighed and bit into my hamburger, expecting it to be cold and dry. Instead it was warm and delicious, and I nearly choked.

Much later in the afternoon, toward the end of the second reel, I noticed Roger Prindel's response to something Tim Duffy said immediately after the final touchdown. During a congratulatory hug Tim soberly accepted Prindel's joyous words, then said something in return that deflated the offensive coordinator's smile. Duffy made one more quick remark, then walked away. The film covered the final kick and the game soon ended.

I shut off the machine and leaned back in my chair. Five hours of scrutinizing film and I had nothing more than I had before. I rubbed my eyes and considered crying. The tears were there, ready to go, but I felt too overwhelmed and confused to succumb to that weakness. Maybe I had seen something after all. Maybe I simply needed some distance in order to digest it.

The activity in the hall outside felt urgent and exclusive. Men bustled by me on trips from one state-of-the-art machine to another. Lost in their work, they withheld any form of greeting, rather fixed me with scolding eyes as if I had unwittingly wandered into the men's room.

I located Ronnie conferring heavily with Dennis and another young man.

Addressing my injured cousin, I said, "You look worse than I feel."

To Dennis, I said, "Can't you give this guy a break?"

"Sure, sure," the editor decided, although—had I not reminded him of the hour and my cousin's overnight stay in the hospital—I wondered whether he would have given Ronnie's condition any thought. Since we interrupted his night's sleep, he probably felt pretty rotten himself.

"Drive me to the train?" I suggested when Ronnie and I were alone in the hall. "Then you can go home and crash."

"Deal." He was grayer and weaker than he had been when the paramedic hauled him off for X rays.

"Didn't find anything?" he finally guessed when we were in his car. The afternoon smelled like snow and the overcast sky had developed a portentous pink cast.

"If I saw it, it hasn't registered yet."

Ronnie grunted that he understood. He had taken half the shots, he knew how many there had been for me to digest.

At the station I leaned back in my door to say good-bye. Neither of us wanted the other to expend any more energy than necessary, we were that exhausted.

"Don't worry about it," Ronnie reassured me from the driver's seat.

"Not over yet," I remarked, mostly because I didn't have the energy to admit defeat or the strength to face Ronnie's disappointment.

"It's okay," he said anyway, causing a lump to barricade the rest of the words in my throat.

TWENTY-SIX

In Philadelphia's Thirtieth Street station I hauled my luggage down the scarcely noticeable hallway that led to the suburban lines, in particular the R5 Paoli Local, the "Main Line" that would take me home. My stop was toward the end, near where the posh communities diffused into ordinary Pennsylvania countryside.

Since it was too early for business commuters, the train was filled with students and Christmas shoppers even more loaded with bundles than I. The car I chose smelled of industrial dirt and overheated wool, and my cramped seat offered a tight baby blanket/papoose feel that invited drowsy thoughts of mother and home.

Empty trees and frosted backyards sped by my eyes. The stone and brick houses I glimpsed were noticeably older than the New Jersey and Virginia ones I had just visited, suggesting comfortable chairs and broken-in slippers. The furniture might well be valuable but it would be nicked and scraped by generations of the same family. Perhaps it would even be dusty, it was so taken for granted. All decors would be subdued unless the house was owned by a couple under thirty-five. Then the walls would be a declarative white with lemon-yellow trim in the kitchen.

Yet each and every house represented someone's snug haven, and oh how I longed for mine. I needed my fading braided rugs and beat-up coffee table, the clutter of mail, and the old *TV Guide*s full of articles I would never quite manage to read.

I paid off my taxi at the end of my drive at the end of our cul de sac. So what if our shrubbery ran wild, or our mailbox tilted, or the shutters begged for paint? This barn-red brick dwelling made my heart flip just because my family was inside.

While I hurried to dig out my keys, Gretsky barked as if I were the British and he Paul Revere. When he finally recognized me, he twirled and leaped and infected me with his joy. I crouched down for the ritual sloppy kisses.

During this love-fest my mother marched down the hall from the added-on family room just past the kids' bedrooms. She wore pink slacks that complimented her rose-colored glasses and a green Christmas sweatshirt depicting an Irish setter wearing a Santa hat with a jingle bell on the end. Gracie politely waved hello from the end of the hall.

"Ginger Struve Barnes as I live and breathe," cooed my mother.

"Hi, Mom. Hi, Gracie," I told Cynthia and her friend. When my mother and I hugged, the bell from the sweatshirt made a painful dent in my ribs. "I'm so glad to see you," I gushed.

"You, too," my mother agreed.

She pinched my chin between soft fingers and grinned, her eyes twinkling with the intensity she reserved for me and my kids. The smile for Rip had an added hint of conspiracy, but the kids and I got unadulterated adoration. I grew up secure in the light of that smile and continued to rely on it.

"Come, come," my mother said. "We're watching *It's a Wonderful Life* on video."

"Thanks, Mom. Just let me get settled, okay?"

Mom nodded and grinned and toddled back to her girlfriend and her sappy movie.

A SCORE TO SETTLE

I dropped my luggage upstairs in my room and Rip's, where the bed was a tousled heap of limp sheets and discarded pajamas. The opened door to our walk-in closet revealed a hamper overflowing with inside-out socks and musty clothes.

Towels half covered the adjacent bathroom floor, and the sink was spotted with toothpaste blobs, water stains, and yes, a few stray whiskers. Also, sitting upright on the old toilet paper spool was a new roll that appeared just as perplexed as I that the mechanics of the spindle still eluded Rip after all these years.

"He missed me," I decided, and when I caught my reflection in the smeary mirror, I wore a pleased, comfortable expression.

Downstairs the contagion continued. Nobody had tidied up the kibble Gretsky spilled when he ate, at least not today. The kitchen sink was littered with pots that needed special attention. An opened loaf of bread spilled onto the counter, and the refrigerator gauge read "E." In the hydrator a piece of fruit, possibly a former lime, had progressed in its decomposition into gray mush dusted with white mold. Also, something in the lunchmeat drawer smelled worse than cheese.

Yet the corner of my eye noticed something colorful through the pass-through to the dining area and the living room beyond. I walked around to check it out, and there in the corner by the patio door stood an ungainly Christmas tree trimmed with gaudy red tinsel rope and gold satin balls. More tinsel with dangling gold balls had been strung across the tops of each window. The mantel of our stone walk-in fireplace also dripped with the ugly stuff as well.

My nose tickled with an impending sneeze. Ashes. A heap of old ashes on the hearth, where in winter I usually kept a fire ready to light. "Hachoo," I told the mess. "I'll get to you later."

The beat-up coffee table so representative of our home sported a bowl of unshelled nuts and a soldier-style nutcracker wearing a red uniform and black hat. "Hello," I told him, for we had not met before. He eyed me with the skepticism of a stranger.

Elsewhere clumps of greens sported shiny ornaments suggestive of dollar day at the local five and ten—late in the sale, after all the attractive stuff had been bought.

My mother's voice startled me. "I hope you don't mind," she said. "We couldn't find your old decorations, but we figured you were so busy helping Michelle that you'd be glad not to have to decorate when you got home."

My tears burst forth with a spontaneous sob and instantly dripped down my face. I said nothing, just hurried over to hug my mother again, uncomfortable bell and all. "It's beautiful," I finally managed.

"Now," my mother said, dismissing my sentiment as if all she had done for me and all I had done for Michelle were to be as taken as for granted as one of those dusty Main Line antiques. "We've got popcorn," she said. "Want some?"

"Of course."

A clamor at the door informed us that Garry was home. Chelsea, I remembered, would still be at volleyball practice.

"Hey," my son greeted me.

"Hey, yourself," I replied, reaching out for the hug he tolerated only in private.

"You ready to see my Ultimate Frisbee tape?" Overwhelmed by the world he was growing into, Garry dealt with its ebb and flow only as necessary. I had been away; now I was back.

Honesty would hurt his feelings, so I opted for a compromise. "I really want to see your video, but my eyes are sore from watching five hours of football film. Soon," I promised. "Maybe tomorrow."

Garry's smooth young face fell, but he managed a gracious reply. "Sure," he said. "The audio's still not fixed anyway."

"What's the problem again?" I asked in an effort to make my interest seem genuine.

To my surprise, Garry's face instantly took on the same intensity as the day we toured NFL Films. This was new, this sustained interest in an occupation, so I paid close attention to my son's reply.

"See, our camera does audio and video on the same tape, so I can't add any of the extra sounds I got with the recorder I put under the bench."

"The little recorder you asked for? The one that needed batteries?"

"Right. But with the main audio and video already together, I can't mess around with the sound the way Ronnie and the sound guy do."

"What do you mean?"

"I mean they've got seven, eight tracks to play around with, plus the audio's completely separate, you know? So they can do anything they want with it."

My eyes widened. I grabbed Garry's shoulders and kissed him smack on the forehead.

"That's it," I said. "You solved it. At least I think you did."

My son gawked. "What are you talking about, Mom? I *didn't* solve it. I told you I *couldn't* solve it. I don't have the equipment they have at NFL Films."

"I'm talking about something else, Gar. The thing I was working on for Ronnie."

"The murder?"

I gulped. "Did Nana tell you I was working on that?"

"No. But you were, weren't you?"

Oh, dear. Honesty? or another compromise?

"Partly. Unofficially," I hedged. "I just asked a few questions. You know how I like to ask questions."

"I know." Garry's expression was too complicated for me to dissect just then, but a quick guess would have included both irritation and pride.

Still, the adultlike ambiguity unnerved me. Was I ready for this new phase? Were both our children suddenly going to become as intricately layered as my husband?

I quickly realized that if I was asking the question, it was already too late. Overnight my son had become a human Rubik's Cube.

"I have to go back to NFL Films," I told him, adult to almost-adult.

"Why?"

"To listen to the audio of last week's game. I think there's something important on it." Garry beamed. "And yes, what you said gave me the idea."

"What'd I say?" he demanded to know.

Behind me, Chelsea came through the front door. "Hi, sweetie," I greeted her with a kiss and hug. "I really, really missed you; but I've got to go back to New Jersey right away."

"Okay," she said doubtfully.

"What'd I say?" Garry asked more loudly than before.

"Exactly the right thing," I assured him.

Running down the hall I called to my mother. "Mom, Mom, I'm going back to Mt. Laurel."

She met me in the doorway so as not to disturb Gracie's movie trance.

We grasped hands. "I think I just figured out something important, and I want to see if it pans out." There was no point in equivocating to her, she always knew the truth anyway.

"Certainly, dear. We'll be fine until you get back."

"I don't have a doubt in the world," I told my mother. Laundry, picking up, vacuuming, scrubbing—all of that could wait. The important stuff continued splendidly on her watch.

"Do you have anything at all for dinner?" I asked, just in case.

"Got it covered," Chelsea said behind me.

Well! Cooking lessons by default.

"Wonderful," I replied without revealing any more self-defeating pleasure than necessary. "Tell Dad I'll call him," I said, trusting that Chelsea would deliver the message as soon as Rip walked in.

Then with one final glance into those three dear faces, I squeezed my mother's hands, let go, and loped up the stairs for a reviving shower and quick change of clothes.

Chelsea handed me a thawed bagel as I threw on my coat, and a minute later I was out the door.

Now all I had to contend with was dusk and the five-o'clock traffic.

Oh, and a killer who didn't realize that for creative purposes NFL Films always recorded the pictures and the sound separately.

TWENTY-SEVEN

The soporific slog over the Betsy Ross Bridge back to Mt. Laurel allowed me to sift through the minutiae of Tim Duffy's death with minimal distraction, and by the time I parked in the twilight shadows of the NFL Films' lot I had tentatively eliminated several suspects and even chosen a murderer-elect.

Everything revolved around what—if anything—I heard on the audiotape from the game. So close to the answer, with so much at stake, my tension could have snapped pencils in half or stared mirrors into shards.

I hammered on the glass front door of NFL Films' office building until someone passing by the Emmy wall on an errand heard me and let me in.

"Geez," he said, censure distorting his face. "You almost set off the alarm."

"Sorry."

"We had the cops here last night. We don't need 'em back," he scolded, but I cut him off.

"Is my cousin, Ronnie Covington, here? Or Dennis, the editor?" I couldn't remember Dennis's last name.

"Yeah, both I think." The man finally showed some interest, but the concern for his ears still lingered.

"Where? This is urgent."

"If you say so." He gestured for me to follow him,

224

then with several irritated backward glances he led me to one of the rooms where the audio was actually mixed. Ronnie and another fellow were there putting the final touches on this week's Green Bay/Miami special.

"Gin," Ronnie exclaimed with surprise.

"Aren't you supposed to be home asleep?" I countered.

"Caught a couple hours here," he admitted. "You know how it is."

I thought I did. Like any of the jobs that captured a person's soul, filming football games for posterity had become my cousin's persona, his identity. I envied him the satisfaction and sense of fulfillment, but right now I couldn't spare the time to tell him that.

"I've got an idea," I announced.

"Come on," he responded, nodding farewell to his coworker as gravely as a reservist who had just gotten the call.

Alone in the hall we huddled like conspirators.

"I think the killer was after the audio," I confided just above a whisper.

"But . . ." Ronnie protested.

"Right. Exactly. The audio is separate, but I don't think the killer knows that."

Ronnie fixed his lively eyes on a spot over my shoulder. "So that's why he wanted the original film. He thought he'd be getting both the audio and video outtakes."

"Exactly."

"Let's go," he said, shrugging off his fatigue and rushing down the hallway. I followed his bandaged head around corners and up stairs and down another hall to the audio archives.

"Mary?" he called into the second of three rooms devoted to copying sound. Like many of the work areas, this too was windowless and sparsely furnished except for electronic equipment. I noticed an old-fashioned record turntable, more space-age consoles with knobs and slides and needle gauges, and two rectangular speakers perched on a wrap-around desk that also held a computer monitor and yet another TV screen.

"She's not here," he concluded, referring to the woman whose domain this was, "but we'll manage."

Off to the left was a small storage room containing reel-to-reel equipment and a low bank of narrow metal drawers that took up the length of the wall. About waist-height, the cabinet top was covered with rows of white labeled cassettes like a sales display that offered only one artist.

Ronnie scowled as he ran his finger down what I assumed were the most recent additions. He lifted out two cassettes labeled with the current year, "Tomcats/Hombres," and the week number of their game.

"You know what you're listening for?" he asked.

"I think so."

If my audio theory was correct, it ruled out everyone except those who had been filmed speaking to Tim Duffy on the sideline. Bobby Frye, for example, had spent the entire game in the owner's box and never went anywhere near the murder victim. Nor had I seen Patrick Dionne speaking to Tim in any of the film I watched earlier that day.

However, Willet Smith, then third- and now second-string quarterback; receiver Bo Shifflett; Roger Prindel, the offensive coordinator; and Walker Cross, the $1.7 million man, remained in the running.

Even kicker Charlie Quinlan or Teal's husband, Morani Todd, could have been suspects, but I temporarily ruled them out because of their body shapes. I had only glimpsed Ronnie's attacker before I closed my eyes to scream, but my lingering impression was that Morani was too large and Charlie too slight. Also,

I hadn't discovered even a hint of motive for either man.

The audio might prove me wrong, but at least initially my money was on Roger Prindel. The way his face had fallen when Duffy came off the field and spoke into his ear stood out as the only misstep in an otherwise flawless afternoon of football sideline behavior.

At the baby shower Debbie Quinlan, the kicker's wife, mentioned how angry Charlie had been when the offensive coordinator sent in a running play that probably would have ruined her husband's last chance for a field goal. Wisely, Tim changed the play in the huddle, electing instead to throw a gutsy pass. The result: a touchdown that just happened to cover the published point spread.

Yet in spite of the insubordination, both the offensive coordinator and the quarterback should have been jubilant; that is, unless one of them happened to be dirty and the other angry enough to throw that dirt back in his face.

One way or the other I needed to hear what Duffy said to Prindel, and I prayed that the audiotape had caught it.

"Just get me wired, and you can go," I told Ronnie.

He watched me fidget from foot to foot and shake my hands. "Yeah, yeah," he agreed testily, but he went ahead and turned on a tape deck, plugged in some earphones with a long cord, and pointed out the applicable controls. "Fast forward, rewind, stop," he lectured.

"Child's play," I said, thinking of Garry.

"Hardly," my cousin disagreed, apparently referring to my formidable task.

He prepared to leave. "You be okay?" He proffered his blanket concern much the same way men press clean handkerchiefs upon crying women, and for approximately the same reason.

"Yeah, yeah." I ungraciously mimicked his previous irritation.

Then, naturally, I immediately regretted being short with him. After all, I had been married for years and knew quite well that men deserved credit for their intentions. So I patted the edge off my rudeness and spoke with a mitigated voice. "You going to be in that same room?"

"Yes," Ronnie responded as if we had been in sync through each turn of thought. "Come and get me," he urged.

I kissed him on the cheek. "Damn straight," I said.

About then some men would have murmured "aw shucks" and trotted off like the hero from an old western, but Ronnie stayed to trade electricity with me a moment longer. He had invited me to joust this particular windmill, and now that my nearly impossible goal actually seemed attainable, we both felt buoyant, like cocky teenagers with the world at our feet.

Soon enough my cousin squeezed my hand and left me to my chore, but our moment lingered like the afterimage on an old TV.

And just as briefly. Twitching, clammy with nervous sweat, I nevertheless felt relieved to be alone with my enormous responsibility, free to do whatever would alleviate my psyche without anyone there to make me feel self-conscious.

First, I turned out all but one dim desk light. Then, after I put tape number two in the player, I fast-forwarded to the middle and picked up the big soft headphones. Eschewing the padded secretarial chair in front of the console, I sat on the floor with my back to the wall and hugged my knees. I did not need comfort; I needed to stifle every sense but my hearing.

A SCORE TO SETTLE

This had to be it. It just had to be. There was nothing else to try. I put the headphones on and closed my eyes.

And popped right up. Too loud.

Yet I did not lower the volume far. Crowd noise still assaulted my ears then fell to murmurs, footsteps, phrases, and grunts. I was a mute, blind listening device. Garry's battery-run tape recorder hidden under the sideline bench—that was me.

And so for ten, fifteen, twenty minutes I listened to every voice, every collision, every *oof*, crackle, or pop the soundman had collected, not the fancy stuff taken off a wired player, for that was on another cassette. I had whatever the boom mike got: beer vendors shouting, coaches' calls to the officials, one- and two-word reactions to what happened on the field, much of this in the abbreviated code of the profession, sound bites only the truly initiated could interpret.

"So if he's in your face, f—ing beat him inside with the swim move."

Or, "When we double Morph, you gotta get in Dwyer's shorts on the flare or circle. If he blocks, take a seam and get a f—ing piece of Singer." Colorful stuff that would never make it into the special.

Hearing it all made my heart pound with vicarious tension; yet without the video to show me the plays, the score, the clock, I was mostly listening to a strange soup of noise with surges of volume and respites of relative silence. Still, I stuck with it, and soon enough I began to summon up my own mental pictures to go with the auditory story.

I heard "All right now," spoken by an unidentified coach, delivered with a nervous clap to a shoulder pad. Then Doug's voice called, "Blue fifty-six. Blue fifty-six. Hut . . . hut . . . hut," across several yards of Astroturf.

Still too early. I needed to fast-forward to the portion of the game after Doug went down and Tim went in.

Initially, I thought I had forwarded too far until another coach's voice shouted for Quinlan to stand by. That meant the Tomcats were either anticipating a fourth-down kickaway, a field goal attempt, or a point after touchdown effort. With any luck I was near the part where Duffy threw the late touchdown.

And so I was. After grunts and thumps and sideline cheers, a brief hush fell, soon giving way to the pandemonium of the score. Footsteps pounded off the field, backs were slapped, congratulations exchanged . . . and then I heard it.

"Don't ever pull that again," threatened the same voice that had called the play on the field just moments before—the substitute quarterback, the murdered Tim Duffy.

"What?" asked a stunned Roger Prindel.

"You heard me. I'm onto you. Don't ever do that again."

I leaped off the floor and punched the STOP button. Throwing the headphones onto the padded chair, I rushed from the room—downstairs, down the hall, around a corner and thirty yards more. Then breathless, half delirious, I interrupted my cousin's work yelling, "Ronnie, Ronnie, Ronnie. I've got it!"

My cousin, whose mind had been totally elsewhere, blinked and asked, "You've got what?"

Hands on my hips, I bent at the waist to breathe and also to select a retort.

"The murderer, of course," I said, straightening up. "Did you think I was up there listening to the Rolling Stones?"

"It's just . . . I didn't think . . ." He had been way way into his world and far far from mine.

"Geez, you sound like Doug," I teased. "What

did you send me to Norfolk for if you didn't think I could do this?"

"It was all I could . . . I didn't really think . . ."

I pulled his hand toward the door and reassured his co-worker, "He'll be back in half an hour. No, wait a minute. Is this where you put audio together with a print and make copies?" More and more of my tour information had become a vague blur.

"No," the kid replied as if one of us was on Mars.

"Gin," Ronnie pulled my hands around, but it was his tone that caught my attention. "I'm with you," he said, much to my relief. "We'll use Dennis's stuff. Just show me what you need."

I squeezed his cheeks in Aunt Harriet's hated manner. "Great!" I said for punctuation, and that was the last word either of us spoke until we were back upstairs.

Wearing headphones as big as earmuffs, Ronnie's expression went from intense concentration, to incredulity, to puzzlement as he listened to the section of tape I wanted him to hear.

"Well?" I prompted.

He rewound the tape, listened again, and scowled, looking even more quizzical and confused.

I yanked the headphones off and almost screamed with frustration. " 'I'm onto you,' " I echoed the tape. "Don't you get it?" I actually stomped my foot. "It's like what's-wrong-with-this-picture? Have you ever heard anybody say anything remotely like that on the sideline before?"

"Well, maybe," Ronnie thought aloud. "It sounds kind of familiar."

"Of course it does," I said through clenched teeth. "You heard Tim Duffy say it to Roger Prindel eight days ago. What's the matter with you?"

"I guess I just thought Duffy was onto the fact

that Prindel was a lousy coach, or something like that.''

"Then you remember absolutely positively it was Prindel he said it to?"

"Sort of, now that you mention it. I still don't think it means anything."

I pulled out the tweed secretarial chair and pushed it behind Ronnie's knees. As he flopped into it, he glanced up at me fearfully.

"Roger Prindel gambles," I lectured, enunciating each syllable as if English were my student's second language. "And he called for a run when a run wouldn't accomplish a damn thing. Don't you see? Prindel was doing a favor for somebody. A big, big favor, Ron. He was risking his career in the NFL by trying to mess with the outcome of a game."

"I don't know, Gin."

I drew in a huge breath and let it out slowly.

"Tim Duffy was an observant guy who'd been around awhile. Right?" I reasoned as calmly as possible. "What if he caught onto Prindel's gambling habit ages ago? Now and then Prindel had to have overreacted to the score of some nothing baseball game or got all excited when Podunk High beat Central Thingamajig in soccer. It wouldn't take a genius to figure out that the guy had money down. But the bets were never on football, so Duffy kept quiet. Who cared? Live and let live, or so he thought until push came to shove.

"The Tomcats/Hombres game was at twenty-one to twenty. Two minutes to go. To everyone's surprise, Doug leaves the game for a second time giving Duffy another opportunity to show his stuff, maybe even dazzle the coaches into giving him back the starting position. He desperately wants to pass for a touchdown, I mean he really really wants to go for it, but Prindel sends in a running play. Once again, who was

to care? Nobody except Tim Duffy and, coinciden-
tally, Roger Prindel. Unless the Hombres could con-
jure up a last-minute miracle, the Tomcats already had
the game in the bag.''

Ronnie almost looked convinced, so I hastened to
clinch my case.

''So what happens? Tim changes the play in the
huddle, scores, and comes off the field both proud as
punch and angry as hell. 'Don't ever pull that again,'
he tells Prindel. 'I'm onto you!' Now do you get it?''

Ronnie's expression remained a little too vague, so
with more than a little exasperation I said, ''Prindel
must've just about had a heart attack. He must have
been terrified Duffy would tell Laneer or Frye or the
league watchdogs that he tried to mess with the
spread. But Duffy doesn't say he's going to do any
of the above, he just lets Prindel know he knows
Roger intended to alter the outcome of a game.

''So,'' I said, pacing and gesturing wildly. ''Prindel figures it's now or never, pop the guy before he
gets really righteous and blows the whistle.''

I clamped both hands on my cousin's shoulders
and spoke to his face. ''Imagine the anxiety. Somebody thinks they know what you tried to do—and
even worse, they're dead on.'' I swung away in order
to resume pacing.

''If Duffy talked, Roger would never get another
sports job anywhere. He'd be ruined, maybe even
jailed.'' I shook my head. ''That's the way it had to
have happened, Ron.''

''I believe you, Gin. I really do,'' Ronnie sadly
agreed. ''But how're the police going to prove it?''

I hadn't had much time to address that problem,
but my cousin's question prompted a thought. ''If
they hurry, they'll catch Roger with the film in his
possession. He can't afford to get rid of the cans before he's sure they contain the incriminating part, and

I'm guessing that requires equipment he won't readily have—at least not until he gets back to the stadium."

"Not even then," Ronnie remarked. "He stole negatives, remember?"

"Right. So for sure he can't have looked at them, and he can't *ever* listen to them because the audio isn't even on there."

"Which he doesn't know."

"Exactly. Now. While I call the police, can you please get somebody to put this audio together with the picture? The print should still be locked in Dennis's desk."

"Sure. I'll do it myself." The bags under Ronnie's eyes had gone nearly blue with fatigue; yet there was a boyish spring to his step, and he turned and threw me a grin and a salute before he headed out the door.

TWENTY-EIGHT

Ronnie's preparation of the combined audio/video-tape for viewing by the police didn't take very long. He just used the equipment consolidated in the central machine room, or CMR as it was labeled on the door, the same spot where the NFL people usually worked on the final edits of shows and on projects with their commercial customers. With considerable trepidation I waited in there for my cousin to collect and deliver our own tough customers.

Detective Schwartz had been especially reluctant to attend our private presentation and almost certainly would be predisposed to dismiss our evidence as fantasy. Ronnie and I would have to be mighty persuasive if we were to convince him to issue a warrant for Prindel's arrest, which we desperately needed him to do. There was no time to bring any other law enforcement people up to speed, and anyway the break-in at NFL Films and the theft of the negatives had occurred within Schwartz's jurisdiction—as had the attack on Ronnie.

"Detective Schwartz, Officer Winthorpe," I greeted the two men as Ronnie ushered them into the narrow room stuffed with electronics. There were no seats, just a tall narrow table running the length of the room. Work units lined both walls left and right.

"Mrs. Barnes." Schwartz nodded formally.

Behind us Ronnie made a show of closing blinds

and pointedly gesturing for the other guy using the room to scoot—a dramatic, take-charge opening I heartily approved.

In response Winthorpe merely sneered, but Schwartz's eyes drooped beneath raised brows in a studied nonchalance that was pure Hollywood. When he sniffed and scratched his nose, I almost laughed.

However, I was much too experienced socially to do anything so inappropriate or counterproductive. Hostess mode, I called it, and by now it fit me like a second skin.

Some lucky headmasters' wives got paid for running the many large social events put on by their spouses' schools each year; but Bryn Derwyn Academy was too young, and its budget too tight. In lieu of cash, I'd been receiving an education in how to handle egos. If I could lead recalcitrant potential donors down the proverbial garden path with ease, how different could it be with a snobby small-town cop?

"Gentlemen," I opened with the grace of Vanna White turning a letter on *Wheel of Fortune*. "I'm sure you'll want to catch Tim Duffy's murderer while he still has incriminating evidence in his possession, so we don't have a lot of time to waste. Please listen carefully before you ask any questions."

Schwartz's soft mouth formed an O, but he narrowed his eyes and quickly closed his lips, a distrustful Little Jack Horner discerning the first hint of the plum.

Ronnie and I agreed that before we showed the film clip, I would explain what it meant so that both Schwartz and his lumbering escort, Winthorpe, would get the impact of Tim Duffy's remarks right away.

I opened with what we knew about Prindel's gambling, supported by the information Pamela Wilkinson provided. Then I added my own reasons for believing that Tim must have picked up on Roger's addiction over time.

"He and Duffy were together long enough for Tim to catch onto Roger's habit; but as long as Prindel wasn't betting on football, Tim probably figured 'live and let live.' He had his own career to worry about."

I glanced around at my audience of three. The cops weren't exactly with me yet, but at least they were paying attention.

Leaving Coren Turner out of it, I related enough history about Doug and Tim to convince my listeners that Duffy desperately wanted to beat out Doug as the Tomcats' starting quarterback.

"So you can imagine that when Tim went into the Hombres game for the second time he was dying to impress the crowd with something big—preferably a touchdown pass.

"Except . . ." I paused for effect, "Roger Prindel sent him in with a running play."

I paced a little and took a deep breath. "Duffy must have been furious," I said, raising a palm. "It was third and twenty-four on the forty-four-yard line with just under two minutes left in the game. Why would Prindel make such a stupid call? A run would use up the clock, but not necessarily enough to prevent the Hombres' offense from pulling off a miracle. The Tomcats might not even get the field position they needed for their own field goal attempt." I stopped and spread my hands.

"The call only made sense when you factored in Prindel's gambling habit. He had to have been helping someone he knew bet heavily on the Hombres to win. I'm guessing that person was his brother, the guy who placed most of Roger's bets for him."

Schwartz nodded to acknowledge that particular conclusion. Any veteran cop would know that the only assured winners in gambling were those who provided the action—the bookies or race tracks or casinos who took their cut up front (along with the state if the betting was legal)—so inveterate players were almost guaranteed to get into trouble sooner or later. In that respect gambling was very much like musical chairs; with something taken out of the betting pool at the beginning of each round, those who didn't cut their small losses early found it more and more unlikely they would ever come out ahead.

So Prindel, a regular longtime gambler, was almost certainly indebted to his brother—if only for hiding his habit from public scrutiny—or their bookie, and probably to both. And, judging by the chance he took with his career—not to mention his freedom—Prindel had to have been aware that the people he was indebted to had bet heavily on the Hombres that week.

I shook my head. "Then opportunity knocked. With one bad call Prindel could have preserved the Tomcats' win while wrecking the spread and paying off his debts. He must have been ecstatic.

"If he ever had to defend the call, he could have argued that he was using the clock or going with the element of surprise. Without the gambling factor, the higher-ups would be forced to write it off as one isolated mental error.

"Except it didn't happen like that. Tim Duffy changed the play in the huddle and successfully threw for a touchdown. Ronnie?" I gestured for him to start the tape, and he turned on one of the monitors crowded in among the wall of electronic equipment.

Schwartz, Winthorpe, and I leaned forward against the tall table in order to watch the ten-second video as closely as possible.

"Again," Schwartz ordered after it finished and gray-and-white snow sizzled on the screen.

Ronnie rewound the tape and pressed PLAY.

For the second time we watched the breathtaking

touchdown catch. Once again Tim Duffy trotted off the field in among a gang of joyous men wearing the blue-on-blue Tomcat uniforms. Yet again he received thumps of congratulation to his helmet, arms, and shoulders from both offensive and defensive players alike, and once again he accepted a proffered hand and Russian-type hug from the diminutive offensive coordinator, Roger Prindel. This time I noticed the boom mike briefly appear behind Roger's head then disappear above the camera shot.

In the final frames Prindel's face had been caught in the center left third of the lens, turned three-quarters forward. When Duffy used the handgrip to pull his coach in closer, the shot showed the quarter-back's profile speaking directly into the coach's ear.

"Don't ever pull that again," threatened Duffy.

"What?" asked a stunned Roger Prindel.

"You heard me. I'm onto you. Don't ever do that again."

"Well?" I asked Schwartz, who had hooked his thumbs in the pockets of his tweed overcoat and rocked back on his heels.

He addressed Ronnie. "Are you prepared to testify that Roger Prindel was the person who attacked you last night?"

My cousin pouted and shook his head no.

Schwartz's own lips pushed out from under his mustache as he turned toward me. "Was Prindel the man you saw leaving the master vault?"

I told him I couldn't say because I'd never actually met the man.

"No? You seem to have met everyone else involved in this case."

I remained silent but refused to cower.

"Oh, well," the detective finally sighed. "I suppose the Norfolk police will have his prints on record."

As a matter of course, all the Tomcats would have been fingerprinted to help identify any prints that did not belong at the murder scene; and fortunately, Schwartz's remark indicated that his thinking went a step further. He wanted to compare Prindel's prints to the ones his technicians took from the vaults that had been breached, particularly (I was pleased to realize) from the knobs of the rolling shelves.

Still, Schwartz continued to rock and pout and cluck. After a long moment and possibly even a belch, he squeezed off a particularly sour pout and said, "Okay, we'll go pick him up," and with that single sentence allowed my lungs to return to work. If there were visions of national fame dancing inside Schwartz's broad, jowly, bureaucratic head, he hid them well.

Then all at once the pout returned and with it the condescending sarcasm I'd grown to detest. "There's just one problem," he said as he skewered me with a glare.

"You don't want to look like a fool?" Winthorpe interjected with a chortle.

"No, John," Schwartz corrected over his shoulder. "I've looked like a fool before and my conviction rate still manages to keep my family fed. No, I'd cheerfully go after this man except for the fact that we . . . don't . . . know . . . where . . . to . . . look!"

His tone fired up a blush—I usually redden up during any sort of emotional confrontation—yet I managed not to slump while I extracted a white slip of notepaper from the pocket of my jeans.

I handed the notation to Schwartz.

"Prindel's at the Claridge Hotel in Atlantic City," I told him. "The Tomcats don't play until next Monday night, so he's not due back at Nimitz until Wednesday."

Delivering the information orally afforded me the

satisfaction of watching Winthorpe's face. It also saved Schwartz from trying to read my handwriting.

The detective had reddened a bit himself. He stuffed my note into his tweed overcoat and turned on his heel.

"I'll be in touch," he said grudgingly as he headed out the door, Winthorpe lagging three steps behind.

"Call us here," Ronnie suggested. "Please. You owe us that."

"Yeah yeah yeah," Schwartz mumbled.

"Good luck," I told the lingering Winthorpe, who shook his head and stared until the door finally pushed him along.

"How'd you find out where Prindel was staying?" Ronnie quizzed me a few minutes later.

We had settled into a booth of the in-house 1950s diner provided for NFL Films employees. There was chrome and Formica and each table even had those little remote juke boxes with pages to turn and buttons to push. Now about 4:30 P.M., a few guys were grabbing an odd-hour meal. Ronnie and I could only stomach coffee, and I wasn't stomaching that very well.

I waved my thick white cup as I answered. "After I knew Schwartz and Winthorpe were on the way, I tried to call the Tomcats' travel department; but they were closed."

Ronnie's light-hazel eyes appeared to be hypnotized by my voice, but then I realized my voice and anticipating Schwartz's call were the only two things keeping my cousin awake.

"So," I said as perkily as possible, "the only person left for me to call was Roger's old girlfriend, Pamela Wilkinson. When I asked her where Roger usually stayed in Philadelphia, she said, 'Philadelphia? Are you kidding? He'll be at the Claridge in Atlantic City!' "

Ronnie shook his head incredulously. "So then you called the Claridge to see whether he was there."

"Right. But it was too risky to ring his room, and the hotel doesn't give out the numbers. Anyway, I figured the police ought to be able to do something for themselves."

Ronnie beamed at me. "You're amazing."

I tilted my head and batted my eyelashes. "I'm a Siddons," I said. "Same as you."

The call came two hours later. Ronnie and I listened to the same receiver cheek to cheek, rendering Schwartz's ebullient voice as thin as an old radio broadcast. Still, we heard him just fine, probably because he was shouting.

"We got 'im. I got a warrant, faxed it down here, and the locals detained 'im for me."

"What about the film cans?" Ronnie asked impatiently.

"Got them, too. Had 'em in the trunk of his car, can you believe it?"

I was dying to ask whether the police had been careful to follow procedures, but Schwartz anticipated my concern.

"Had the hotel photog take pictures left and right," he said. "Of course A.C. had their own gal, but I wanted my own set. Got a shot of the warrant, one of me wearing rubber gloves turning the trunk key. Strictly kosher. We got the sucker, by God." *We're going to be famous* was the unspoken correlative.

"Congratulations," I told him, but he was too sky-high to remember his manners in return.

"Oop. Gotta go talk to the TV." And off he went.

"You're welcome," I muttered.

"They'll give you credit in the papers," Ronnie assured me with the usual Siddons optimism.

A SCORE TO SETTLE

And that proved to be true. "Ronald Covington, a cinematographer for NFL Films, prepared the pivotal evidence in the case against Roger Prindel, reported Detective Schwartz of the Mt. Laurel police. . . . The crucial film segment was originally brought to Mr. Covington's attention by a concerned citizen."

TWENTY-NINE

"**T**his is good," Didi proclaimed referring to my lasagna. She was eating off a leftover Christmas paper plate balanced on the knee of her narrow magenta slacks. Her complementary print blouse remained spotless—so far—but the way her dog, Chivas Beagle, tore around the family room (followed closely by Gretsky) a tomato stain on someone was inevitable. The only surprise would be who and when.

"You mean it?" I pressed.

"Yes. It's good. Take a compliment for once in your life."

"On my cooking?"

Didi tsked with disgust. "You're too damn modest."

Was there such a thing as being too modest? "Impossible," I decided out loud.

"Whooee," my mother and Chelsea chorused with a reprise of "Did you see that?" and "Good one, Duke. Atta boy."

We were all of us watching professional wrestling while eating my most flexible meal: spinach salad, dinner rolls, and the aforementioned lasagna. About half an hour ago Rip had called to say Doug's plane was late. Then when Garry complained that he felt faint and my mother admitted she was pretty hungry, too, I abandoned my notion of a cozy family meal before everybody went over to Bryn Derwyn together.

But now it was nearing seven, and I was becoming twitchy nervous worrying about the crowd of people who were probably already gathering for tonight's event. Doug's arrival had been billed for 7:30 P.M.— early enough for kids, late enough for commuting parents, Friday night—family night. Our own week's snow, a mere two inches, no longer coated the roads; so attendance would probably be the maximum—especially since Rip had invited every other private school in the Delaware valley to help dedicate Bryn Derwyn's new gym.

Chelsea, who all but ignored her second cousin-in-law on Thanksgiving, had determined that plenty of boys her age could be counted on to come to hear a professional quarterback speak. With that in mind she began changing clothes immediately after the school bus dropped her off. The present outfit, a very après-ski getup featuring angora elks grazing in a field of blue, had lasted twenty minutes so far and would probably win by default.

When a beefy man wearing skin-tight pirate rags got pinned by another steroid specimen in red, white, and blue, my mother flung her arms high. The piece of roll she had been nibbling flew from her fingers and landed on the braided rug. Chevy, our four-legged houseguest, gobbled the tidbit on the bounce.

"Just out of curiosity," I inquired of my best friend, "what made you decide to bring Chevy along tonight?"

Didi did a slow turn from profile to full forward. Her expression questioned my intelligence. "She loves parties. You know that."

I blinked in preparation for a good, old-fashioned stare-down; but just then the uninvited beagle ran by again, followed closely by our own family pet. Rudely close, actually. Gretsky's snout hung low enough to get slapped by Chevy's wagging tail.

"At least somebody's glad to see her," Didi observed. She engrossed herself in the effort to cut a perfect-size bite of lasagna with her fork.

"Garry!" I called to my son. "Why don't you take the dogs outside for a few minutes?" Give the rest of us some time to eat.

Didi lifted her fork and pretended to watch the wrestling.

Chevy rounded the sofa again and blindsided her owner. The paper plate flipped off Mommy's magenta knee and landed upside-down on our family room rug. The only remaining lint-free bite of Didi's dinner was suspended near her opened mouth.

"Oops," she said.

"Garry!" I hollered.

"Okay, Mom," he sang back, which either meant I had just suggested something he actually wanted to do; or Doug's appearance tonight had elevated our son's stature in the sixth grade enough to make him temporarily magnanimous.

I went and got cleaning materials from the kitchen; and when my best friend held out her hand for the rag and soapy water, I relinquished them. Didi was family. At her house I might have had to fetch my own soap and water.

"Get 'im," my mother told the TV, lips firm, fist clenched.

I sat down out of Didi's way.

"What is it with the wrestling, Mom?" I asked because I had no clue. The pageantry, the passion— I just couldn't take it seriously.

My mother squinted at me hard before turning back to the show.

"That one has a nice butt," Didi observed, pointing with the drippy rag.

I squinted at her à la Cynthia, and from the arm of the sofa Chelsea calmly answered my question.

A SCORE TO SETTLE

"It's Everyman, Mom. Good versus evil."

"I beg your pardon?"

Chelsea sighed. "Wrestling's a morality play that lets you cheer for the Mountie in the white hat and boo the villain wearing black. The plight of Everyman. What's not to get?"

Unsure of how to respond to that, I simply closed my mouth.

"Of course," my thirteen-year-old added with deference to my best friend, "the one in black really does have a great butt."

The front door opened just then, and Rip ushered in the evening's guest of honor. We all congregated in the hall for hugs and kisses. Gretsky, Chevy, and Garry clamored in, too. with Gretsky demanding his hello while his girlfriend jumped and barked. My mother effused. Didi hung back and smiled, while Chelsea and the angora elks stood on their dignity slightly away from the wet dogs.

I sniffed. Along with the smell of slush-soaked fur was the questionable odor of soggy boy. Garry looked to be a garbage collector just finished his first day.

"I slipped," he admitted.

"Go change—down to your socks," I told him. "And hurry. It's already ten after seven."

"Got anything to eat?" Rip inquired. As usual, his shock of dark-brown hair drooped toward his left eyebrow in a boyish clump. Catching my glance, he raked it back. "They didn't offer Doug much on the plane."

Recalling the beverage and thimbleful of peanuts they gave me on the flight up from Norfolk, I assured Rip I would fix two plates—he needed dinner, too— "but you guys really have to hurry."

On my way into the kitchen I whispered in my mother's ear. She nodded and thanked me before waddling down the hall to the bathroom. I also got her coat out of the closet for her. She liked her hat and scarf just so, and that tended to take more time than it used to.

While the men ate microwave-reheated lasagna standing up at the counter, I checked on Garry's makeover, let the dogs out for business rather than pleasure, locked up, and secured the extra dinner food from critters. Then I brushed my acorn mop into a static phenomenon, found my own hat, and generally nagged everybody out into the van we borrowed from school—all by twenty after seven.

Only then did I turn in my seat to say, "Hi, Doug. How's the baby doing?" Jody had been released from the hospital just last week.

"She's great. Eats all the time." Which, translated, meant she was gaining weight like she should. It probably also meant she did not yet sleep through the night.

"Ask Michelle to call me when she isn't napping, will you? I miss those two."

"You bet."

Parking at Bryn Derwyn had spilled over from the three modest-size lots onto the lawn. In among the other vehicles I spotted a network news van, white with the prominent channel logo.

Stragglers walked up the slight slope toward the main entrance then crossed the front of the sprawling brick school to the huge new gym on the right.

Remembering that our family once lived on the exact spot where the gym now stood usually gave me a pang, but the regret always passed when I reminded myself that our present house was bigger and better. The mortgage was mountainous, but eventually the place would belong to us rather than to Bryn Derwyn.

"Wow, it's big," Didi remarked of the gym, which had been decorated with green and white banners and lighted to look like a Christmas package.

"Beautiful, isn't it?" Rip responded proudly. The project had been a burden to him ever since he took the job as head of school, and he sometimes felt as if he had laid every cement block himself.

Unfortunately, stucco wasn't very aesthetic even when it was painted, but Didi tactfully agreed that the building was gorgeous.

Rip's secretary, Joanne Henry, caught our eye as soon as we entered the gym. "Yoo-hoo." She waved to us. "Up here."

Her beige hair looked slightly dented from the effort of saving seats for our whole family, and this was the first time I ever saw her in slacks. Beside Joanne my mother looked like laundry, yet Cynthia's face drew you in while Joanne put you on probation pending proof of merit.

The crowd recognized Doug with a collective murmur, and our progress to the front of the room caused the clusters of people chatting among the folding chairs to scurry into their seats.

Ronnie, Aunt Harriet, and Uncle Stan had driven over from New Jersey together and rose to greet us. When I introduced Ronnie to Didi, both of them narrowed their eyes with skeptical indifference. Obviously no love match there.

Meanwhile, Rip and Doug proceeded directly to the riser and podium placed at the inside edge of the basketball court. Bleachers left and right were filled with people of all ages, including more men than a school event ordinarily attracted. And of course, the gym floor was stuffed with chairs and more audience.

"Thank you all for coming tonight," my husband said into the microphone. Bright light coming from the front left corner made us all aware of the TV camera.

"I'm exceedingly happy to welcome you to the dedication of Bryn Derwyn's brand-new gym," Rip continued. "Already it has enhanced the student life here tenfold, and we look forward to many years of valuable instruction and competition within these four walls.

"As most of you know, it's been a lengthy process to bring us to this point, but rather than make it any lengthier, allow me to introduce our guest of honor, Mr. Douglas Turner, quarterback for the Norfolk Tomcats. Doug . . ."

"Thank you, Mr. Barnes, Rip . . ." Whistles and cheers. "Thank you," he said to the audience.

"Now, I'm sure you all expect me to talk about sports and how important they've been to me"—more hoots—"and you'd be partly right. Sports—football—is my livelihood, and it's bringing me a great deal of satisfaction. Naturally, I'd like to be able to say we beat the Eagles—at least once—but that, too, will come—eventually.

"What I'd really like to talk about tonight is something that's more important to me than football . . . my family."

The room had been quietly settling down before that; but, except for groans from a few disappointed youths, the audience now totally hushed. Even the youngsters quickly resigned themselves to enduring yet another boring adult speech. Maybe Doug would get to the good stuff later.

"That's right, kids. There is something more important than beating the Eagles, even more important than winning the Super Bowl. I want you to look left and right and take a good look at your parents, your brothers and sisters, maybe even your aunts and uncles and grandparents if they're here.

"They're what matters, kids. You may not think so right now, but I'm here to tell you that's the truth.

"Recently I went through a very rough time. An old friend and rival of mine was killed. In addition to that, my wife was expecting a baby, and she almost lost it. Who came to our rescue? Not Barry Sanders. Not Desmond Howard, although he might have come if I had called.

"No, my wife's brother, Ronald Covington, phoned his cousin, Ginger Barnes, and she called her mother, Cynthia Struve. Cynthia took care of the Barnes family while Mrs. Barnes literally came down and saved mine.

"You should have seen her tonight. She was just being a mother, probably exactly like your own mother, but it was amazing how she took care of everybody, thought about everybody . . ."

Without realizing it I had sunk lower and lower in my chair until I was slouched halfway to the floor. *Please please please please shut up*, I mentally begged the man with the microphone and the attention of probably three hundred and fifty people, not to mention an indeterminate TV audience.

". . . I'm here to tell you, if it weren't for my family, I wouldn't be here tonight—probably *couldn't* be here tonight. So listen up, kids. I want you to treat your family as well as you treat your friends, and treat your friends as if they were family . . ."

"Ouch," Didi yipped, probably because I had kicked her.

"Ask him."

"Ask him what?" she hissed back.

"The question I gave you. For just in case. Hurry up."

"Why can't you just, ouch, oh, all right."

Didi raised her hand, but she didn't wait to be called upon. Doug finished a sentence, something about ". . . and you'll have a rich and rewarding life," and she interrupted as deftly as a professional interviewer.

"Excuse me, uh, Doug," she began with only a

slight glance toward the television camera aimed her way. "Can you please tell me—if you're going to run a pick play, which is better, lining up in trip? or motioning into it?"

Doug took a breath to mask his surprise. Then he said, "Go with the motion, Didi. Give the defense something extra to think about."

Laughter sliced through the tension, stifled the yawns, and relaxed the entire gathering, or so I thought. For sure the change of subject relaxed me. Pretty soon I was even sitting up in my chair.

A large teenage boy, probably a football player, piped up next. "What's it feel like playing in the NFL?"

"Wonderful, if you don't mind the bruises." And so the questions and answers continued until Rip sidled over to bring the program to a halt. Forty minutes by my watch, and it took about half that time for the sizzling in my ears to recede.

Rip reclaimed the podium. "Now there is one more announcement some of you have been waiting patiently to hear: the winner of the Bryn Derwyn mascot contest. So now, for the very first time, allow me to present the one, the only—Bryn Derwyn Dragon!"

A trio of boys in a rented Chinese dragon costume slithered from the nearby locker room door. Their antics, both deliberate and accidental, caused much disruption and amusement among the audience.

Rip called for a hip-hip-hooray for the donors who made the gym possible and again for the contractors who did such a fine job. The "head" dragon raised gloved fists to lead these cheers, and finally the crowd rose and began to disperse.

Doug was mobbed by kids and dads, of course. The women mostly mooned from afar. Ronnie ushered our older folks out of traffic to wait for Rip and me. A flurry of friendly women patted my hand and murmured their appreciation of Doug's remarks, especially the "treating family like friends" and vice versa remark, which, much to Didi's disappointment, was all that made it onto the eleven o'clock news.

During the ten minutes it took Rip and Doug to wrap up their conversations, I amused myself watching people. Off and on there was Didi, visually separating the single men from the herd like a virtual-reality cowgirl looking for somebody to brand.

But mostly my eyes wandered back to a young man of a certain age who was monitoring every movement made by our daughter. The boy was still slender, soft and fair, with thick-lashed eyes and a stylishly sloppy haircut that kept him from being too beautiful. I figured he shaved maybe twice a week.

And, unless I missed my guess, he would have Chelsea's name and phone number before his next shave.

Some answers are much easier to come by than others.

Here are excerpts from other Main Line Mysteries by Donna Huston Murray—all available from St. Martin's Paperbacks!

THE MAIN LINE IS MURDER

My hand flew off the doorknob. The soft click of the door latch spooked me further into the room. I was alone with Richard's corpse.

Suppressing the need to run, I hugged in a deep breath then whistled it out through pursed lips.

Calm your breathing, that's right. Then try to think.

Okay. Finish looking. Finish looking and then you can go.

The position of Richard's body appeared benign, as if his death were a passing whim of fate. One second he had been sitting at a table collecting a pile of papers, the next he was sprawled forward, his skull shattered, the papers again in disarray.

Moved by sympathy, I reached toward Richard's arm, my hand anticipating the rough tweed of his brown sport jacket even as I brought myself up short. Television police forever warned about disturbing a murder scene.

Murder. My mind grappled with the incomprehensible. How could anyone do this—ever?

Soon I would force my frozen body to leave, to report Richard's death and set the process of the law into motion. Meanwhile, my heightened sensitivities continued to record the room. Although I probably spent only half a minute assimilating Richard's appearance, those thirty seconds had made an indelible impression.

Now I noticed that the most visible paper on the table bore the name of the couple who was delinquent with their tuition payments. The box of extra large T-shirts remained on the table at the same angle as before I left. The pencils and erasers and bag of scarf rings—everything appeared untouched.

Only the groundbreaking shovel was out of place. Looking incongruous and unnaturally clean, trimmed with a large, loopy bow in the school's trademark dark green, it had originally rested in the corner near the box of brochures.

Now it lay on the floor near where I'd been working. A small smear of blood suggested it skidded or bounced a few feet after the killer flung it behind him. Or her. I was not an especially large woman, but with a nicely balanced little shovel, I could cause plenty of damage if . . . if what?

It was time to get the hell out of there and call the police. Let them ask if, and what, and why.

I pulled my jacket cuff down over my hand before I opened the door. Then I sprinted down the hall into the lobby, nearly colliding with Jacob, the maintenance supervisor.

I put both hands on his chest to steady myself, to reassure myself he was real.

"What's wrong?" he asked.

"Something terrible, Jacob. A man's been murdered. I'm going to call the police. Please stand at the front door and keep everybody here."

Jacob's complexion had turned ashen all the way back to his remaining band of dark hair. Sweat beaded his upper lip.

"Who?" he asked. "Where?"

Already jogging toward the main office, I answered over my shoulder in a hushed voice. "Wharton. Richard Wharton. He's in the Community room. But don't say anything. Just guard the door and tell everyone Rip will be right out."

Jacob wiped his lip with his hand and nodded solemnly. When I glanced back again, he had stationed himself between the two main doors. He wasn't much bigger than me, but if I had come face to face with him just then, I would have stayed put—if only to find out what was going on.

Joanne and the teachers who had been with Rip had scattered around the outer office, one reading mail, two chatting quietly. Joanne spoke into the phone.

"Stay here," I told them all. "Don't move an inch."

I entered Rip's office and shut the door tight behind me.

My husband rose slowly from his chair. "What's wrong?" he asked. Instinctively, he gravitated toward me.

What I said stopped him like a slap. His eyes widened and stared. His body swayed slightly, and he spread his fingers on the desk top to steady himself.

He said nothing, just reached for the phone with the same stunned expression, punched 911 and handed me the receiver. Then he tightened his tie and straightened his back and opened the door to the outer office.

Just as our emergency call was answered, I could hear the gasps of shock from the people Rip informed. One of the women began to cry.

The crying braced me, toughened me. It's been that way ever since Chelsea was born. Somehow I learned to cope first and crumble later—preferably in private. I calmly and succinctly told the dispatcher there had been a murder at Bryn Derwyn Academy, adding that the people on the premises were being asked to stay until the police arrived.

After that, I made a second call to our house. The kids would see and hear the police roar into the school driveway, and they needed to be warned. To my relief, Chelsea answered; being the younger of the two, Garry might have panicked just from the stress in my voice.

"There's going to be a bit of commotion over at the school," I said as calmly as possible.

"What?" Chelsea interrupted.

I took a deep, time-consuming breath. "Something happened to Mr. Wharton, and the police have to check it out."

"Is he dead?" I could visualize my daughter's face wide with awe, flushed with the thrill of life's drama. She did not sound scared. Tell her the truth?

"Yes, Chelsea. I'm afraid so."

"Ohmigod."

"Dad and I are fine. Everybody else is fine. Please just wait at the house for us. We'll tell you whatever we can when we get home."

"Like, how did he die, Mom? Was it a heart attack or something?"

"Probably not."

"Then what, Mom? Mr. Wharton was old, but not *that* old." Fear was infusing itself into her voice. I could almost hear her thoughts: If somebody Mr. Wharton's age could die suddenly, so could anybody.

"It was more like an accident." The expedient white lie.

"Look," I added before Chelsea could quiz me further, "I've got to go now. Just hang in, and I'll be there as soon as I can."

When I got home, I would obliterate the white lie with the whole truth, and probably spoil some additional innocence as well. It wouldn't be easy, and I felt certain both kids would require generous portions of reassurance for weeks to come.

My eyes rested on the familiar cover of Bryn Derwyn's present-year directory, tucked under Rip's phone for handy reference. It reminded me that, for my husband, there would be 239 students, their parents, the faculty, the board and the whole alumni body to reassure.

"Phew," I remarked to myself. "Lucky thing Richard was a bachelor."

Was a bachelor. I began to tremble, but one more glimpse at the directory shamed me out of that.

When I emerged from the office, the three waiting teachers ambushed me for more details. Joanne saw my face and held them back like a no-nonsense crossing guard.

I proceeded into the lobby, a robot now with only so much juice left to operate my limbs.

When he caught sight of me, Rip stopped speaking with Jacob and just watched.

There was an oak bench along the far wall. I went to it and began to pull. Rip recognized what I was doing and helped me close off the hallway leading to the Community room.

Then wordlessly, we sank onto the bench side by side. Rip covered my hand with his. I allowed myself to meet his greenish-brown eyes just a second, just a second for sustenance, and that did it. Next thing I knew I was sobbing into his shoulder.

After I had finished venting, finished wiping and blowing, while all of us who had gathered in the lobby seemed stuck in that suspended-time state of waiting, it occurred to me that I had always considered Richard Wharton educated scum.

I disliked him the day we met, and nothing he had done in the six months since had improved my opinion.

FINAL ARRANGEMENTS

A bump in the road bounced Mother's chin off her chest and opened her eyes. She grimaced at the light thrown by my elderly Nissan station wagon.

"Good morning," I said.

"Umph," she replied.

When she seemed alert enough, I said, "Tell me again. Why are we doing this?"

She sighed. "You know Sylvia planned Alfie's retirement party months ago. I couldn't very well let her down."

I downshifted for a curve.

"That part I understand." For an early start, ordinarily Mother would have stayed overnight with Rip and me. The party meant I had to be at Mother's at 5:30 a.m., drive to Bryn Mawr to pick up her friend Winifred "Iffy" Bigelow, then hurry along to the Civic Center so Iffy could do an entry in the Philadelphia Flower Show. Apparently competition goes on all week.

"What I'd really like to know is why your friend Iffy offered us maintenance passes."

"Because I don't drive, and I was sure you'd love to go."

I shook my head. "No, Mom . . ."

"I beg your pardon, you practically jumped at the chance."

I wagged my head. "What I actually said was, 'If you need me to drive, I'll take you.' "

Mother stiffened. "Well, I'm terribly sorry to put you out. I thought you'd be delighted to avoid the crowds."

I spread my hand in a mollifying stop signal. "Yes. Yes, you're absolutely right. I hate seeing the flower show an inch at a time. But what I'm trying to find out here is exactly why we were offered not one but two maintenance passes. People who belong there have trouble getting them. Why did this 'Iffy' person offer them to you?''

"What do you mean, why?"

"Why? W-H-Y. Why?"

"Her car is in the shop."

I braked a little hard for a red light. "Let me put this another way. Who the hell is Iffy Bigelow?"

Mother blinked. "She came to the funeral." I understood her to mean my father's funeral since it was the only one we had attended together in the last decade.

"Mom, nobody said more than a sentence to us that day. Sometimes less."

"You'll remember," she told me confidently. She recalled details with ease; and since she considered me to be the new-improved product of Cynthia and Donald Struve, naturally I would retain whatever she had and more. "Iffy Bigelow," she prompted. "We were in high school together."

Surely I wasn't expected to remember that! I stretched to make some connection, if only to finish the conversation.

"Is her husband named Arthur, by any chance?" A few years back I took an investment course from a dry stick named Arthur Bigelow, until I caught on that you needed money to make money. Discerning my frustration, Arthur had invited me for coffee and suggested a couple ways to start a college fund for the kids. I thanked him, and we parted company. Nice enough guy, but stiff as starch.

"That's right." Mother gloated.

I tempered my astonishment. "Small world," I said, "but I still don't remember Iffy."

"You will," Mother assured me. "You will."

While my car coughed itself out in the driveway

of the Bigelows' hulking brick Tudor, I squinted at the two women silhouetted by the front door light. Mother's friend had to be the short lump with the hat, but all I recognized was the set of her shoulders and the way her purse hung from her fist. She was loaded for bear.

"Oh, good," Mother remarked. "I thought we might have to pick up Julia."

"Julia who?"

"Iffy's niece. We'll be looking after the girl while Iffy's busy with her entries."

Before I could press for more, Mother began relocating to the back seat, leaving the amenities to me. I rolled my eyes and climbed out into the chilled March air.

Iffy Bigelow shouted, "You're late," with a voice that could singe paint.

I glanced at my watch. Five fifty-five a.m. According to Mother's schedule, we were early. When I got close enough to speak normally, I tried to correct the injustice.

"We're okay by me. Should we have synchronized watches?"

"Don't get flip with me, young woman." Mrs. Bigelow ignored my outstretched hand, so I swung it toward the younger woman cowering behind her.

"Ginger Struve Barnes," I said, maintaining my friendly expression. Not really the "girl" mother described, like me, Iffy's niece was at least thirty, yet her ingenuous expression spoke of a sheltered life.

"Julia Stone," she mumbled, hesitantly accepting my handshake. Little puffs of breath condensed and dispersed around us.

I willed a little extra kindness onto my own face; adults just don't look that uncomplicated without a reason. Lord knows there were complications and undertones written all over her aunt.

Winifred Bigelow tapped a foot, and Julia jumped to retrieve a cardboard box from the stoop.

"Julia, give that to her," Iffy snapped, efficiently insulting Julia and reducing me to a flunky with one succinct phrase.

I accepted the carton with a sympathetic smile.

Meanwhile, Iffy collected a bulky potted plant off the step. Its leaves were a fistful of splayed green belts. From the center rose a tall stalk sporting a pompon of orange trumpets.

"It's a clivia," Iffy announced protectively, adding, "in perfect condition," as she cringed away from her niece.

Julia clutched her coat closed at the throat; and we all paraded toward Mother, who wiggled her fingers hello through the rear window.

"Julia! Open that back door," Iffy barked.

I practiced projecting saintly patience as I slid the open carton of arrangement equipment and carefully wrapped plant materials into the rear of the car.

Julia leaned close. "I'm just out of the hospital," she confided with pride. "My psychiatrist said I was ready for an outing."

My eyes widened, and my smile went stiff. Clinical depression? Paranoia? Schizophrenia? You can't help wondering, but you don't dare ask.

"Congratulations," I said, hanging onto that smile.

We each climbed into the Nissan thinking our own thoughts.

"No expressways," commanded Mrs. Winifred Bigelow.

I risked a questioning glance. No wink, no joke. She actually wanted a whistle stop tour of the Main Line.

This was developing into quite a morning.

SCHOOL OF HARD KNOCKS

As I untied Barney from the red maple, the mail truck passed by, its brakes squeaking to a stop at the end of each drive. Since I knew Letty often appeared soon afterward, I decided to approach her about her yard so I could scratch that onerous chore off my list.

Right on time, my next door neighbor emerged from her house like a mole from its burrow, blinking at the light while scanning her surroundings for danger. She wore yet another shapeless house dress under the brown cardigan. Her toes shuffled forward in order to accommodate her loose black shoes. Her palm batted the weeds that encroached upon the driveway ruts as she passed.

Barney easily accomplished what I set out to do. He tugged me toward the old woman as if I was missing the social event of the day—and would I please get the lead out?

Letty, the dog, and I arrived at her mailbox simultaneously. Our Irish setter eagerly reacquainted himself with the smells on Letty's skirt and shoes, plus every flavor on her hands.

"Barney," I scolded, hauling him a polite foot away by force of his choke collar, a temporary and not very effective gesture.

"Oh, let 'im be," Letty remarked. She seemed tired and careworn today, as if she had not slept well last night. The gnarled fingers she ran around the dog's muzzle moved more slowly than before, and she lowered her face for a friendly licking as if her joints were stiff.

I watched carefully for a signal of how to accomplish my mission. Honesty seemed to be my only choice.

"Letty," I began. She apparently liked dog kisses,

because she endured Barney's licking much longer than I would have.

"Lord, he's a mess, in't he?"

"Yes. I'm really sorry."

"No matter." She was smiling wearily, her plain white face a swag of cheek wrinkles and thin lips. Her ears protruded from wispy strands of mostly gray hair confined by yet another blue rubber band. I could see now that the dress had been brown and white striped in previous years. Of the ten buttons down its center front, one was misaligned and one was missing.

"Letty," I began again. "Letty, I have something I have to ask you."

Her eyebrows rose, or I should say the flesh where eyebrows usually were arched with mild surprise.

"You got somethin' to axe me?"

"Yes, Letty. Some of the neighbors were wondering if you would mind maybe cleaning up your yard a little."

The non-eyebrows arched as she cast silver/black eyes across the mess that was her domain.

"What for?"

Oh, dear. "Well, your property doesn't exactly look like most of the others on the street . . ."

"So?"

". . . and a couple of the families are trying to sell."

"Yeah?"

"So they're hoping you will agree to pick up the trash and cut the weeds out front, at least from the wall out to the curb. Twenty feet. That isn't much." That wasn't all they asked, but it would be a start. At least the rest of the jungle would remain behind the front wall.

Letty's fists set on her hips and her eyes stared at asphalt. Her scowl could have been consternation, but

I thought it best to finish my spiel before finding out.

"If the work would be too strenuous for you, my kids and I would be glad to help."

"Nope."

"I'm sorry. Do you mean no, you don't need help?"

"I mean nope I ain't gonna do it."

My jaw went slack.

"Me and me friends likes the place just as she is," Letty elaborated. "Ain't that right, doggie?" She patted the top of Barney's head and the turncoat grinned back at her.

I sighed, imagining myself repeating Letty's answer to Wendy and Gail. "What friends?" they would retort. "The old bat doesn't have a friend in the world as far as we can see."

It pained me anew that of the people on Beech Tree Lane I was the most sympathetic toward our eccentric neighbor, and here I was stepping on her proprietary toes.

She reached into her mailbox as if our conversation was over.

Remembering how I had portrayed her to the complainers—as a penniless recluse—I spoke somewhat more softly than before. "If it's money you're worried about . . .'"

"What? What did ye say?" Her eyes snapped like a Sunday school teacher demonstrating the wrath of God. She clutched a handful of junk mail to her breast. I spread my hands and backed off, physically and metaphorically. My face burned. My heart hammered.

"Letty, I'm truly sorry. I hated giving you their suggestions, but I had to let you know how they feel around here. I hope there aren't any hard feelings . . ."

She backed up her drive until her heel hit a rock,

then she spun and scurried as if pursued by antagonists from every angle. I was sorely sorry to be numbered among them, but at the time I could think of no way to separate the messenger from the message.

I hurried home to nurse my guilt—and anger that I had allowed myself to be pushed into such a position in the first place. Later I realized I should have told Letty about Liz so she could be on the alert. If others suspected, as Wendy and Gail did, that Letty had money stashed somewhere in her house, the old woman might be in danger.

NO BONES ABOUT IT

My only choices were a) admit defeat and phone Linda, my dog trainer friend, or b) try my last idea.

The trouble was, Linda and her ex-husband Karl shared custody of a German shepherd named Tibor, a paragon of a dog who—had Lincoln been indisposed—probably could have written the Gettysburg Address and delivered it, too. When Linda used him to demonstrate perfection at our beginner's class, the snobby shepherd sneered at the other dogs the way Zeus probably gazed down from Olympus.

So far, our new Irish setter, Gretsky, named after the astonishing hockey player Wayne Gretzky (aka The Great One), exhibited only one attribute, i.e. a prodigious capacity for affection, which he insisted be returned. *Insisted* was the operative word.

After lunch, while I tried to relax with coffee and the morning paper, he barked at me for half an hour. He did not need to go out. He wasn't even hungry. Swatting him produced no effect. Ignoring him? No effect. Gretsky just wanted to see me jump through hoops for the fun of it.

"Okay," I challenged him. "Let's find out who's Alpha Dog around here."

I climbed up on the living room coffee table. I put my hands on my hips. I glared at the pushy young animal yapping for my attention. Then, trying to simulate a Great Dane, I barked right back at him.

Gretsky paused to blink at me. He was a beautiful dog, really. Shiny auburn red. That sculpted head shape peculiar to setters. At four months of age he had already become a leggy young adult with a deep, narrow chest and sparse fringing on his legs and tail, He reminded me of the legendary chestnut thoroughbred, Secretariat. Except, of course, horses don't bark.

The pause ended, and Gretsky joined me in a ridiculous duet of opposing wills. I'm sure I looked and sounded like a total idiot, but I was too angry to care. Luckily, both kids were off at Bryn Derwyn Academy's day camp, and Rip was there doing the zillion things headmasters do in the summer.

Having failed with my Great Dane imitation, I stopped making noise. Gretsky, however, continued. Woof, woof, woof. Yap, yap, yap, yap. If his objective was to get under my skin, he was a runaway success.

As I climbed down from the coffee table, I experienced a guilty pang of nostalgia for our previous Irish setter, Barney.

Barney and I had a rapport. If I so much as thought about walking him, he would shimmy with joy. When the kids' bus was late, he would raise an eyebrow of concern. And the morning he bolted for the house next door, I knew for certain there was an emergency involving Letty MacNair, our reclusive older neighbor. Unfortunately, Barney's heart gave out shortly after that episode. All four of us Barneses cried for days.

We acquired Gretsky more as a diversion than a replacement. With time and luck, maybe that special rapport would come.

Meanwhile—aspirin. I rummaged around in the kitchen junk drawer for two Bayer. Then I downed them with water straight from the tap. Mercifully, Gretsky had gone off on his own *silent* mission.

Initially, I did everything right—obtained a list of reputable breeders; called a few, asked lots of questions.

Then I did everything wrong. All we wanted was that silly Irish setter personality, not a living art object worth hundreds of dollars. So after school one day, my son Garry and I answered a local newspaper ad.

A Lancaster County farmer had bred his own two setters. He described them as "hunters" rather than show dogs and priced them accordingly.

Both the man and his wife agreed that Gretsky's mother possessed a sweet, affectionate disposition, but his father was . . . husband and wife exchanged a glance, "We almost got rid of him," said the woman. One more litter, said the husband's nod. The condition of their living room conveyed that they needed the money. I cheerfully handed it over.

As I drove out their lane with our beautiful red puppy snuggled in Garry's lap, Daddy Dog pranced through the rain alongside our car, head held high like the champion he reputedly had been. Surely that glint in his eye was just pleasure over his freedom.

It was.

I glanced at the kitchen phone. Linda once mentioned that anyone in the beginner's class was free to call and discuss specific problems, so technically I wouldn't be imposing upon our friendship. Of course, right that moment Gretsky seemed to be behaving himself.

Wrong. Our Great One scooted past me with something light blue in his mouth and his daddy's glint in his eye.

My underwear! The little scamp had stolen a pair of my panties. Head throbbing, I set off after him.

We circled the living room coffee table. He zigged when I zagged. I lunged. With four legs to my two he merely trotted to avoid my grasp.

Prancing lightly, knees up like a Lippizaner, he exited the living room and proceeded down the hallway past our two kids' bedrooms toward the added-on TV room just beyond.

"Come on, Gretsky, *give*," I begged as I lumbered after him.

He glanced back as he entered the family room

where a sofa rose like an island centered in front of the television. We both knew he could do laps around it until I fell flat on my face.

To close off his escape, I shut the door behind us. Then I laid a wooden chair barrier-style between the back of the sofa and the bookcase.

Gretsky gracefully leaped over it on his way by.

I extracted a broom from the closet, planning to swipe the dog's hip in the vain hope that he would pause long enough for me to retrieve my unmentionables.

The broom fanned the dog's rear from a distance of eighteen inches, but Gretsky's eyebrows straightened with dismay. He oozed forward like Secretariat eying the stretch. I promised myself never to miss the clothes hamper again.

"Drop it," I demanded through a very tight throat.

A fast glance and another leap over the chair.

I climbed over the back of the sofa forgetting entirely about keeping my sneakers off the upholstery.

The four-legged Great One faked right and bolted left. From my high position on the seat cushions I thrust the broom in front of the oncoming dog. He stopped just long enough to entice me to the floor then rounded the broom, flew over the chair, and stood with his back to the wall like a gunfighter covering every option.

I flopped onto the sofa, arms folded over my heaving chest, and glared at him while I caught my breath. Gretsky refused to meet my eye.

Instead he sidled over to the door, which unfortunately had bounced half an inch out of the totally-latched position. Our canine Einstein easily nosed the door open wide enough to shoulder his way out of the room.

"The hell with you," I shouted down the hall after him.

I rubbed the back of my neck and contemplated the phone resting on an end table. Linda really had invited her students to call anytime with questions.

Did "Help! Help! Help! Help! Help!" qualify as a question?

"Would it be possible to schedule another private session?" I asked as soon as my friend and I had exchanged hello's.

Her response was so uncharacteristic that my own problems fled from my mind.

"Sorry, Gin. I just . . . no. Sorry," she told me with a quivering voice.

"What's wrong?" I asked with apprehension.

Linda took a slow, ragged breath.

"Karl's dead," she said. "Tibor did it."

Be sure to read all the books by
Les Roberts
featuring Cleveland private eye
Milan Jacovich

THE CLEVELAND CONNECTION

Who hated an old man—a veteran of World War II—enough to kill him? When an old Serbian immigrant is murdered, Milan Jacovich must follow the old blood ties that lead to a world of hidden violence, family secrets—and old hatreds that die hard.

_____ 96218-5 $5.99 U.S./ $7.99 Can.

COLLISION BEND

When a television reporter is found strangled in her own home, Milan Jacovich's ex-girlfriend asks him to clear her current love as the chief murder suspect. But as Jacovich goes behind the scenes to uncover all the scandal and intrigue of big-city television, he comes closer to making the evening news—as a murder victim.

_____ 96399-8 $5.99 U.S./$7.99 Can.